HOUSE OF
B

DARK LEGACY

LUANNE BENNETT

Copyright © 2020 Luanne Bennett
All rights reserved.

The Word Lounge, Atlanta, Georgia
No part of this book may be reproduced, distributed, or transmitted in any written or electronic form without permission from the author, except for quotations and excerpts for articles or reviews.

This is a work of fiction. Names, characters, places, and incidents portrayed in this book are fictitious. Any resemblance to actual persons, living or dead, or events is entirely coincidental.

luannebennett.com

Cover by Deranged Doctor Design

CHAPTER 1

The Hamptons, New York
Fall 2019

The wind picked up as the waves rolled over the sand, inching closer while the tide pulled higher. The temperature had dropped when the sun set, but Katherine Winterborne felt oddly warm standing naked on the beach, her fair skin glowing from the light of the moon, the doubt that she'd made the right decision no longer swaying her thoughts. She'd finally made peace with the gods.

It had only been a few minutes since she'd swallowed the potion that would allow her to walk into the ocean and never return, giving her dominion over her destiny before it manifested completely and destroyed the people she loved. But taking your life when you're immortal is nearly impossible without the aid of dark magic. Without the potion, she would merely breathe in the sea and spend the evening trying to expel the salty water from her lungs. A curse or a blessing, depending on your intent, and her intent at that moment was to disappear under the waves and leave no trace of her indiscretions and the nightmare those flawed decisions had set in motion decades earlier.

A hazy feeling of warmth spread through her limbs as she walked toward a spot where the sea bled into the dunes. She dug her toes into the sand and glanced back at the house, thinking of her brother. He'd hate relinquishing control to his niece, but he'd eventually accept that although Morgan was young, she was the rightful successor to the House of Winterborne. Heir to the helm of an empire, her daughter would reluctantly accept her station and show them all the powerful witch inside that was already beginning to wake up. Then the clan would accept Morgan as their queen.

As Katherine's symptoms had started to progress rapidly, she'd given her daughter more responsibilities within the company. But time was up. Morgan would be thrown into the lion's den with only her birthright and intuition to guide her through a gauntlet of ambitious immortal men looking for the weak spot in their new leader, undoubtedly deeming her inadequate. The Elders would look for any opportunity to convert their matriarchy to a patriarchy. To give the power to a son. But not while Katherine still had the right to designate her daughter as her heir, her last declaration as the queen of Clan Winterborne.

Her thoughts were suddenly distracted as she tried to remember if she'd gotten rid of the evidence. Dark magic used to end a life was a high crime, even if it was your own. The stigma would leave a mark on the House of Winterborne and possibly give the Elders grounds to pronounce her unstable and incapable of appointing an heir. She relaxed when she remembered throwing the empty bottle into the ocean after drinking the powerful potion, before she sat on the beach and waited for it to enter her veins and render her mortal just long enough to drown. When the deed was done, the gods would carry her out to sea and pull her to the bottom of the ocean for eternity. The evidence would never be found. It was just a bottle of seawater if it washed up on the beach, and Katherine Winterborne would be one of the thousands to go missing in New York City every year.

But an immortal never really dies; an immortal transitions.

Katherine walked closer to the ocean and felt a cold wave roll over her feet and wash against her ankles. She looked down at the sea foam covering her toes and caught a terrifying glimpse of her cold skin. It had gone stark white and gave off a blue tone against the moonlight. Her veins pulsed beneath the surface, turning black before her eyes, and her breath grew heavy as a gnawing hunger in her throat reminded her of why she had to do this.

Looking back at the beautiful summerhouse for the last time, she followed the wave as it receded, her mind filled with random thoughts as she walked into the dark water until it reached her waist. Her hair floated up and fanned across the ocean surface as she continued deeper. Then she plunged beneath the waves and took a deep breath, sucking the water into her lungs. But instead of drowning her, the water seemed to oxygenate her blood.

The potion wasn't working.

Suddenly her lungs began to burn. She panicked and tried to swim for the surface, but her limbs wouldn't move. They were frozen. A few seconds passed, and her fear began to melt away as the haziness returned and a tingling sensation raced across her skin. The murky water had become crystal clear, giving her a view of her fingers as they began to dissolve into tiny particles, carried off by the ocean like dust disbursed to the wind. The sensation continued up her arms and across her shoulders, engulfing her until she couldn't feel or hear anything but the cold water calling her deeper.

Katherine Winterborne's secret had drifted with her out to sea.

CHAPTER 2

Manhattan
A Month Later

"Who is that?" I asked my brother, nodding to a man sitting on the other side of the room. He'd been staring at me since he walked in and took a seat, and it was making me uncomfortable.

With zero discretion, Michael turned to look at him.

"Don't be so damn obvious," I whispered, as if the man could hear me from across the room.

"Who cares. We get a free pass to act as uncouth as we want today." He studied the man for a moment before shrugging. "He probably works for us." Then he pointed to a guy leaning against the wall. "Tell you what. You find out who *he* is for me, and I'll check out your stalker over there."

My brother had a thing for blonds. The kind who were too good-looking. Pretty boys who were guaranteed to break your heart. Prospecting for his next distraction always took priority, even at our mother's memorial service.

"Jesus, Michael. Not today."

"Come on, Morgan. Mom would have hated this morbid shit. She would have preferred a party. In fact, I recall her saying, 'When I die, I want my children to throw me a damn party.'"

"You're right about that," I said, envisioning the great Katherine Winterborne shaking her head from wherever she was. Funerals and memorial services were for the living, and she wouldn't have wanted either.

My mother had disappeared a month earlier, and a weekend trip to the Hamptons had turned into a search party. She'd said she was going out to the beach house to unwind for a few days, but when she never called me that first night and wouldn't answer her phone, I knew something was wrong. To make matters worse, I hadn't gone with her that time. I usually did, but on that particular weekend I'd already had plans. She also hadn't asked me, which was odd, but it'd saved me from explaining that a night out with my best friend was more important than spending a weekend in the Hamptons with her.

God, I felt like shit.

"It wasn't your fault," Michael said, reading my mind as he always managed to do.

"Yes, it was. If I'd gone with her—"

"Yeah, and if I'd gone with her, or Ethan or Avery." He let out a heavy sigh and lowered his voice. "For God's sake, Morgan, our mother was one of the most powerful immortals in this city. You don't really think whoever or whatever got to her could have been stopped by one of us? We don't even know if she's actually dead. They haven't found a single strand of her hair, let alone a body."

I tensed at the thought and stood up to head for the bar on the other side of the room. I wanted her back so bad I couldn't breathe at times, but to suggest that she might not be dead was too much to consider. Did he think she just ran off and deserted her family? Of course she was dead. Every member of our clan had known the moment she took her last breath on this earth. We'd all felt it. Her energy had been ripped from each of us, leaving a hollow well in the center of our chests, tearing a gaping hole through the web of our universal bond. And the way the owls had screeched over Central Park at the exact moment that we all sat up in our beds and knew she was gone… It was awful, the sound they made.

The night we felt it, my brother Ethan had driven out to the island. I still resented him for not waking me up and taking me with him, and since we all lived under the same roof, he had no excuse. All he'd found when he arrived were her clothes on the beach and footsteps leading toward the water, not yet washed away by the tide. We believed she'd walked into the ocean and somehow drowned. How was still a mystery.

My clan owned an entire block on the Upper West Side of Manhattan. The Winterborne was a prewar apartment building named after our family. Most of us lived there, my sister being one of the few exceptions. Avery preferred to dwell like an "ordinary" New Yorker and lived in her own apartment on the Upper East Side. But she had no problem accepting an obscene salary as a regional director for the luxury real estate division of Winterborne Holdings.

I sagged with relief when I spotted Jules heading for me.

"Sorry I'm late." She asked the bartender for a shot of Jameson and surveyed the room. "Couldn't catch a cab to save my life. I was about to stand in the middle of Broadway and lift my skirt."

"That would have been interesting," I mumbled over the rim of my glass. "You should have called me. I could have sent a car."

She glanced at the guests milling around the room with

drinks in their hands and handkerchiefs to blot their teary eyes. "Looks like I missed most of the service."

"Yeah. It's about over. We had a pretty good turnout."

We'd decided to have the memorial service in one of the large rooms at the auction house we owned and operated. Since our "religion" didn't exactly involve worshipping a god in a church, the clan thought it would be best to hold it in a neutral location. It was really for the employees and shareholders though, and a high-profile family like ours had to put on a show for the media. But the real memorial service for Katherine Winterborne had already taken place in a chamber hidden deep within the walls of the Winterborne Building where we lived. The Elders had officiated the ritual that sent her spirit off to the gods, so now we were just going through the motions expected of a family who'd lost one of their own.

"How are you holding up?" Jules asked, downing her drink and holding her empty glass out to the bartender for a refill. "The bar was a great idea, by the way."

"My mother wanted a party instead of a funeral or memorial service, so we compromised with an open bar."

She raised her fresh drink in the air. "That's Katherine. She's the best."

It didn't bother me to hear my best friend speak of my mother in the present tense, but she got an awkward look on her face when she realized she'd done it.

"It's fine, Jules. I'll probably talk to her for months like she's still in the room."

Jules, short for Julia, and I had been fused at the hip since high school. She was the smartest girl I'd ever met, but she acted like she didn't give a shit about anything. It turned out she was just bored. There wasn't a class she couldn't ace, but her parents refused to let her skip a couple of grades because they wanted her to be a "normal" child. The only reason she'd taken a liking to me was because she'd picked up on my talents. That girl had spotted me from a mile away and never flinched when I told her about my family's unusual heritage. Winterbornes are immortals, and though my immortality was still five years away, I was a rare witch born to our line once in a blue moon. Not the kind that casts spells or stirs cauldrons—Winterborne witches are more subtle in our endeavors. Our powers are more practical, manifesting in autonomous ways, like the time I stopped a car from hitting me as I crossed Park Avenue after leaving school—with my bare hands. That was the day Jules decided we were to be friends for life.

"Have they named you yet?" Jules asked, referring to my impending "coronation" as we jokingly called it.

I'd known for some time that I was my mother's successor. It was tradition for a female to head up the clan. Avery was the obvious choice, being the oldest daughter, but my mother had recognized my powers early on and made no apologies for choosing me as her successor over my sister. What was right for the Winterbornes was all that mattered to her, and Avery simply didn't have what it took to lead the clan, nor did she have any desire to do so. Neither did I really, but it was my mother's wish and I planned to honor it.

I groaned and took a sip of wine. "The council has called a meeting tomorrow morning to officially announce it. Ethan's going to love that."

"It's not like he doesn't know," she said over the rim of her glass.

He did know, but the council formalizing it was another thing. Both he and my uncle Cabot would smile supportively, all the while thinking it was time to change tradition and let the men of the clan rule for once. I'd be seen as young and lacking the killer instincts of a true leader. My mother had been one of those killers. She'd been kind and loving, but she would cut you off at the knees if you threatened her clan or company. Obviously she'd seen those instincts in me, even if I didn't.

Right on cue, Ethan came through the crowd and joined us at the bar. He ordered a double scotch and eyed Jules. "Nice dress, Jules."

She leaned back against the bar and gave him a cocky grin. "Oh yeah? See something you like?"

"Watch out for the wolves," he said, laughing as he grabbed his drink and made his way back toward his date on the other side of the room.

I watched Jules watching Ethan walk away. "You two need to just get it over with."

She continued to watch him as he reached his date and ran his hand down her back. "Your brother's good-looking, but sleeping with him would be so… wrong."

"Yeah, I don't think I'd ever look at you the same way again." I snickered and looked around to see where Michael had gone. "Shit. Not again."

"What?" She perked up and followed my gaze.

I downed the rest of my wine and nodded to the other side of the room. "You see that guy in the corner?"

"The tall one with black hair?"

"He keeps staring at me, and I'm about to go over there and ask him why."

She huffed a laugh. "Have you looked in the mirror? Half the guys in the room are staring at you. Probably has a thing for redheads."

"I doubt it," I said, shaking my head. "He's giving me the creeps. I don't even think he was invited."

"You think he crashed the memorial service for the open bar?" She set her glass down and straightened up. "I'll just go have a word with the man."

"No," I said, calling her off. "I have a better idea."

CHAPTER 3

Jules filled a corn tortilla with steak and cheese and stuffed half of it in her mouth. "Damn, this is good," she mumbled around her mouthful of food with a trail of green salsa running down her chin.

"That good, huh?"

"You kidding me? Best tacos in the city."

The memorial service had ended, so I'd grabbed Jules and we'd slipped out the back entrance and headed down to the Village to get something to eat, leaving my stalker behind.

It was nice to get out for a few hours. I'd been sequestered in the house for weeks, grieving my mother, barely setting foot outside the walls of the Winterborne fortress. That would all change when I officially assumed my role not only as head of the clan but also as the future CEO of Winterborne Holdings. The clan owned one of the most prestigious auction houses in the world, along with a luxury real estate division. We brokered everything from fine art and antiquities to slick new penthouses around the globe. At twenty-five, I wasn't anywhere near ready to take over the corporation, but I had several years to prepare myself, and I'd be lying if I said I was confident about leading a clan of immortals as of tomorrow morning.

We finished our food and Jules ordered a margarita. I stuck with tea. With the council meeting in the morning, the last thing I needed was to face the Elders with a hangover. They'd be looking for any flaws, so why make it easy for them?

The waitress returned a few minutes later with our drinks.

"You're too young to be so boring," Jules said, taking a sip from the salty rim of her glass.

I grinned and stirred a little honey into my cup. "Don't worry. I'll be fun again before you know it."

A few years back, we would have headed straight for the bar across the street, and we still went out every now and then. But for the most part, those days were over.

She downed half her drink and pushed her glass away. "I need to call it a night anyway."

A loud crash got our attention before I could rib her about not finishing her drink. I turned around and saw one of the waiters running down the length of the bar with a metal object in his hand. It looked like one of those giant forks you skewered a turkey with. On the floor next to the bar was a pile of broken plates and glasses with food scattered everywhere. The waitress who'd dropped the tray had climbed on top of a table to escape whatever the waiter was chasing.

"What the hell is going on?" I said.

Jules's face curled into a grimace. "Looks like rat stew is about to be on the menu." She shuddered dramatically and pointed across the room.

The bar area cleared out, and several customers jumped out of their chairs and moved away from the commotion. A woman shrieked and headed for the front door. Her dinner companion got up and threw his napkin on the table. "I'm not paying for this," he yelled before following her out.

The creature must have run behind the bar because the waiter circled around it and came back down the other side. A second later, something flew out from behind it and headed for the window on the far wall. It hit the glass and fell to the floor, stunned and barely moving.

I jumped out of my chair. "That's not a rat. It's a bird!"

"What are you doing?" Jules said as I ran across the room.

It was too late. The waiter threw the fork across the room and hit the bird, skewering one of its wings to the floor. Then he headed toward it like he planned to finish it off.

"Don't you dare!" I gave him a warning look as I cut him off. "It's a harmless bird." I hated nothing more than a bully. Especially those who tormented animals.

He brushed past me a little rougher than necessary and yanked the fork out of the bird's wing. As he raised it into the air to deliver a deadly blow, a single word slipped from my mouth. "*Stop!*"

Jules was staring at me when I looked over at her. "Shit, Morgan," she said as she glanced around the restaurant at all the frozen faces. "What did you just do?"

With the exception of the two of us, everyone in the room seemed to be suspended in place, frozen as if time had stopped, and I had no idea how I'd done it. The bird was also unaffected and was flapping around the room with its wing stretched out and covered with blood.

"Go into the kitchen and find something I can put it in."

She just stood there, looking around in disbelief.

"Go!" I yelled, getting her full attention this time. "The spell is about to break!"

She snapped out of it and ran through the swinging door that led to the kitchen. A minute later she came back out with a box big enough to hold a cat. "This is all I could find. What kind of bird is that?"

"It's a crow. It must have flown in through the back door."

The terrified bird had stopped moving. It lay on its side with its eye and mouth open, its breathing so shallow I wasn't sure it would survive the cab ride uptown.

"The loading door is open," Jules said, stepping closer to get a better look at it as I gently picked it up. "Is it dead?"

I shook my head. "But it will be if I don't do something soon." I put it in the box and stood up.

"You're not taking it home with you?"

I pinned her with a look. "Well, what would you suggest? Should we wait for the server to unfreeze and finish the poor thing off?"

She glanced at his awkward form. "We might not have to."

The waiter twitched, and I knew it was time to go. Whatever I'd done to him was beginning to wear off, and I didn't dare try to reinforce it.

I threw some money on the table and headed for the door. Time was running out for the poor crow.

∼

I MADE it home in less than thirty minutes, looking in the box every now and then to see if the bird was still alive.

Jakob stood up as I entered the building. "Can I help you with that?" he asked, nodding to the box in my hands.

"Thanks, but I've got it. It's lighter than it looks."

Jakob had been the doorman for the Winterborne Building since it was built by the clan in 1886. He was an indentured immortal who'd been given his freedom nearly a century ago but had chosen to stay on in exchange for a small apartment on the first floor. He also helped raise me and my siblings when my father left after Michael was born.

When I reached the elevator, I stopped and listened for

sounds in the box. I had a fifty-fifty chance of finding a dead bird inside when I got upstairs. "Jakob, have you ever dabbled in necromancy?"

The look on his face answered my question. Then he glanced at the box. "Do I dare ask why you would inquire about such a forbidden subject?"

It had been a reckless thought. "I think it's best if we just pretend I didn't," I said, stepping into the elevator. "Good night."

I hit the button for the penthouse that I'd continued to share with my mother after graduating from college. There was a nice apartment for me a few floors down, but the penthouse had an attached conservatory, which was just a fancy name for a greenhouse, that housed my orchid collection. Not to mention the spectacular views of Central Park.

"Good evening, mistress," a refined male voice said as I stepped off the elevator and headed for the living room.

"Don't call me that, Otto."

"Very well, mistress."

My jaw tensed. "Don't make me replace you with Alexa," I muttered, immediately regretting it. The voice went silent, and I knew I'd be apologizing to my astral assistant in the morning.

I set the box on the coffee table and sat down on the sofa, dreading what I'd find inside. It was just a bird, but it had broken my heart to see it tortured by that asshole waiter. The strays, the horses that pulled the carriages around the park, they all got to me.

When I opened the lid and found the crow still alive, I sighed with relief and gently scooped it out of the box and laid it in my lap. The poor thing had lost a lot of blood, and the stress of being chased around that restaurant had probably taxed its tiny heart. A moment later, it began to convulse and its eyes closed. It was dying.

"Hold on, little guy." I got up to get a towel from the kitchen. "Otto, call Jakob up to the penthouse. Quickly."

"Yes, mistress."

I heard the elevator door open as I came back into the living room, and Jakob came rushing in. "What's wrong? Otto said it was dire."

"I need a few drops of your blood."

He stared at the safety pin in my hand. Then he noticed the black feathers sticking out from the folded towel I was hugging to my chest. "What are you up to, Mora?" He'd called me that since I was a kid. "What's in the towel?"

"I don't have time to explain, so don't make me compel you."

He snickered. "I'd like to see you try." When I unfolded the towel, his eyes lit up. "Is it dead?"

"It will be if you don't start bleeding within the next few seconds." I shoved the pin at him. "Necromancy will get us into a lot more trouble than this."

"Us?" he said, throwing his hands up. "Slow down. This is unorthodox, to say the least. Do you have any idea what will happen to that bird? Because I certainly don't. And I don't relish the idea of what will happen if the clan finds out you fed it immortal blood. *My* immortal blood."

"Come on, Jakob, It's the only way to save it. No one's going to find out, and I doubt the crow will talk."

He sighed and took the pin. "All right, but this is all on you if it goes badly." A drop of blue blood welled up on his fingertip as he stuck himself. "Happy now?"

"Ecstatic." I took his finger and placed it at the edge of the crow's gaping beak. "Some asshole tried to kill it. I can't explain why, but I have to save this bird."

He grinned and cupped his other hand against my cheek. "Of course you do. You're my Mora, mother of beasts."

The crow stirred as Jakob's immortal blood touched its

tongue. Its eyes fluttered and its punctured wing began to heal immediately.

A wide smile spread across my face. "It's working."

"Did you doubt it? Now all we have to do is make sure it doesn't claw our eyes out when it comes to and sees a couple of giants hovering over it."

I hadn't thought about that. "Do we still have that old birdcage?"

"I believe it's in the basement."

He headed for the elevator to get the cage I'd kept a couple of cockatiels in when I was a kid. It had doubled as a rehab center for injured pigeons over the years as well, and I was surprised my mother hadn't gotten rid of it. The plan was to keep the crow in the cage overnight while it recuperated and release it in the morning if it was well enough to fly.

Before stepping into the elevator, Jakob stopped and turned around. "This is a first for me," he said, his forehead puckering. "Sharing my blood with something mortal, I mean. An animal, no less. Be careful tonight, Mora. We have no idea what we just created."

CHAPTER 4

Something crashed in the living room around three a.m. I sat straight up in bed and listened for more sounds.

"Michael?" I called out when the house went silent. It wouldn't be the first time my brother raided my refrigerator in the middle of the night.

Another sound came from right outside my bedroom. I got up and tiptoed toward the door and heard a commotion in the living room like someone was stumbling and bumping into furniture. Then I heard a soft clicking sound. A rattling.

I stepped into the living room and saw a large shadow in the corner near the terrace door. As I tried to reconcile what it was, a set of golden eyes slowly opened and looked at me. A moment later they faded to shiny black and continued to watch me as I circled the room toward the cage that had fallen on the floor. The bars were bent and broken.

"I guess I don't have to worry about you anymore. Looks like Jakob's blood did the trick."

The crow's wings suddenly spread. It flew across the room, knocking over a lamp as it came toward me. It was the size of an eagle and stopped to hover in the middle of the room as it studied me with its mirrorlike eyes.

I stumbled backward and hit the ground when it suddenly flew closer, cawing and flapping its wings as its talons reached out.

"Stop!" It worked back at the restaurant, but not this time.

The crow hovered and cocked its head, my attempt to freeze it a mere distraction. I glanced at the row of windows and its eyes followed mine, that soft clicking sound coming from it again.

I jumped up and ran for the terrace to throw the door open. The crow sailed past me into the night sky, its silhouette gleaming from the lights of the city hitting its shiny feathers. It turned and flew back toward me, stopping a few feet from the terrace and holding its wings out like a phoenix, growing larger before my eyes until it was taller than me. Then it let out a deafening caw and headed toward the park.

The breath I'd been holding came rushing out as I watched it disappear. "Goodbye, crow. Have a nice life."

When I shut the door and headed back to bed, I couldn't shake the feeling that that crow would come back to haunt me. There were no rules about using immortal blood on animals, but I should have known better. I'd definitely hear about it from the council if they ever found out.

I climbed back into bed to sleep for a few more hours before the big day got underway. It was just a bird. A menacing-looking bird the size of a man. Who would notice?

∽

SOMEONE SAT on the edge of my bed and shook me awake.

"What are you doing here?" I rolled over and ignored my brother.

"Get up. It's almost nine thirty. Today's your big day."

Michael and I were almost as close as twins. He was only a year younger than me, so we'd grown up with a lot of the same friends and gone through similar teenage angst together. My mother was a saint to have raised us successfully.

"Do me a favor and make breakfast while I jump in the shower."

He got up and headed for the door. "What the hell happened in the living room? There's a mangled birdcage on the floor."

"Don't ask."

Twenty minutes later, I came into the kitchen wearing my robe and sat at the counter.

Along with his talent for painting, Michael was an excellent cook. He'd spent a year in Paris training at a world-class restaurant, only to come back to New York and realize he didn't want to be a chef at all. He loved the cooking part, but the idea of actually working in a restaurant turned him off. Something about too much cigarette smoke and odd hours.

"Thank you," I said, a little disappointed by the plate of scrambled eggs he slid in front of me. I was hoping for one of his amazing omelets, but at least he'd made coffee.

He grabbed an apple from a bowl and leaned against the counter. "So, what happened in the living room?" he asked, biting into the fruit with a loud crunch.

"I brought an injured bird home last night. It knocked the cage over and went a little berserk."

I could see his bullshit detector firing up. "That was a mighty strong bird to bend those bars."

"Yeah, no kidding." I changed the subject to spare him from becoming complicit in my crime. "What time does the party start?"

"You're asking me?" He straightened up and tossed his half-eaten apple into the trash. "Get dressed and let's go find out. I have a date afterward, so I'd like to get this formality over with."

After taking a couple of bites of my breakfast, I went back to my bedroom to get dressed. I glanced at the clothes hanging in my closet and tried to imagine what my mother would have worn to such a meeting. Katherine Winterborne was a fashion maverick. New York designers loved her because she was tall and beautiful. But it was her money and influence that they really loved. They'd probably be clamoring to clothe me next. I finally settled for an appropriate blue dress. Conservative but not too stuffy. We were immortals who sold art for a living, not accountants.

After applying a little lipstick and mascara, I walked back out and did a spin for my fashion-savvy brother. "Do I look all right?"

"Specfuckingtacular." He tossed the book in his hand back on the table and stood up. "Let's go raid the chambers. Shall we?"

We got on the elevator and pressed the button marked CC. The elevator stopped and the door sprang open, revealing a large room with a very long table. At the far end was an ostentatious chair reserved for the head of the clan. The walls were lined with shelves holding hundreds of books, each one containing a part of our history. The dustier ones documented the clan's bylaws. As children, we'd been forced to sit down and read them as punishment for getting on our parent's last nerve. An immortal's version of a belt.

A booming voice got our attention as we stepped off the elevator. "Ah… the future of the clan has finally decided to grace us with her presence." It was Ramsey, the senior Elder.

Michael and I glanced at each other. "I guess we're late," he muttered.

Since no one had actually set the meeting time other than to say "in the morning," I felt no guilt for showing up when I did.

The room was filled with family members and Elders, the latter being the ones who'd written those dusty old books on the shelves. Enforcers of the bylaws.

I suddenly thought about the crow. As far as I knew, there was nothing in those books that indicated Jakob and I had done anything wrong by saving it with immortal blood, but then again, there were a few volumes on those shelves I hadn't gotten around to reading yet.

Ethan and Cabot were seated at the far end of the table, near that ridiculous chair we'd nicknamed "the throne." My sister Avery was farther down, looking bored and inconvenienced as usual. She wanted as little to do with clan business as possible. In fact, she would have given up her immortality if it were possible. But it was something we all experienced when we reached our majority, whether we liked it or not.

Majority was reached at the ripe age of thirty, but we stopped aging and maturing at different times, women at thirty and men at thirty-five, with men needing a little more time to bake. Hence the reason for our youth. You could be looking at a hundred-year-old clansman and have no clue.

Of course, it was impractical for the world to see a Winterborne unchanged forever, so we retired fairly young. Uncle Cabot had transitioned a decade ago, but with a little gray hair dye at the temples, he could work for another ten years before having to step down from the company. Plenty of time for him to battle for his new position as CEO. A position he was expected to relinquish to me in a few years when I was ready.

My cousin, James, was grinning at me like a fool from across the table. He'd recently turned thirty-five and had gone through his final transition, which meant he would look like a movie star for eternity. So would his twin sister, Olivia, who'd stopped aging five years earlier. They'd both chosen to focus on development of their magical skills in lieu of working in the mundane world, which was perfectly acceptable.

I walked around the table to sit next to James so I could wipe that grin off his face, but one of the Elders stopped me.

"Over there, Morgan." It was Ramsey's booming voice.

Not wanting to argue on my first day as clan leader, I took a seat in the awful chair.

"We are all saddened by the loss of your mother," he continued, unwilling to say *death* because most of them couldn't wrap their head around the idea that their queen had killed herself. Dark magic hadn't been confirmed, but there was no other way she could have done it. I think they were all hoping she would just show up one day. Like she was returning from a long vacation. "The law of the clan dictates that we appoint a new—"

"Don't say queen," I said. I couldn't stand the title. It was the twenty-first century, and my first executive order would be that no one called me that. "Just refer to me as the head of the clan." That I could live with.

Ramsey stared at me for a moment, disapproval written all over his face. I wasn't worthy of the title, and the Elders made no effort to hide their disdain for handing over the fate of the clan to a woman who hadn't even reached her immortality yet.

"Very well." Ramsey took his seat and opened a large book where the transition of power would be documented. That book would then be placed back on the shelf to draw dust until the next generation of children was forced to take it down and read it.

He put on a pair of wire-rimmed glasses and commenced with the formalities. "In light of the tragic passing of Katherine Abagail Winterborne, we are here to witness the transition of power to her secondborn daughter, Morgan Winterborne, as was her directive." He glanced at Avery, who was sitting at the other end of the table and avoiding eye contact with me. Another female wasn't much better in the eyes of the council, but at least Avery was immortal. Barely, but still immortal. Too bad for them she would have rather died than assume the role.

Michael slumped in his chair and glanced at his Rolex.

Ethan looked at our younger brother and raised his brow. "Are we boring you?"

"A little," Michael replied.

I forced myself not to smile.

Michael straightened up and looked at Ramsey. "Sorry. Please continue."

Murmurs filled the room as everyone pretended to be annoyed by the distraction, but they all wanted to get this over with as much as I did.

"I don't mean to be disrespectful," I said, trying to move things along, "but I have a meeting at the auction house this afternoon."

Ramsey groaned and let out a long sigh. "Since we all have lives to get back to, I'll speed this up." He wrote something in the book and then stood up. "Morgan Winterborne, do you accept your position as head of the clan and swear your allegiance to the House of Winterborne?"

It reminded me of a wedding, which in a way it was, with me as the new bride of the House of Winterborne. "I do."

"And do you swear on your very life to hold the clan above all else? To fiercely defend the integrity and honor of your people? To fall upon the tip of a sword should you fail?"

"Yes." I suddenly felt a little claustrophobic and needed to get out of the room.

Ramsey picked up the book and plopped it down in front of me, placing his finger on a line. "Sign here."

I quickly signed my life away and stood up. "If we're done, I need to get to work." I turned to leave before the council could drag the meeting out and turn it into a town hall of clan business.

"Wait," Ramsey said. "There's another matter we need to discuss."

Here it comes. They know about the crow.

The room went eerily quiet as everyone waited for me to turn around.

When I did, Ramsey was holding a folder in his hand. "There's been an increase in activity from the Night Walkers."

A collective gasp filled the room as Ramsey opened the folder and pulled out a photograph. The Night Walkers were the clan's sworn enemies. Vampires who'd walked the earth before the House of Winterborne even existed. That was our other little secret. The clan had hunted them for centuries. It was our mission. But I'd never actually seen one, having never been on a hunt.

"How do you know that?"

He laid the photo on the table and turned it around so I could get a good look at it. A jolt shot through me as I gazed at a picture of a man with black hair and brooding eyes. It was the man from the memorial service.

Ramsey watched me closely. "This one has been spotted sniffing around the auction house. He's one of their most deadly assassins. A vampire called the Reaper."

"Damn carrion," one of the other Elders muttered.

I continued to stare at the picture. "Does he have a name?"

"I'm sure he does, but we don't know it."

The room buzzed with chatter, and then it went silent as everyone looked to their new leader for a statement. My uncle seemed amused by my attempt to appear confident and authoritative.

I steadied myself and took on the challenge. Blindly, I had to admit, but I had to say something or leave an indelible first impression of a weak young woman who had no business trying to lead. "Do we know what they're up to?"

Cabot hijacked the conversation. "What they're always up to. They want control of this city. They already own Chicago and Los

Angeles, but the Winterbornes have stood in their way of talking over New York. But now that Katherine is gone—"

"They think we're an easy target." I lifted my eyes from the photo to look at him. "Then they're underestimating us. I'm the daughter of the woman who's kept them at bay all these years."

"Until now," Ramsey said.

"Then I guess we'll have to send them a message to let them know the clan is still in charge of this town. Nothing has changed."

A cocky grin appeared on Cabot's face but quickly disappeared. "How do we do that?"

"I haven't figured that out yet, but I will. Right now I need to get to the auction house for a meeting. We'll talk about this later."

"Very well." Ramsey lifted the book off the table and snapped it shut. "You can keep the picture."

"I don't need it. I've seen him with my own eyes. The man in the picture was at the memorial service."

Michael must have realized I was talking about the man who kept staring at me yesterday afternoon, because his expression went from bored to shocked.

"I thought vampires fried in sunlight?" I said as I gazed at the picture on the table and remembered the late-afternoon service.

"That's a little racist," James said. "Lumping all vampires into the same category as your garden-variety bloodsucker." My cousin was ridiculously handsome and charming, quickly putting me at ease with a flash of his brilliant smile.

Cabot clarified the differences. "There are many races. Some have become tolerant of sunlight while others do… *fry* when exposed. This Reaper has obviously evolved." He leaned back in his chair and studied me for a moment. "You'll learn about that soon enough."

With the other Elders in tow, Ramsey headed toward the back of the room.

"Did you hear what I just said? He was at the memorial service."

He replied without turning around. "Yes, we know. Where do you think we took that picture?" Then he slid the book onto the shelf before disappearing through the back wall.

I jumped when Michael placed his hand on my shoulder. "I need to get out of here," I whispered, feeling as if my legs were about to give out.

He must have smelled the fear threatening to unhinge me because he took my hand. "Come on. Let's go before you melt down in front of everyone. Wouldn't want to give Cabot any ammo." He took the picture from my hand and looked at the Reaper's face. "No denying it. Your stalker is definitely a vampire."

As he led me toward the elevator, it all sank in. The responsibility of the entire clan was on me. On *my* shoulders.

Suddenly the scrambled eggs Michael made me for breakfast threatened to come right back up.

CHAPTER 5

I went back up to the penthouse and estimated I had another hour before I had to leave for my meeting at the auction house, which was a good thing because I was still suffering from a mild case of shock over what I'd just signed up for.

It was the same feeling I'd gotten the night before starting my current position at Winterborne Auctions. I'd grown up on the auction floor and had held many jobs there over the years, but when I worked my way up to the position of director of the Rare Objects Division, I couldn't shake the impostor syndrome and barely made it through the front door on my first day. That same syndrome was paralyzing me as I stepped off the elevator and leaned my back against the wall.

"Is something wrong, mistress?"

I laughed at the sound of Otto's voice. "I'm fine, Otto. Thank you."

After taking a deep breath and shaking off my irrational fear, I headed for the terrace to spend a few minutes in the one place where I could clear my head.

The thick humidity and warmth of the conservatory wrapped around me as I stepped into the jungle of orchids and ferns. *Catt-*

leyas, *Paphiopedilums*, and a vast collection of mounted orchids lined every inch of the space. Many of them had been my mother's, and her green thumb had been passed on to me. I used to be more of a collector, but once I started working full time for the auction house a few years back, my time in the conservatory had been limited.

Something had bloomed and filled the air with an intoxicating fragrance that reminded me of jasmine and roses. But it was the smell of earth and water that settled my nerves and brought on a desperately needed feeling of calm. I was an earth sign. My mother used to call me her little seed. Said I needed the garden to grow.

The sound of running water drew me deeper into the tangle of foliage. I parted the giant fronds of the bird's nest ferns and continued toward a spot I hadn't bothered to visit in ages. It was a place beyond the city that really had no name, another realm, the real reason the conservatory was so special.

The deeper I went, the thicker the mist became, and the trickle of water turned into a cascade. Something fluttered against my arm, and a luna moth settled on a wide leaf and opened its large wings. Just beyond it was the waterfall guarded by a stone statue of a frog the size of a Thanksgiving turkey.

My brows furrowed and then arched when I recognized him. "Monoclaude?" The statue's eyes fluttered. "*Monoclaude? Is that you?*"

The surface of the statue began to craze and crack until it resembled an old antique vase. Its eyes moved as if trying to break the stone seal keeping them shut. And then they popped open and looked at me.

"I thought you were dead."

The frog shook himself like a wet dog, sending bits of stone flying in every direction, the debris vanishing into mist. "I feel dead sometimes, but I'm always here, Morgan. You're the one who disappeared."

His skin began to bloom with a bright green color, and I tried to remember the last time I'd seen him.

"Oh my God, it's been years," I muttered to myself.

Monoclaude had been my guide since I was old enough to remember. My advisor and teacher. My mother used to leave me with him for hours, and it took me years to understood why—he was my familiar. But by the time I entered high school, my visits with him had all but stopped. Eventually he just disappeared. At least that's how I remembered it.

"You haven't needed me for a long time," he said, staring at my bare neck. "I see you no longer wear the pendant."

He'd given me the pendant the first time we met. It was an alchemy sign that symbolized transformation. A symbol of our alliance. I'd taken it off years ago when I left for college. And since I thought he was gone, I never put it back on. It was buried in my jewelry box under a mountain of other things I hadn't worn in years.

"I'm sorry," I said, feeling like a fair-weather friend. "I went off to school and…"

"You owe me no explanation. But look at you now. The queen of Winterborne House."

The title made me cringe. "I wish people wouldn't call me that. It makes me feel like a fraud. An impostor."

"Really?" He sounded uninterested in my self-deprecation. "And why is that?"

"Because I don't have a clue how to fill my mother's shoes."

"Perhaps you shouldn't try. Katherine would turn over in her watery grave if she felt you dipping your toes into her Louboutins. Perhaps you should focus on filling your own shoes."

"Watery—" It hit me like a sledgehammer. "You know what happened to her."

His steady gaze sent a chill through me. Then he turned away and muttered something under his breath.

"You're not going to tell me, are you?"

After a few seconds of silence, I realized he wasn't going to say anything more about it. His loyalty to my mother ran too deep because he was her familiar before he was mine. I also knew better than to think I could compel him to talk. That frog didn't do anything against his will.

He shifted around to face me again and started to ball up and shrink. "The darkness is coming for you, Morgan. A threat like no other. Your mother knew it too."

"Threat? What threat?"

His skin began to harden as his eyes grew cloudy and gray.

"I'm sorry I left you before," I said. "I wish you would stay, because I could really use some wisdom right now."

"You didn't leave me, Morgan. You just didn't need me anymore." His voice faded as he started to turn back to stone. "But don't worry. I've found you something better than an old frog."

I left the conservatory with a monsoon of emotions threatening to wreck me for the day. I couldn't believe he was still in there. After all these years, he was still there.

After pulling myself together, I walked back into the house to get ready to leave. I wiped a tear from my face and smoothed my hair into a neat ponytail. Then I decided to change into a more conservative dress. It was time to let everyone know I intended to fill my own shoes.

"Otto, have the car brought around."

"Yes, mistress. Shall I fetch the elevator?"

I applied a bold color to my lips and gave myself a hard look in the mirror. "Yes, Otto. Fetch the elevator. It's time to act the part," I added under my breath. Then I grabbed my bag and left, my nerves kicking in again as I descended to the first floor.

Jakob eyed me as I stepped out of the elevator and headed for the front desk. He got up to hold the door open for me and winked. "You remind me of your mother, wearing that dress. I trust the meeting went well this morning?"

"Well they didn't chase me out with torches and pitchforks if that's what you're asking. So I guess it's time to start looking like a Katherine Winterborne protégée."

He took another look at my dress and shiny pumps. "I'd certainly step out of your way if I ran into you in the hallway."

"I'll take that as a compliment."

He laughed. "Go get 'em, tiger."

As I headed for the car, he called out to me. "How's our little friend doing this morning? Fit as a fiddle or…?"

I started to laugh, but the thought of that giant crow was anything but funny. "Fit as a crow on steroids."

He lost his smile and gave me a questioning look. "Something I should know about?"

"We probably need to talk about that," I said. "The bird has been safely returned to the sky, but we did have a little glitch in the middle of the night. I have a meeting to get to, so I'll tell you about it later."

The driver got out to open the door for me. It was Edward, my mother's private driver. "Where's Louie?"

"He's driving Ethan today," Jakob said. "Edward will be your driver from now on."

I guess I'd inherited more than my mother's title.

Edward spoke up. "If that's all right with you, Ms. Winterborne."

"It's all right on one condition. Stop calling me Ms. Winterborne. It's almost as bad as ma'am. You're fired if you call me ma'am."

He tensed up for a moment.

"I'm kidding, Edward." I shook my head and got in.

As we headed up Central Park West, I tried to focus on my meeting with Wilson Woodard from Estates. As the name suggested, his division handled assets commissioned from clients selling off estates, usually from wealthy, deceased relatives. All I knew was that something had been commissioned with the express condition that I handle the sale of the item personally. It was an unusual request, so my curiosity had been piqued.

We turned onto Seventy-Ninth Street and headed through the park toward the Upper East Side. Traffic was a bear, so by the time we pulled up to the auction house, I was a few minutes late.

Edward parked in front of the building and got out to meet me as I climbed out of the back seat. Then he started to walk me to the revolving doors.

"You don't have to escort me, Edward."

He seemed a little embarrassed and backed off.

"It's nothing personal," I said, smiling to put him at ease. "You'll find out pretty quickly that I'm not big on formalities, but I'd like for you to continue driving me."

He perked up when he seemed to realize he still had a job. "Thank you, Ms.— *Morgan*. Call me when you're ready to leave."

It felt like every person I passed on the way to the elevators was staring at me. I'd been on leave for weeks, and this was the first time I'd been back since my mother's departure. Although she hadn't been declared legally dead, it was assumed by the board of directors and probably every employee in the building.

I got off on the second floor and headed straight for Wilson's office. It was empty when I walked inside. My gaze immediately went to the table near the window and the old wooden box resting on it. With a cup of coffee in his hand, Wilson walked in and nodded to it.

"That's it?" I dropped my bag and jacket on a chair and walked over to take a look at the box. It wasn't unusual for Winterborne's to handle a single item from an estate, but it was usually something considerably more valuable than a wooden box.

He joined me at the table and sipped his coffee as he looked at it. "A longtime colleague of mine was hired to represent the seller. He says it's quite valuable, although I'm skeptical about that. But since the instructions were for you to handle it personally, I thought I'd let you decide if it's worth our time."

The box was about fifteen inches long and half as tall. The grain of the wood twisted and turned in an elaborate flow of symbols that reminded me of hieroglyphics, but they all connected into a continuous design that covered the entire surface as if it had been wrapped in decorative paper.

"Is it carved or painted?"

He handed me a pair of gloves. "See for yourself. The design almost looks like it's part of the wood grain."

"Now that would be unusual. It is beautiful. What is it, maple?"

"I don't think so. Maybe an extinct wood. All I can tell you for sure is that it's very old."

After slipping the gloves on, I ran my hand over the surface to feel for grooves, but it was smooth as silk. "Well it's not carved, that's for sure." I gently turned it on its side and heard something move. "What's inside?"

"That's a very good question. We can't get it open. The lock seems to be a mystery. I had Beth in Antiquities take a look at it, and she can't find the lock either."

"It has to have a lock somewhere," I said, trying to lift the lid myself with no luck. "It's just well hidden." It wouldn't be the first time the auction house encountered a tricky lock on an old trunk or chest.

I took a step back and continued studying it. "A colleague of yours, huh? Who is this client of his?"

"He doesn't know. He was hired by the seller's attorney. Very hush-hush for some reason."

"I guess we can auction it off as a mystery box with its unknown contents inside and let the buyer worry about getting it open." People love the idea of buying a bargain and finding a hidden gem inside. "But if we can authenticate that it's an extinct wood, it could go for a fairly high price to a collector. What do you think?"

Wilson shrugged. "I think I'll be dreaming about what's inside that box for weeks."

"Yeah, me too." Deciding to take another look, I lifted one side and ran my finger under the bottom, hoping to trigger a latch. As I did, I felt something. "What's this?" I turned the box over and stared at the name. MORGAN WINTERBORNE was engraved along the bottom edge.

"Christ," he said, taking a seat. "I swear that wasn't there before, and Beth would have said something if she'd seen it." Wilson was one of the few trusted mortals who knew what we were, so he'd seen some pretty strange things over the years. But my name mysteriously showing up on the bottom of a box he'd previously examined seemed to startle him.

"It's all right, Wilson. I doubt you're losing your mind. Can you ask your colleague to find out who his mystery client is?"

He shook his head. "I already asked him, but the attorney won't say."

I stared at my name engraved on the bottom of the box. "I don't get it. Why would someone do this?"

He let out a heavy sigh. "I suspect the answer is inside that box. I know one thing for sure—it was meant for you."

CHAPTER 6

My first day back at work and I'd spent less than three hours in my office. I didn't even get there until after one o'clock, but what was I supposed to do? Work until seven or eight in the evening with that box staring at me from the table in my office? I certainly wasn't letting it out of my sight.

Edward brought me home around five o'clock. Jakob met me at the car and carried the box inside. It wasn't heavy, but I had my hands full of documents I'd brought home to look over that evening, so he carried it up to the penthouse for me.

"What's in the box," Jakob asked, setting it on the dining room table.

"I wish I knew. It came into the auction house this week and no one can get it open. I thought I'd bring it home and give it a shot." I left out the part about my name being engraved on the bottom because I didn't want him thinking some psycho had left me something dangerous inside, which was a distinct possibility.

He squinted at me. "You're not telling me everything."

"Damn it, Jakob. How do you do that?"

"I'm immortal, and I can spot a lie from a mile away."

I gave him an indignant look. "Are you calling me a liar?"

"Yes, I am. And by the way, you still need to tell me about this *glitch* in the middle of the night with that crow."

I relented and went into the kitchen to get a bottle of wine and two glasses.

"Have a seat," I said when I returned. "This might take a while."

He glanced at the bottle in my hand and then at his watch. "It's a little early for that, don't you think?"

"Don't judge me, Jakob. I've had a strange day, and I still have to get through another six or seven hours of it."

He took the bottle and glasses from my hands and poured the drinks. "Let's start over. What's so special about the box?"

"See for yourself," I said, nodding to it. "Turn it over."

He set his glass down and carefully flipped the box over, its contents shifting inside. "What's this?"

"It's exactly what it looks like. An anonymous client commissioned it with the express instructions that I handle the sale personally. Jesus, they carved my name on the bottom of it. If that isn't messed up, I don't know what is."

"Whoever commissioned the box obviously wanted you to have it."

"My colleague said the same thing. They could have just sent it to me like a normal person."

He got a cautious look in his eyes. "Unless its contents are important enough to ensure that no one else gets their hands on it. Packages do get lost in the mail."

"Let's see if we can find out," I said. "You might want to stand back." Lockpicking spells are nothing special, but my magic had a mind of its own and it was best to give it a wide berth.

Jakob seemed skeptical but decided to comply. The power of the spell involved forcing the intent inside the mechanism of the lock. Not an easy thing to do when I couldn't actually see the lock.

When my attempt to manipulate the lock failed, I poured every ounce of my will into envisioning the lid opening. I pointed to the box and directed my intent toward it, but instead of the lid popping open, the wood began to smoke. "Well, that was humiliating," I said, shaking the excess energy from my fingers.

"That's it," Jakob said. "You're about to incinerate it." He headed for the kitchen and came back out a minute later with a chef's knife in his hand.

"Forget it, Jakob. You're not hacking it up."

"Of course not. I'm going to find that lock." Before I could stop him, he slid the sharp edge of the knife under the lid and ran it along the length of the box, but it slid smoothly all the way across. He pulled it out and scratched his chin. "That's odd. There's no bolt holding it shut."

"Did I mention that our experts at the auction house have already done that? They thought it might be hidden. Wouldn't be the first box we encountered with a trick lock."

He shook his head. "I don't think that's it. I'm starting to wonder if it even has a lock. Something tells me that box just doesn't want to be opened."

If Jakob was right and there was no physical lock, I'd have to resort to something a little more drastic. "Maybe it just takes a different type of key." I picked up the box and headed for the terrace. "Get the door for me please."

He held it open with a bewildered look. "Where are you going?"

"To the conservatory. If I can't open it, I know someone who can."

Without waiting for me to ask, he opened the conservatory

door and followed me inside, through the thicket of giant plants. We continued beyond the mundane walls until the waterfall came into sight. Monoclaude was perched on the boulder where I'd left him that morning, stone-cold and inanimate.

"Is that…"

"Monoclaude? Yes."

Without an explanation, I aimed the box toward the pond beside the waterfall. Jakob instinctively reached out to stop me, but the box flew from my hands, plunging into the water where it sank like a lead weight, leaving only a froth of bubbles at the surface as it descended toward the bottom of the deep pool that appeared deceptively shallow.

He gave me a horrified look. "What did you just do?"

"Put your hand in the water," I said.

After staring at me for a few seconds, he dipped his fingers in the pond. I motioned for him to reach deeper, and he plunged his entire hand below the surface, including the tip of his sleeve. "Now what?"

I shrugged. "Pull it out."

He retracted his hand, and the water disappeared completely from his skin. He did it a second time and stared at his bone-dry hand. "How did you do that?"

"I didn't do anything." I grabbed his wrist and felt his sleeve. "Your shirt is dry too. It's not allowed to leave the pond."

"What's not allowed to leave? The water?"

I nodded and turned back to the pond. "Undines, open it!" The undines were the elementals of water. There were few things capable of outwitting the elemental spirits, and I doubted that box was one of them.

"Mora?"

"Let's see how that box holds up against the forces of nature."

"But it'll be ruined!"

"Look at your hand, Jakob. That box and its contents will be completely dry once it leaves the pond."

The water began to roil, and suddenly the pond erupted into a thick cloud of bubbles. The box was coming back up. We peered closer but stepped back as it broke the surface at the top of a geyser that sent it catapulting into the air. It flew over our heads and landed next to Monoclaude, completely dry and still sealed shut.

I ran toward the box to see if the lid would open, but as I reached for it, the surface began to crack. The wood lost its beautiful old finish and started to turn a dull gray, and within seconds it had hardened. The box had turned to stone.

"No," I groaned.

Jakob walked up behind me and stared at the stone box fused to the same boulder as Monoclaude. He stood there looking dumbfounded, and then he began to laugh.

"I'm glad you think this is funny."

He finally stopped laughing and cocked his brow. "What did you expect, Mora? You don't bark an order at an elemental. You ask nicely."

I glanced at the stone box again before heading out of the conservatory. "Obviously. At least I know it's not going anywhere. I'll show it to Cabot tomorrow and let him try to open it." On my way out, I started to giggle.

"I thought it wasn't funny?"

I held my stomach as I turned to look at Jakob, tears welling up from my uncontrollable laughter. "It's not," I barely managed to get out.

We walked back inside the penthouse and let our laughter subside. "I haven't had a good laugh in weeks," I said, wiping my face. "It feels good."

Jakob gave me a hug. "It'll get better. I promise."

My phone rang as we headed over to the table to retrieve our wine. It was Jules.

∼

I wasn't in the mood for drinking, but it was time to get back to some semblance of a normal life, and Jules had begged me to come out. Since my mother had disappeared, I hadn't allowed myself the luxury of a real night out. There was something about drinking and laughing and actually enjoying myself that made it feel like I was betraying her. Like I'd moved on the second the memorial service was over. But I knew she would want me to live beyond my grief, and tonight I would try.

It was eight o'clock when my car pulled up to the club. Early by New York standards, but I planned to have one drink, maybe two, and then call it a night.

After checking my face in the mirror, I got out and glanced at the long line of people standing out front. One of the luxuries of being a Winterborne was not having to wait to get into popular clubs like this. For some reason I wasn't looking forward to going in there.

Bypassing the line, I headed straight for the door, feeling a little guilty from all the looks I got from the people waiting to get in. "Busy night?" I asked one of the bouncers I knew.

"It's Friday," he said, shrugging. "Your girl's at the bar." He gave me a peck on the cheek and ran his hand slowly down my backside. I didn't mind. He was harmless and not hard on the eyes.

The music amplified tenfold when I walked inside, vibrating relentlessly through my body. It had only been a few months since I'd been here, but I wondered if it had always sounded this obnoxious.

As I made my way toward the bar, I pushed past a group of

guys who reeked of sweat and bad cologne topped off by the stench of beer and cigarettes. One of them decided to grab my ass and tried to slip his fingers into the crack of my thighs. I resisted the urge to ram the heel of my palm into his throat when I whipped around, a move I'd used before. He was just some drunk college kid who wouldn't remember being an asshole in the morning, but he would remember taking a hit to his windpipe. I gave him a look instead that was enough to make him back off.

I turned back to the bar and spotted Jules waving at me. She looked like she was nine feet tall, but then I realized some guy was holding her up in the air so she could get my attention over the crowd. She'd be getting everyone's attention if she fell over and crashed on top of the bar, having had a two-hour lead on drinking.

The bartender handed me a shot of tequila when I finally managed to squeeze my way over. Either he had an exceptional memory or Jules had ordered it for me. I downed it and asked him for another, my first and last drinks for the night.

"Pace yourself, woman," Jules said.

I snickered and leaned my back against the bar to survey the crowd. The music seemed to turn down a notch, but I think my ears were just getting acclimated to the damage being done to them. "Who's your new boyfriend?" I asked, nodding to the guy buried in some other women's breasts, the one who'd lifted her into the air.

"Mike?" She glanced over at him and grimaced. "Hell no."

"Well that's good, because I think you have competition."

Jules was like a chameleon, but instead of changing her clothes or the color of her hair, she changed her preference in men to suit her mood. She went from man buns to Wall Street suits in the blink of an eye and tended to dump her latest quarry as soon as he showed any signs of wanting to stick around. I think her aversion to commitment stemmed from the string of asshole stepfathers who merely tolerated her but loved her mother's money. Mrs. Wells attracted leeches like flies, and it was best for Jules not to get too attached.

My best friend was one of the most confident people I'd ever met—and the most fragile.

The music suddenly cranked back up a notch. Jules downed her drink and slammed her empty glass on the bar, beckoning me toward the dance floor. At first I resisted, but she grabbed my wrist and pulled me into the crowd. I finally let go of everything except the music coming out of the speakers, feeling free for the first time in weeks as the alcohol loosened me up and clouded all thoughts of that box and that eerie crow and the vampires stalking the city. I even forgot to feel guilty for enjoying myself.

I danced through the sea of people with my arms swaying above my head and my eyes closed, scared to open them. Scared to come back to the pain of loss and the pressure of my new reality. When I did decide to finally open my eyes, to see where Jules was, they landed on a guy sitting on top of one of the amplifiers. I wondered how he'd gotten up there, the amplifier being a good ten feet up on the stage. He was just sitting there with a bottle of beer in his hand, his jeans-clad thighs spread wide, making no attempt to hide the way he was watching me.

I swallowed hard as he sipped his beer without taking his golden eyes off me. Who had eyes that color?

He grinned when he saw me looking back at him, and my confidence went right out the window. This guy was *too* good-looking. The kind I preferred to steer clear of.

Without looking back, I left the floor and headed for the ladies' room, more to catch my breath than anything else. I think the day had finally caught up to me, and that damn box was back on my mind. As I rounded the corner to head down the hallway, I slammed into someone.

"Sorry," I said, looking up at a set of golden eyes. "How the hell did you—" *Get around the corner before I did?* I had to crane my neck to see his face, and I was five foot nine.

He took my hands—which were still pressed against his chest from colliding with him—and managed to lace his fingers between mine, intimately, like we were more than complete strangers. Then he leaned closer and took a deep breath.

"What are you doing?" I pulled my hands away and stepped back, startled by the way his touch affected me. "Do you always grab strangers like that?"

I shoved past him and continued toward the bathroom door, looking back before pushing it open. He was leaning against the wall, running his hand over his face like he was catching my scent on his skin. I should have been creeped out, but instead I was on fire. Jesus, I was on *fire!*

He smiled and combed his hand through his spiked blond hair. "I won't hurt you."

"Damn right you won't." I shoved the door open and headed inside. As it shut behind me, I glanced back but he was gone.

I came back out a few minutes later and glanced around the club as I headed for the bar. If he was still there, he'd lost interest in me.

"Where the hell did you go?" Jules asked as she came up behind me and wiped the sweat from her forehead. Her neck-length black hair was plastered to her cheekbones, and her doe-like brown eyes were half-shut from the alcohol. Tall and thin, she reminded me of one of those unconventional models people didn't quite get but couldn't look away from either. Tough but soft underneath her *fuck you* facade.

"Don't get mad," I said as I got ready to burst her bubble and end the evening. I'd put in my appearance, and I was done for the night. "I have to go."

Her shoulders sagged as she slumped dramatically against the bar. "You're dumping me?"

"Yeah, and I'm taking you home." I wasn't about to leave her there half-drunk.

She ignored me and asked the bartender for another drink, but I shook my head to warn him not to. Then I called Edward and steered her out the door.

CHAPTER 7

The sound was muffled, but it was enough to wake me and make me sit straight up in bed. It was a banging noise that sounded like it was coming from the other side of the penthouse. My phone on the nightstand said 2:36 a.m. New York was never quiet, not even in the early morning hours, but the sound that woke me wasn't the familiar white noise of the city.

Slipping on a pair of sweatpants, I listened for a moment to see if I heard it again. The banging continued at a measured pace, dull and repetitive at equally spaced intervals.

On my way to the bedroom door, I opened a small chest on the bookshelf in the corner of the room and pulled out a doubled-edged knife sheathed in a leather scabbard. My athame. I felt a little guilty even touching it, having ignored it for so long. My mother had insisted I own one because every proper witch had an athame, a psychic shield. The fact that I didn't know how to use it properly didn't help, but it was coming with me. I just prayed I wouldn't need it.

As the banging continued, I walked into the living room and glanced around the dark penthouse illuminated only by the city lights. The sound came again from just outside the terrace door. Someone was out there.

With the knife gripped firmly in my hand, I slowly walked across the room toward the door, holding my breath as I reached for the handle. Through the glass, I spotted the door to the conservatory flapping open and shut from the wind.

Relieved, I exhaled my pent-up breath, but a second later my calm vanished. Even unlocked, that door was solid as a rock. The highest winds had never pried it open.

I walked outside and into the conservatory, chilled by the cool, damp air circling me. As I walked deeper into the jungle of ferns, I sensed something foreign, something out of place.

"Monoclaude?"

There was no response as I walked deeper into the inner realm toward the waterfall. The stone effigy of Monoclaude was gone, but the box was exactly where it had landed when the pond expelled it, although it had turned back to wood and was still sealed shut.

I shoved the athame into the pocket of my sweatpants and picked up the box to bring it inside the house just in case it decided to turn to stone again. On my way out, I stayed focused on my surroundings because something still had the hair on my neck standing on end.

When I stepped outside the conservatory, I set the box down to make sure the door was firmly shut. After yanking the handle a few times, I turned around and slammed into someone, then stumbled backward before hitting the ground. The athame flew from my pocket and skidded across the patio before coming to a stop against the terrace wall.

It was the guy with the blond hair from the club.

"What the hell are you doing here?" And how had he gotten up here?

He reached down and offered me his hand, but I backpedaled as fast as I could, glancing at my athame several yards away.

"Just take my hand." His voice was deeper than I remembered, but his eyes were just as bright. "Don't be so stubborn, Morgan. Let me help you up."

"Don't touch me!" I knocked his hand away as I climbed to my feet. Jesus, I couldn't think straight, and a witch who can't think is as good as dead when cornered by a wolf, and this guy smelled of wolves. He was also standing between me and that blade. "How do you know my name," I asked, glancing at it.

He came closer and reached out to touch my hair. I shook it away from his fingers and stepped back. Staring at the spot just below his chest, I directed some well-focused energy at his center of gravity, which should have at least sent him flying backward, but nothing happened.

With his brows knitted tightly together, he glanced down at where I'd aimed, the brightness in his eyes turning dark as he looked back up at me. "Why did you do that? I told you I wouldn't hurt you." His voice was calm, but his words came out with a slight growl—that wolf I'd smelled a moment earlier.

A cold chill ran through me the moment my instincts kicked in. I darted past him and ran for the door.

He grabbed ahold of me around my waist and carried me to the edge of the terrace, pressing me against the short wall that served as a meager barrier between me and the sidewalk below. "You'll forgive me for this eventually, but I can see there's no other way."

The upside-down view of the city was the last thing I saw as he pushed me backward and sent me tumbling over the edge. As I fell toward the street, dozens of images bombarded my mind—my mother's face, the cold concrete below waiting to break my fall, my skull cracking against it, a bird.

Suddenly the wind stopped beating against my face and I

started to fly upward. The air I sucked back into my lungs shocked me into opening my eyes, to see the sky getting closer and to feel something gripping me from behind. It all happened so fast I wasn't sure if it was real or if I'd slammed against the sidewalk and was ascending toward the afterlife.

The answer came when I landed on the terrace with a thud and saw the intruder's reflection in the glass door as he stood behind me. Then the athame caught my eye. It took me less than a second to reach it and another to have it at his throat.

"Who are you?" I demanded. "*What* are you? And don't even think about lying to me, because I'll know."

Without as much as a flinch, he calmly replied, "If you're planning to slit my throat, it won't work. You'll have to take my head clean off."

I pressed the blade harder to his throat, careful not to nick his skin because a witch's athame is forbidden to draw blood. I knew that much about it, but I hoped he didn't. It was a dangerous bluff. "I'd prefer not to cut you open with this blade, but I will kill you if you don't start talking."

"Easy, love. There are certain things you can't take back. Killing me is one of them."

"You haven't told me how you know my name." I continued to hold the blade firmly against his neck, but I had a feeling it was the strange surge of energy coming from my hand that was causing him discomfort.

He winced and let out a weak laugh. "You're the daughter of Katherine Winterborne. Your family has been all over the news since your mother—"

My guard eased up from the shock of hearing him say my mother's name, and the tables were turned. He knocked the athame out of my hand and backed me against the conservatory glass, cupping my jaw with his palm. "Morgan Winterborne. Witch and queen of the House of Winterborne. I knew who you were the second I saw you in that club. I could smell you." He lost his confident grin and stepped back, giving me room to breathe. "But I didn't come here to hurt you."

"You keep saying that, but throwing me over the side of a building says otherwise."

"You're still breathing, aren't you?" He huffed a laugh. "If I wanted to harm you, you'd be plastered all over that sidewalk right now."

Based on his cocky expression, I think he'd actually convinced himself that the death-defying stunt wasn't the act of a psychotic.

"You seem to know a lot about me," I said, my mouth dry. "But you still haven't told me who you are."

He got up in my face again and leaned one of his forearms on the glass, pinning me against it and staring down at me with his obscenely attractive eyes. "My name is Hawk."

"Hawk? What kind of name is that?" I tried to come off confident, but he had me shaking inside. He obviously wasn't human. For all I knew, he'd been sent to kill me by one of the clan's enemies. With my mother out of the way, we were ripe for an attack. Or maybe my power-hungry uncle had resorted to murder.

His eyes grew darker and his chest expanded, nearly touching mine as his breathing quickened. I could feel his power as he hovered over me and inhaled my scent like he had back at the club. And then his audacity emboldened me when he leaned closer and brought his lips so close to mine I could feel his breath.

"Don't even think about it."

He cocked his head and pulled back to look me in the eyes. "Don't flatter yourself."

The light from the sky hit my eyes when he suddenly pulled away from me. I looked up as something black crossed over the moon, turning the sky dark. A moment later the light returned as the shadow passed overhead and continued toward the Hudson River. When I looked back at Hawk, he was gone.

I spotted the box sitting next to the conservatory door and grabbed it before running inside. When I turned around to slam it shut, the giant crow was perched on top of the wall, staring at me with its glossy black eyes. Its wings fanned out a good ten feet as it lifted into the air and headed straight for me. Unable to take my eyes off its talons as they splayed wide and reached toward the open door, I stumbled backward and tripped, hitting my head against something hard.

Everything went black.

~

A WAVE of nausea woke me. My head felt like it was spinning and being punched at the same time. I ran into the bathroom and hugged the toilet, vomiting the drinks from the night before. But since I'd only had two shots, I suspected the nausea was from the throbbing lump on the back of my head.

I climbed to my feet and walked back over to the bed, trying to clear my thoughts long enough to remember what had happened. My T-shirt was soaked and my brain was so foggy I wasn't sure if the memories of the night before were real or if they'd been a bad dream. Then I spotted my athame on the dresser.

A spike of fear hit me square in the chest when I remembered the box. I stood back up and ran into the living room to look for it. The terrace door was closed and locked, and the penthouse looked pristine, but where was the damn box?

"The crow," I whispered, remembering its massive wings sailing across the terrace with its talons aimed at me.

After frantically searching the room, I figured it was gone. Then I heard a little voice in my head telling me it was still in the house. I could feel it. I followed that voice and headed for the kitchen, spotting it on the breakfast table, the lid wide open.

For a few seconds I just stared at it from a distance, terrified I'd find it empty. When I did finally get up the nerve to look, I was surprised to see a book inside. A black leather-bound notebook to be exact. Such a large box for such a small thing.

Lifting it out and setting it on the table, I noticed the blank cover. Before opening it, I grabbed a pair of white gloves from a drawer, a habit from handling rare and fragile books and manuscripts at the auction house, something I should have done before even touching it.

I carefully opened the cover and looked at the inscription on the first page. It appeared to be a journal, and the handwriting nearly took my breath away. The journal on the table in front of me was written by my mother, confirmed by her signature in the upper right-hand corner.

Lost for words and feeling like I'd just been given a rare gift from the gods, I sat down and stared at it, wondering who had opened the box—Hawk or the crow?

CHAPTER 8

Katherine Winterborne
November 20, 1994

It was brutally cold this morning, so I threw a wool scarf around my neck and brought a pair of gloves just in case. When I was at the library a few days ago, my hands nearly froze. Try writing or turning the pages of a book when you can't feel your fingers. The house has been buzzing with visitors for the past week with Thanksgiving only days away, so I was relieved to be able to slip out for a few hours.

I arrived at Columbia U just before noon and headed straight for the third floor of the library. I found an interesting book the last time I was there that delved into Eastern European death rites. It was part of the collection on Magic in Antiquity in the Special Collections section, and it looked like it might provide some information on a matter I've been researching. Unfortunately, the library was closing by the time I found it, so I made a point of getting there earlier today.

With the holiday approaching, the place was nearly empty except for a few people sitting at the other end of the room. After the librarian fetched the book for me, I sat down and found the section that had caught my eye the other day. It was a chapter titled "Contamination of the Dead." I'd seen something about this in one of the other books I researched, but the information was too basic, only containing references to the practice of making sure the dead stayed dead.

Before diving in, I flipped through a few pages and came across a picture of a wild animal. It looked like an unnatural cross between a wolf and a bear, with fangs that dripped blood.

I almost shut the book and changed my mind about reading it, but then I probably would have left and not met the man I'm having drinks with tomorrow. His name is Ryker, and he's fascinating in a dark and dangerous sort of way. The kind of man who doesn't waste words. I thought he worked at the library, the way he navigated the stacks without making a sound, shuffling books around and keeping his eyes on anyone who entered the collections room. I don't know what got into me, but we played a game of eye contact before he eventually came up behind me and peered over my shoulder to see what I was reading. Then he asked me if I wore my scarf and gloves to bed at night. I guess because I was wrapped up so tight in that cold room. Isn't that the most ridiculous line you've ever heard? I nearly jumped out of my skin when I felt his breath against my cheek, but then I got a look at his spectacular eyes and my common sense flew right out the window. I did give him a hard time about sneaking up on women in libraries before inviting him to sit down though.

We talked for at least an hour, so I never did get to read that book. He's an art dealer, of all things. Can you imagine how wide I grinned when he told me that? I could barely contain myself while I let him educate me on the ins and outs of spotting valuable pieces. Halfway through our chat, I finally told him about the family business. I think he was a little embarrassed, but he got over it quickly and invited me for a drink tomorrow night at a club in the Village.

Did I mention that he's gorgeous? Icing on the cake.

It's getting late and I'm exhausted, so that's all for today.

"She was having an affair?" I muttered to myself.

I started the coffee and was about to dive into the next entry of the journal when I heard the elevator door open. "Jesus, I've got to change that elevator code." The courtesy of calling first before stepping into my apartment was a foreign concept to my family. It was my mother's fault. She'd had an open-door policy with the clan—literally. That had to change.

My sister walked into the kitchen with Michael, her symmetrical chestnut bob clinging to her jawline as if glued in place. "Good God, Morgan, what happened to you?"

Avery didn't have a filter, so I was pretty sure she was being completely honest in telling me I looked like shit.

Hawk and that frankencrow happened to me last night.

"Tequila and Jules," I replied. A convenient lie, because I'd left the club long before I could do any real damage with alcohol. I glanced at my brother, who looked a little rough himself. "Don't tell me you two are having breakfast together."

Michael and Avery loved each other, but they didn't actually like each other very much. It probably had something to do with her constant berating of his lifestyle. She was practical and independent, and he was the polar opposite, choosing to supplement his meager income with the family fortune. My sister, on the other hand, would have jumped off the Brooklyn Bridge naked if it would release her from her immortality. She craved a mundane existence, as long as she got to keep her high-paying Winterborne job of course.

"Don't be absurd," Michael said with a smirk. "Avery hates me."

"Not true," she said, narrowing her eyes at him. "If I hated you, I would have drowned you when you were a baby."

"Aww, you two are so sweet together." I forced a grin and tried to shove the journal back into the box before they noticed it and got curious.

It was too late for that.

Avery glanced at the box. "What's that?"

"Nothing." I shrugged and closed the lid.

"Hmm." She pursed her lips, trying to decide if I was lying. But then she mercifully lost interest when she spotted the fresh pot of coffee. "I hope you have soy milk. I've given up dairy."

Michael and I glanced at each other and tried not to snicker. Last month it was wheat. Before that it was anything white like rice or bread.

"Half-and-half is the best I can do."

"Maybe you can pour a little flour in your cup," Michael said. "It'll thicken it up and give it a nice creamy texture."

I admonished him with a look before picking up the box to take it to my bedroom.

When I returned to the kitchen, Avery was gone and Michael was leaning against the counter and glaring at me. "Did she head over to Starbucks to get her soy milk latte?"

"She left, so now you can tell me what's in the box."

Trying to avoid eye contact because he could spot my lies from a mile away, I poured myself some coffee. "It's just a box, Michael."

"You're full of shit."

"Well, that is often true," I said over the rim of my cup. I trusted Michael more than anyone in the family. Our secrets were like a trip to Vegas, and I had enough of his for leverage. "Can you keep your mouth shut to you know who?"

"To whom? Ethan?"

I snorted a laugh. "Especially to Ethan. And Cabot." They'd both barge in here and tear the place apart looking for the box if they knew what was inside.

He tilted his head and did his best to look offended. "I think you know me better than that. So tell me before I beat it out of you."

"I found Mom's journal inside. I was reading the first entry when you two walked in."

He stood there with a puzzled look on his face, like he couldn't wrap his head around the concept that our mother would partake in such a mundane activity like journaling. "Our mother kept a diary?"

"Apparently." I felt the lump on the back of my head starting to throb again when I tried to remember who opened the box and put me to bed. At least I was wearing clothes.

"Are we talking about *the* Katherine Winterborne? The tiger lady? Where did you find the box?"

"Believe me, it surprised me too." I came up with a convenient lie to buy more time. "I was going through her things and found the box under her bed. Just promise me you won't tell anyone about the journal until I have a chance to read it. In fact, I order you to keep your mouth shut."

"Hey, my lips are sealed, but I have just as much right to read it as you do."

"I'll let you read it, but not until I do." I hadn't had time to digest the first entry, but the date on it suddenly fixed in my mind. "Something doesn't make sense," I said, cocking my head in thought. "Do you remember when dad left?"

He thought about it for a second and confirmed what I already knew. "Right after he knocked Mom up with me, so it had to be around 1996. Why?"

"The first entry in her journal talks about her meeting a man at the Columbia University library. She was gushing about him and how they were having drinks the next night. The date was November 1994, but she was married at the time."

"You sure about that? Maybe all that tequila jumbled your brain."

I went to the bedroom to get the journal and show him the date. "See. It was Thanksgiving week, 1994. A year before *I* was born."

"Let me see that thing." He tried to grab it from me, but I held it out of reach.

"Not until I finish it." I shut the journal and sighed. "She was having an affair, Michael. Or at least thinking about it."

He snickered and rubbed a lock of my hair between his fingers. "We all wondered why you were the only redhead in the family."

I mussed his perfectly coiffed head and noted the auburn streaks mixed with brown. "I see plenty of red in here too."

"Love children?" he said with an arched brow.

We lost our grins and stared at each other as the possibility set in. Did we know our mother at all?

Neither one of us had known our father. I'd been a toddler, and Michael hadn't even been born yet by the time he was gone, so while the suggestion was a little shocking, it really had no impact on our feelings for a father we never knew. Just another skeleton in a crowded closet.

"I'm still trying to take it all in," I said. "Jeez, you think you know who you are, and then smack! The rug gets pulled right out from under you."

"Yeah, imagine the scandal if it's true. I guess we should be upset about it, but we never knew our father anyway. And," he said, holding up his index finger, "we don't know if it *is* true. She probably just had a fling with the guy and ended it."

"I can tell you this," I said. "I'm damn sure going to read the rest of that journal as soon as I get a chance, but right now I have to get to work. We're auctioning some rare letters this morning."

He grabbed a banana from the counter and stuffed half of it into his mouth, mumbling something about DNA testing.

"By the way, why are you here?" I asked.

He tossed the other half in the trash and wiped his hands on his sweatshirt. "I ran into Avery on her way out of Cabot's apartment. She said she was heading up to say hello and to tell you that Cabot wanted to talk to you, so I thought I'd tag along. Why? Do I need an invitation?"

"Not you, but a warning before Avery shows up and sucks the oxygen out of the room would be nice." I was only half joking. My sister was one hell of a psychic vampire at times. "I'll call Cabot from the auction house."

"Wise move." He headed for the elevator, probably to go back down to his apartment and sleep for a few more hours.

Before he disappeared around the corner, I asked, "Did Mom ever mention an interest in death rituals, or… voodoo?"

He looked at me like I'd lost my marbles. "Why the hell would you ask me something like that?"

"Forget it. It was a stupid question." Not really. She'd been researching something to do with old magic and the dead.

Michael got on the elevator and headed back down to his apartment, and I headed for the bedroom to get ready, my head swimming with questions. Now I had to deal with Cabot on top of everything else. But first I had an auction to attend.

CHAPTER 9

The halls of the auction house were buzzing when I arrived around ten a.m. Our special auctions always took place on the weekend. This one was much smaller than usual, and it wasn't required that I be there, but I chose to attend for one particular item that could possibly break a Winterborne record. Today's featured item was a set of rare letters written by George Ivanovich Gurdjieff, a Russian mystic who founded the Institute for the Harmonious Development of Man. The auction had been heavily promoted in Europe because of the author's connection to Russia and France, and a bidding war was guaranteed.

"Morning," I said to my assistant, Kerry, dropping a couple of tickets on her desk.

"No! You got them?"

She'd been dying to get tickets for a sold-out show at Madison Square Garden.

I grinned and headed into my office. "Enjoy."

Wilson walked in behind me, rubbing his hands together with a devilish grin on his face. "God, I love this feeling. I can smell blood in the air."

"I take it we have a lot of deep pockets in attendance today?"

He laughed quietly and paced the room. It was his usual reaction to auctions like this. The man lived for the sight of paddles lifting into the air and the sound of excited whispers spreading through the crowd when an item sold for double or triple the reserve price. So did I.

"By the way," he said, his glee turning to curiosity. "How'd it go with the box?"

The question caught me off guard. I had to think for a second because I wasn't ready to tell him what was inside. Finding out that it contained a journal written by my mother would put him in an awkward position because ultimately he reported to Cabot. He'd feel compelled to either convince me to tell my uncle about it or to tell Cabot himself. Why take the risk?

"I haven't figured out how to open it yet, but I'll let you know when I do." I hated to lie, but as long as I wasn't hurting anyone, I could live with it.

"You can't just…" He twirled his finger.

"Wiggle my nose and throw some incantation at it? Sure, if I want to risk destroying it in the process." That part was true.

Kerry stuck her head through the doorway. "The auction is starting in fifteen minutes, and thanks for the tickets."

"You're welcome," I said. "We'll be right down." I took my jacket off and sat down to quickly check my email. "So, who's the heavy bidder today?"

He took a seat and began to brief me on the celebrities in attendance, celebrities meaning the bidders with the most money. "We've got three on the floor, including Jonathan Henderson, who's made it very clear he wants those letters."

"Henderson? I guess we can all go home now." Jonathan Henderson was filthy rich, and he didn't like to lose. At the very least he'd push the bidding past the hefty reserve.

"Not so fast. We have five bidders on the phone and two more on the floor, all interested in the letters."

I glanced up from my laptop. "Oh yeah? I guess our promoting paid off. Who are the other two on the floor?"

He pulled a small notepad from his pocket. "Margo Kemp from Boston and a man named Caspian."

"Hmm. Margo Kemp doesn't stand a chance against Henderson. Who is this Caspian guy?"

Wilson got up and buttoned his jacket. "He's never been here before and no one seems to know much about him other than he's wealthy. All I could find out is that he likes to win as much as Henderson does. A colleague at Christie's in London said he's never lost a bid."

"Did his credit and bank references check out?"

"Spotlessly. No one seems to know where he gets his money from though."

I shut my laptop and stood up. "As long as he's good for it, I don't care."

We took the elevator down to the lobby and headed for the room where the auction was starting, not an empty seat on the floor. I glanced around for our mysterious guest, but I recognized every man and woman lining the front row where we seated our high bidders, the ones who required vetting before allowing them to bid on an item costing as much as a house.

"Where did you seat Caspian?"

He shook his head. "Nowhere. We offered him a seat down front, but he said he preferred to mingle with the crowd. Probably a bidding strategy. You know, throw the competition off because they don't see you coming."

"Or he's trying to keep a low profile. Maybe his money is dirty, so he doesn't want to be seen spending it."

The auctioneer spoke into the microphone to get everyone's attention, and the crowd settled into their seats. The first lot—a rare Patek Philippe pocket watch from the early part of the twentieth century—appeared on the large screen that descended from the ceiling. The bidding opened at one thousand dollars. The watch was estimated to sell for seven times that amount. Paddles immediately started to go up, and a few minutes later, the bidding ended. It went to a phone bidder for nearly ten thousand.

"I need to make a call." I headed for the back room to call Cabot to see what he wanted. With the sound of the auction barely muffled behind the closed door, I dialed his number. "You hear that?" I said when he answered on the first ring, holding the phone up to the noise. "That's the sound of money on the floor. I hear you were looking for me this morning."

"Yes," he replied. "And you only waited two hours to call me."

I ignored his sarcasm so I could get off the phone as quickly as possible. "What is it, Cabot?"

He cut to the chase. "It's time to convene the Circle."

There it was. I'd known it was coming. After taking an appropriate break to mourn my mother's passing, it was time to gather the Circle and get back to business. The business of eradication. I took a steady breath and tried to sound like a leader even though the thought of sitting at the head of a table and planning the hunting and extermination of the enemy sent a cold shiver through me. It would be the ultimate test of my ability to lead the clan, and there was no time for easing into my role as executioner.

"When?" I asked.

"Let's have lunch to discuss it. Say... one o'clock?"

The auction was important, but so was discussing the clan's mission. "I'd like to hang around until we sell the Gurdjieff letters, so let's make it a late lunch. Around two?" Weekend auctions usually took up most of the day, but today's auction was limited to a much smaller number of lots that would be sold within a few hours. The letters were going up for sale sometime after noon, and I didn't want to miss it.

We agreed on the time and place and I hung up, feeling a sudden rush of nerves. Cabot had a way of making me feel small. Immortals were good at that, but I was determined to sit across from him at the restaurant and hide those nerves.

I had about an hour to go back up to my office and try to relax before the letters came up for sale, and then I had to face my uncle. When I reached my office, the door was open, but I distinctly remembered locking it on my way out. I always locked my office on auction days when the building would be filled with strangers and potential office creepers.

"Kerry, did you unlock my door?"

She stood up and shook her head. "I was downstairs for a few minutes and saw it open when I came back up. I thought it was you in there." She frowned and started to fiddle with her hands. "Should I call security?"

The office looked fine. The drawers to the desk were shut, and I could see my handbag sticking out from under it. Maybe I had been careless.

"It's fine," I said, waving it off. "I probably just forgot to lock it."

I checked my bag for my wallet just in case. I found it with all my cash and credit cards still inside.

Wilson walked in a few minutes later. "There you are. I wondered what happened to you."

"I need to relax for a few minutes before the letters come up." I sank into my chair and glanced at him sideways. "I'm having lunch with Cabot afterward. That's who I went to call."

"Ah, I see," he said with a knowing grin. "It's not like you to disappear when the heat turns up, and we just sold a vintage Rolex Submariner—never worn and in its original box—for triple the expected price."

"Well, I would have liked to have seen that."

He glanced at my desk. "What's that?"

I followed his eyes to a small box next to one of the picture frames. It was sage green with a white ribbon wrapped around it. I straightened back up and reached for it, shaking it gently before untying the bow, the sound of pennies or some other small objects rattling around inside. "You sure you didn't set it there and forget about it before we went downstairs earlier?"

He gave me an amused smile. "I think I'd remember misplacing a Van Cleef & Arpels box."

My hand started to shake as I reached for the lid. The week was getting stranger by the second, and I knew I wasn't going to find some loose change in that box. "Here," I said, shoving the box at him. "You open it."

He took it from me and lifted the lid. "Earrings. Very nice earrings." He took them out of the box and placed them on the desk.

I leaned forward and looked at them. There were two rubies on each side, connected by filigree platinum crafted into a delicate design. I knew that because they'd belonged to my mother.

"Morgan?" He placed his hand on my shoulder when I didn't respond. "Are you all right?"

"Someone's playing games with me," I said, still staring at the jewelry. "Those are my mother's."

He gawked at me for a moment. "Katherine's? Why would someone—" He stopped and thought about it for a moment. "Are you sure?"

"I've never actually seen them, but there's a portrait of her in the penthouse. The painting was commissioned before I was born, and she's wearing these earrings. She told me they were custom made for her." I pulled my eyes away from the brilliant rubies and tried to think of who would leave them on my desk and why.

"They're about to auction the Gurdjieff letters," Kerry said, sticking her head inside the door. "In ten minutes."

I snapped out of it and looked at her. "Thank you." Then I put the earrings back in the box and shoved it in my bag as I grabbed it and headed for the door. "Do me a favor and don't mention this to anyone."

Wilson looked confused but nodded. "Of course."

We made it back downstairs just in time for the auction of the letters to begin. Since they'd been heavily promoted and anyone interested in bidding on them already had all the history and background they needed, the auctioneer only gave a brief description before beginning. There was an absentee buyer who opened the bidding at fifty thousand dollars. Having already been outbid, Margo Kemp got up to leave, obviously annoyed at not getting a bargain today.

"This should be fun," I said.

Wilson grunted. "And we're just getting warmed up."

"I have ninety thousand," the auctioneer said, referring to the one remaining phone bidder who decided to throw in a high bid. "Do I have ninety-five?"

Jonathan Henderson raised his paddle with a smug grin on his face.

Henderson barely broke a sweat as his paddle kept up with his rival. The bidding continued until it reached one hundred and fifteen thousand, but eventually the phone bidder dropped out.

"I have one hundred and fifteen thousand. Do I hear one hundred and twenty?"

The auction floor went silent as we waited for the gavel to drop. The letters had already exceeded the estimated price of seventy-five thousand.

"Two hundred thousand," someone said.

Jonathan Henderson's eyes went blank, and I swear he lost all color in his face. A collective gasp filled the room when he started to raise his paddle. But he seemed to come to his senses and changed his mind, lowering it back down to his lap.

The gavel eventually hit the desk when the bidding stopped, and it was over. I looked at the man leaning against the back wall, recognizing him instantly. It was my stalker. The man from my mother's memorial service, the vampire from the picture Ramsey had shown me, had just bought the letters.

"Is that him?" I asked Wilson.

"Yes. That's Ryker Caspian."

My heart began to pound and the sound of the voices in the room muted as I looked over the sea of people.

His name is Ryker, and he's fascinating in a dark and dangerous sort of way.

The words from my mother's journal filled my head as Ryker Caspian stared back at me, his eyes growing darker as a knowing look appeared on his face.

"Morgan?"

I pulled my eyes away from him to look at Wilson. "I have to get out of here."

As I headed for the door, the pounding in my ears intensified. When I got outside, I leaned my back against the side of the building and pulled out my phone to call Edward, but when I looked up, he was parked at the curb.

"Thank God," I whispered as the faint feeling started to subside.

Edward lost his sunny smile as I approached the car. "You're white as a sheet. I should get you home." He opened the rear door and ushered me inside.

"I'm meeting my uncle for lunch." I gave him the address of the restaurant and sank back into the seat, trying to rationalize what had just happened. Ryker wasn't a common name, but in a city with eight million people, there had to be a few.

Edward kept glancing at me through the mirror. "Are you sure I can't take you home?"

"There's no place I'd rather be right now," I said, feeling like the city was closing in on me. "Just take me to the restaurant please." I just needed to hold it together for a few more hours, and then I could go home and look for the name Caspian in the journal.

We pulled up to the restaurant fifteen minutes early, giving me just enough time to down a glass of wine before Cabot arrived.

"Good afternoon, Ms. Winterborne," the maître d' said as I walked inside. He grabbed a pair of menus and headed for a table at the back of the room. "Mr. Winterborne hasn't arrived yet."

"Perfect," I muttered under my breath.

He seated me and placed the menus on the table. "Can I get you a drink?"

"Cabernet sauvignon, please."

A waiter delivered my wine a few minutes later, and I wasted no time drinking half the glass before Cabot walked into the restaurant. My uncle was a handsome man. Tall with the same sable hair as Michael. He had a classical face and some of the bluest eyes I'd ever seen. He didn't need his immortality to attract women, and I was pretty sure he kept a few in the city.

He bent down and kissed me on the cheek. As he sat, he noticed the half-empty glass in my hand. "Am I late?"

"You, late?" I smirked. "That'll be the day." Cabot was the most punctual person I'd ever known. He was the perfect male specimen, and he expected that same perfection from everyone else. I sympathized with his direct reports at the company.

Impatient as usual, he signaled for the waiter the second he sat down. "I'll have the T-bone and a scotch. My niece will have the filet mignon. Rare."

"I'll just have the spring salad," I told the waiter.

"And bring my niece another glass of wine."

"I'm good," I said. I needed to take the edge off, not give him more fuel for the fire by telling the Elders that I had a drinking problem.

After the waiter walked away, Cabot got down to business. "We need to convene the Circle immediately. The Walkers are showing up all over the city. The cocky bastards are getting bolder."

I'd known this conversation was coming, but until now I'd been spared from participation in Circle business. Few mortal clan members actively participated in the hunt, Ethan being one, but my mother had prepared me for years, knowing that one day I'd be sitting right where I was now, with Cabot telling me it was time to serve. The Winterborne clan had one mission as far as the gods were concerned—to live among the mortals and stop the biggest threat to the city—the Night Walkers.

The waiter returned with Cabot's scotch. Then he set a glass of wine in front of me, because what Cabot asked for he always got.

"How did the auction go?"

"Really, Cabot. Small talk? You know exactly how it went." The auction house was probably on the phone with him a second after the gavel dropped. "We made a killing on the letters."

Taking a sip of his scotch, he studied me for a few seconds, unnerving me with his laser-beam stare.

"Jesus, Cabot, what?" I finally said, breaking the tension. "Let up on the staring please."

He finished his drink, and his grin disappeared. "Get used to it. If you can't handle me staring at you, you'll be dead the first time a vampire locks eyes with you."

I shook my head and looked away. "Can you just tell me why I'm here? I need to get back to work."

He laughed quietly, but it sounded bitter. "Work? You're not going back to work today. The Circle is convening tonight, and you're going to need a few hours to pull yourself together and act like you're not scared shitless. You want a bunch of immortals to follow your lead, then earn it!" He was angry, finally showing me all the animosity he'd been harboring since my mother designated me as clan leader.

Two waiters approached the table with our lunch, one carrying Cabot's T-bone and another with my salad and that filet mignon I didn't want, seared for about thirty seconds on each side.

"Can I get you anything else?" the waiter asked.

"We're fine," Cabot said, waving him off.

"You know I'm not going to eat that," I said, irritated by his arrogance and a little shaken by the way he'd just tried to put me in my place.

He leaned over the table and looked me in the eye. "You'll eat every bite of that bloody steak. Then you'll go home and dig as deep as it takes to find the killer inside you. If the Circle perceives you as weak, it's over." He pulled away and grabbed his fork and knife, that patronizing smile on his face again. "Can't have the clan questioning your ability to lead," he said, raising his brow and taking a bite of rare meat.

Looking down at the pool of blood circling the edges of my unwanted steak, I decided to start acting the part by being direct. "By the way," I said, spearing a forkful of my salad while shoving the steak away. "The man who bought those letters this afternoon is a vampire."

CHAPTER 10

Jakob pick up on my dark mood when I walked into the lobby and squinted his eyes at me. "Did something happen, Mora?"

Cabot had put on a real show at the restaurant, nearly getting us kicked out. If we hadn't been Winterbornes, I'm sure his slamming his fist down on the table and berating me in front of all the other customers would have gotten us banned for life. He was furious because I'd failed to call him immediately to let him know about Caspian, but I defused his anger by telling him I hadn't realized who the man was until the auction was over and I was heading out to meet him.

"Have you had lunch yet?" I asked on my way to the elevator. I'd barely gotten a bite of my salad at the restaurant before Cabot laid into me. "Come up to the penthouse with me. I have something to show you."

When we got off the elevator, I headed straight for the bedroom to get the journal. If I couldn't trust Jakob to keep my secret, I couldn't trust anyone. Michael knew about it, but I needed to speak to someone who could advise me on what to do with it. I needed an immortal on my side.

He had a loaf of bread in his hand when I walked into the kitchen.

"Can I trust you?" I asked, knowing it was a ridiculous question.

He dropped the bread on the counter and gave me a pointed stare without wasting his breath on an answer.

"I just need to hear you say it."

"If you have to ask, you shouldn't trust me." He opened the refrigerator and rummaged through it. "Do you have anything besides turkey in here?"

When he pulled his head out and straightened back up, I held out the journal. "I got the box open. This was inside." He stared at it for a few seconds but said nothing. "It's my mother's journal."

"I know what it is!"

I nearly dropped it when he snapped at me. Jakob rarely raised his voice, but today I was on the receiving end of everyone's anger.

"I'm sorry," he said, his face strained. "The sight of it triggered me. I guess I'm not over losing her yet."

I'd never get over losing my mother, and I knew Jakob wouldn't either. But how did he know about her journal? "You've seen it before?"

A long breath shuddered out of him as he rubbed his eyes. "Do you think you're the only child in this building I practically raised? Where do you think she got that journal? Take a closer look at it."

My fingers roamed over the black leather. "Oh wow. I didn't even notice that before." It was the clan's insignia embossed into the grain, so faintly I could barely see it.

He took it from me and ran his hand over the cover. "It was a gift a long time ago. There used to be a shop on Broadway that made custom stationery and journals." He opened it but quickly shut it again and handed it back to me. "Have you read it?"

"Just the first entry. I was planning to read more tonight, but Cabot has called a meeting to convene the Circle. Said it's time for me to serve, so I was hoping you could tell me what to expect so I don't walk in there blind and make a fool out of myself."

He went back to making lunch. "Turkey or turkey?"

"I'll have turkey please, and don't change the subject."

He finished making the sandwiches and offered me one. "You know what the Circle does, and I know your mother prepared you well. What makes you think I can add anything you don't already know?"

I took the sandwich and leaned against the counter next to him. No one ever spoke about it, but our doorman was more than just an indentured immortal who'd worked off his passage to this world by serving the clan. He was a tracker. A hunter with the ability to sniff out a Walker before anyone saw it coming. Jakob was a legend, and then one day he wasn't anymore.

"You were one of them once." I shrugged and walked over to the sink to pour a glass of water. "Come on, Jakob. You know I don't have her killer instincts. Can't even step on a bug. Cabot and Ethan will have a field day with me tonight."

He joined me at the sink and wrapped his arm around my shoulders. "Your uncle and brother are ambitious, but they love you."

"But they don't respect me."

"Then make them. Show them what you can do." He walked over to the large glass bowl on the breakfast table at the other end of the kitchen. "Show me what a little fire starter you are. Go on, Mora. Start a bonfire in that bowl."

He used to call me that when I was a kid because I'd had a bad habit of nearly burning the building down on occasion. Not on purpose. I discovered my talents early, but it took a while to understand that starting blazing fires in the middle of the living room was inappropriate. I was six when I destroyed the sofa and finally made the connection between fire and devastation. That was when my mother introduced me to Monoclaude, who'd put the kibosh on my fire skills. To this day, I've never gotten them back.

"Don't waste your time, Jakob. I couldn't light up the kitchen if I tried."

He looked like he was about to drop the subject, but suddenly he clenched his teeth and reared back, twisting his hand as if he were gripping an object. Then he flung something at me, a ball of flames that grew as it hurtled across the kitchen toward me. My instincts kicked in, and I raised my own hand and released a sphere of light that collided with the fire. I just stood there staring at the wall of flames that it created between us in the middle of the kitchen. The fire reached the ceiling and spread to the north wall, racing down to the floor.

"Stop!" I yelled, instantly extinguishing the flames before they could spread and destroy the kitchen. My hands wouldn't stop shaking. "I think you just undid twenty years of mastering control over my pyromania. I could have burned the place down."

"But you didn't." He had a surprised look on his face. "It looks like your fire skills have evolved. It appears you're an energy witch now."

I glanced at my hand and remembered the strange feeling I'd gotten when I held my athame to Hawk's neck the night before. It was like a surge of power. A surge of energy.

"Don't ever let them forget who you are," Jakob said, his voice stern. "You are Morgan Winterborne, queen of the House of Winterborne. Just now, you did exactly what you needed to do to defend yourself, because you're *just* like your mother."

He winced briefly and pulsed his hand as if releasing the

excess heat that must have burned in his palm. "You've unlearned too much in this mundane world. We do our children a grave disservice by numbing them to the magic they're born with, and it's time you got yours back."

I glanced at my hand again. "Where do I start?"

"Right there," he said, nodding to the scorched ceiling. "I thought it would be harder to provoke you though."

"So you planned this?"

For a moment he just stared back at me with his brow pulled tight. "Did you think I would let you walk into that den of lions with nothing but a pep talk and a few pointers? You *must* wake your killer instincts, Mora."

"Funny," I said with a slight laugh. "Cabot said the same thing at lunch today. He just wasn't as nice about it as you." I headed for the living room, shaking my head.

Jakob followed me. "He's right. You'll find that out tonight when the Circle convenes. In fact, I'm sure they have something planned that will erase any doubt about that." He took my hand and traced the lines of my palm. "You're a kind person, Mora, but you were born to be an executioner. That's the price for all this." He motioned around the penthouse, with its elegant interior and Central Park views.

The building, the auction house, the money. It was all payment for the clan's services. Compensation from the gods for ridding the world of devils.

"Some people would say those two traits can't coexist. But make no mistake, you can be kind and a killer. Your mother was. And don't forget for a second what the enemy is. They're abominations that wouldn't think twice about killing every member of this clan. Man, woman, or child!"

I pulled my hand away and took a deep breath. "You're right, but I'm still not looking forward to it." Most of the clan couldn't wait to reach majority so they could join the Circle. The only reason I was being admitted prior to my thirtieth birthday was because I was now the head of the clan and expected to participate in the hunt. I was one of the few mortals allowed in, Ethan being the other because his transition was only a few months away and the Circle needed new blood. It was time to accept my responsibility and make sure I didn't get myself killed.

Thank God for Jakob and his provocation of my dormant power.

"So," he said, taking a seat on the sofa. "Tell me about the crow."

"Is that what it is?" I muttered.

He lost his smile. "What do you mean?"

"I mean I think we've created a monster. It showed up last night and nearly came through the terrace door after me. That bird is huge!"

"Did you provoke it?"

I didn't dare tell him about Hawk showing up on the terrace and the crow appearing out of the blue to chase him off. "I didn't do anything to it. I was leaving the conservatory last night and it was perched on the wall. I ran inside and shut the door before it got in." I was getting good at lying, which I wasn't proud of.

"Well, if it wanted to harm you, that door wouldn't have stopped it."

I glanced at the terrace door. "You don't think it would have shattered the glass, do you?"

He shook his head. "It wouldn't have to. My blood is inside it, so it's immortal. It would have passed right through it."

Now I really wondered which one of them had opened the box and put me to bed the night before.

"Call me next time it shows up."

"I was hoping it *wouldn't* show up again."

"I'm afraid it will. Immortality can be a jarring experience when it's fresh. Another immortal is usually there to help navigate through the transition. That bird seems to be confused. I can help it find its way."

Otto's voice suddenly carried across the room. "A letter has arrived for you, mistress. It's on the table in the foyer. Shall I read it for you?"

"I'll read it myself, Otto. Thank you."

I got up and retrieved the envelope that had mysteriously appeared on the table. Inside was a card with a handwritten note. "I've been formally invited to the Circle meeting tonight," I said, looking twice at the location. "It says we're meeting in the grand suite at eight o'clock." The grand suite was where my grandparents lived. They'd been in the Winterlands for the past month, mourning my mother's death, and as far as I knew they were still there. "This can't be right."

Jakob took the card from me and read it himself. "I guess they're back."

You didn't just come back from the Winterlands like you were hopping on a plane and returning from Palm Springs. It took time to come back. The Winterlands existed on the astral plane. It was a place of mourning where immortals went to heal and grieve. But the choice to go there was never taken lightly because there was no guarantee of ever getting out. When you entered the Winterlands, you left your immortality at the gate, often requiring the help of another immortal to get you out. But there was no other place in the universe where you could shed torturous grief that threatened to destroy you, and my grandparents had been gutted by the loss of my mother. Against the clan's advice, they'd chosen to take the risk.

"Why didn't anyone tell me?"

Jakob handed the invitation back. "I'm sure Cabot didn't want to get your hopes up. You know the odds of coming out of that place. He probably wanted to surprise you."

"Well, he succeeded."

He got up to leave. "I guess I should be getting back down to the lobby before a band of thieves wanders in and ransacks the place. I'll just clean up the mess in the kitchen before I leave."

I laughed. "Yeah, right. A very unfortunate band of thieves if they pick this building to vandalize." We had no need for a doorman, but Jakob refused to accept his room and board without earning his keep. As far as I was concerned, he was family and could live here as long as he wanted, free of charge.

"Never underestimate the power of stupidity."

I beat him to the kitchen. "You cooked; I clean." I shooed him away from the counter. "Now get out of here."

"It was a turkey sandwich," he said, tying the bread bag. "I didn't even put mustard on it."

"Exactly. There's no mess to clean."

I wish I could have said the same for the ceiling and walls. Of all the magical talents we Winterbornes had, I couldn't think of one of us who could fix the place without calling a contractor.

I tossed the turkey in the refrigerator and walked Jakob to the elevator. "When's our next magic lesson?" I asked as he stepped inside.

After a moment of chuckling, his face went somber. "Are you planning to tell Cabot about the journal?"

"That's funny. I lured you up here for lunch to ask your advice about that very thing. But I think I've already made up my mind. Michael knows about it, but I'm going to wait awhile before telling Cabot or anyone else. I'd like to actually read it before he confiscates it."

He sighed, looking relieved. "Promise me something, Mora. Promise me you won't show it to Cabot until you've read it. All of it."

CHAPTER 11

※

Katherine Winterborne
November 22, 1994

I've gone and done it now. I'm officially a bad person. I guess I'm being overly critical of myself, but technically I'm still a married woman. Phillip has been out of the apartment for months, but I was raised to honor my marriage until the divorce is final. That might be difficult to do with Ryker though. Does a hand on another man's arm count as adultery?

Ryker and I went to the most interesting bar last night. When I met him in the Village, he suddenly changed his mind and suggested something different. Imagine my reaction when he hailed a cab and gave the driver an address on 121st Street. When we got out and headed down a dark stairwell, I thought he was taking me to someone's basement. But then I heard music and my nerves settled. I would have hated to put him in his place with a little magic before I even had a chance to get to know him.

We drank bourbon all night, and I actually smoked a cigar! Well, I took a few puffs and handed it back to the gentleman sitting to my right at the bar, a lovely man who later got up and played the saxophone with the band. God, it was fun!

At the end of the night, Ryker got me a cab and was the perfect gentleman. The man didn't even try to kiss me, which was a bit of a disappointment. It probably would have just made me feel even more like a wanton woman, but I wanted that kiss.

I'm seeing him again this weekend, after Thanksgiving. I thought about it all night and let guilt do a number on my head. I almost called him this morning to tell him I couldn't see him again, but I can't stay away. I have to see him. I've never felt like this before. No man has ever made me feel the way he does. I know it's only been a couple of days, but Ryker Caspian has put a spell on me.

I read the sentence one more time to make sure I wasn't seeing things. If there was any doubt that the man who'd been following me was the same man my mother had an affair with twenty-six years ago, it was gone now. The most shocking part was knowing he was a vampire, which explained his youthful appearance after all these years.

Had she known?

My phone rang as I turned the page to continue reading. It was Jules.

"You're not going to believe what just happened," she said without a greeting. "Your stalker walked into my shop a few minutes ago."

Jules had passed up a college education and opened a vintage clothing boutique down on Broome Street in the East Village, funded by her rich mother for the first couple of years. It was a lot cheaper than Harvard and all the other Ivy League schools she'd been accepted to. If you needed a leather jacket or a T-shirt with some interesting history attached to it, you shopped at 6Seven8, a reference to her favorite decades, even though she wasn't alive during any of them. I was convinced she was the reincarnation of some dead rock star from the seventies.

Ryker Caspian?

It took me a second to find my words. "The guy from the memorial service?"

"Yep. The same guy."

That meant a vampire was in her shop, and she was in danger. "Jules, you need to get out of there right now."

She huffed into the phone. "Please. No one's chasing me out of my shop. Besides, he seems pretty harmless to me."

"Seems? Is he still there?" I whispered.

"Why are you whispering? You think he can hear you?" It made her snicker. "Don't worry, he's long gone. Didn't buy anything either, but he left *you* a gift."

"Me? What is it?"

"I'm walking into your building right now, so you can see for yourself."

I hung up and sat down, stunned. I was easy to track down. With the clan's name on the building, everyone knew where the Winterbornes lived, but he also knew where to find my best friend. This whole thing was spinning out of control.

"Ms. Robbins is on her way up."

"I know, Otto."

When she walked into the living room a couple of minutes later, I blurted it out. "He's a vampire."

She dropped her bag on the coffee table and headed for the kitchen. "Got any wine?"

"Did you hear what I just said?"

"Yeah. Hence my need for alcohol." She came back out with two glasses of wine and handed me one. "He does kinda look like a vampire. You know, with his dark hair and eyes. Sun doesn't seem to bother him though."

"I'm not kidding, Jules. He's a card-carrying vampire."

She took a sip of her wine before digging into her bag to retrieve a small box. "I peeked," she said, handing it to me. "Congratulations." My first name was written across the top in perfect calligraphy. "He didn't say a word. Just handed it to me." She guzzled the rest of her wine. "The guy's got some creepy eyes."

After hesitating for a moment, I opened it. There was a ring inside. "What the hell is this?"

She shrugged and sat down on the sofa. "A proposal?"

"That's not funny, Jules." I took it out of the box to get a better look at it. "And since I'm pretty sure he had an affair with my mother twenty-six years ago, that would be *so* wrong."

"What?"

I spared her the details about the box that mysteriously showed up at the auction house, but I told her about the journal and what I'd read about Ryker. "She was married to my father at the time, but she mentioned that they'd been separated for months."

"Let me see that thing." She grabbed the ring and looked at it closely. "It's probably white gold, and I'm guessing the stones are rubies."

"It's platinum." I got up to fetch the earrings from my bag. The filigree design matched the carving of the ring perfectly. "These were my mother's, and someone left these on my desk at work this morning in a box with a bow." I walked over to the painting hanging on the living room wall. "See. She's wearing them in the painting."

Jules joined me to see for herself. "Yeah. They're definitely the same earrings."

"It was him, Jules. His name is Ryker Caspian, and he paid two hundred thousand dollars for a set of rare letters at the action house today."

∼

I KNOCKED on the door of the grand suite a few minutes before eight o'clock. When the door opened, a strange woman was standing on the other side. "I'm looking for— Who are you?"

The old woman gave me a wide smile. "Morgan!"

"I'm sorry," I said, sidestepping her outstretched arms to look over her shoulder at the group of people in the living room. "Do we know each other?" She had to be in her late sixties or early seventies and had a familiar look in her eyes.

She chuckled and put her hands on her hips. "Don't you know your own grandmother?"

"Uh…"

"Is that Morgan?" An elderly man joined her at the door, and this time I couldn't avoid the onslaught of hugs.

They pulled away and looked at each other.

"She doesn't recognize us," the man said.

"Well, of course she doesn't." The woman stepped aside and invited me in. "It's Grandma and Grandpa. We're just a little older now."

Ethan walked up and handed me a glass. "We're having champagne to celebrate their return."

"Can someone please explain what's going on?" I said, happily taking the champagne flute. Like every other immortal in the clan, my grandparents had stopped aging in their thirties, so while these two people had familiar eyes, they definitely did not look like Grandma and Grandpa.

"That's the problem with the Winterlands," the man said. "You leave your immortality at the gate. Every day—every minute really—that you stay there, your mortality starts to catch up with you."

The woman shook her head. "I looked at my husband one day and barely recognized him. That's when I took a good look at my hands and realized we needed to get out of there before it was too late. Mirrors are forbidden in the Winterlands for a reason." She leaned in and whispered, "They like to keep people."

The man—I mean my grandfather—continued. "Steep price to pay for lifting grief. We had no idea how quickly it would happen. No disrespect for the land of sorrow eaters, but I think that's exactly what they intend to do when you enter—feed off your residual immortality until there's nothing left but your old, mortal bones."

"You'll get used to looking at us old farts," my grandmother said with a grin.

If it didn't bother them, which it clearly didn't, it didn't bother me. I kind of liked the idea of having grandparents who actually looked like grandparents.

Ethan took a sip of champagne and pointed at them. "I warned them not to go. The Elders managed to get them out just in time. Another week and they'd have probably been dead."

I followed them to the living room where everyone was congregating. Cabot was deep in conversation with Ramsey and my cousin Olivia, and James was sitting by the window with some guy who looked a little dazed and confused by whatever they were discussing. Knowing my cousin's over-the-top presence, I suspected the poor man was just trying to keep up with James's overwhelming mind dump of a conversation. He was probably reciting his thoughts on ceremonial magic or some other pet topic he liked to expound on to unsuspecting victims.

James and Olivia's father, my uncle Samuel, lived in Edinburgh, Scotland, but my aunt Charlotte had stayed behind with the twins. She was quiet and shy, not at all like her children, who were usually the life of the party. You'd think they were Cabot's children. But he had a child of his own, a daughter with some serious magical abilities. Even at nine years old, Georgia could put most of us in our place if she ever developed half of her father's ambition, which I think we all secretly prayed she wouldn't. That child was a force. Dangerous if guided in the wrong direction.

And then there was my aunt Rebecca, Cabot's wife. Now there was a woman with ambition. Rebecca enjoyed living like a queen. In fact, her father was the head of a prominent clan that controlled Paris. If she'd been married off to a French immortal, she'd probably be a queen today, and I never lost sight of her ambitions for her daughter. Neither had my mother. I think that's why she insisted on naming me as her successor before I reached majority. Had she died without naming me, Cabot would have stepped into the role while his wife quietly groomed Georgia to someday rule the clan.

Knowing that Rebecca wouldn't miss a gathering of the Circle, I wondered where she was. She'd been conspicuously absent from the meeting to formally announce me as the new head of the clan, and I hadn't heard from or seen her since the memorial service.

Right on cue, she walked into the living room with a bottle of Dom Pérignon dangling from her hand. She was wearing a tight red dress that hugged her perfect figure and matched her lipstick. Her blond Hollywood-glam hair fell over her shoulders like lacquered waves that barely moved as she walked toward me with a forced smile.

"Don't you look lovely," she said, giving my conservative slacks and blouse a once-over. "I'm sorry I missed the council meeting yesterday morning. I hear it was eventful. Your first day as queen and you're already spotting the enemy."

I would have preferred a snub rather than her condescending greeting.

"Don't worry about it," I said, waving it off. "There'll be plenty more for you to attend."

We locked eyes for a moment before she raised the bottle to my glass. "I couldn't take another drop of that Bollinger swill. Would you like some real champagne?"

"I'm fine," I said, taking a sip from my full glass.

My grandfather headed for the terrace door when the Elders appeared on the other side of it. It wasn't necessary for them to wait for him to open it, but as a courtesy they rarely let themselves into someone's house without an invitation. The Elders were long past the point of needing doors.

"Good," my grandmother said. "We can start now. Who's hungry?"

Apparently we were having a dinner meeting, which was fine with me because I was starving.

We followed them into the dining room and headed for our usual seats. "Not there, Morgan." My grandfather pointed to the chair at the head of the table. "That's your chair now."

I hesitated. My mother had never sat at the head of the table in her parents' house, and neither would I. It was disrespectful. I sat down next to my grandmother before Grandfather could make a fuss over it.

"Very well." He reluctantly took the seat I refused to sit in and motioned for the stranger James had been chatting with to sit directly across from me. "Mr. Miller, this is my granddaughter. She runs the place."

Rebecca's eyes threw daggers at me when I glanced at her

across the table. "It's nice to meet you," I said to Mr. Miller, who was seated next to her. "I'll shake your hand when we don't have a table between us." Everyone laughed at my comment, which wasn't really funny. "How do you know my grandparents?"

He opened his mouth, but nothing came out. The man's eyes looked dazed, the same way they had when he was having that conversation with James.

"Mr. Miller has agreed to help the Circle," my grandfather said with a cheerful smile. "But we'll get to all that later. First we eat."

I leaned over to Ethan, who was sitting on my other side. "Where's Charlotte?" Of all my relatives, my aunt Charlotte was one of my favorites. She was kind and had been a good friend to my mother, nothing like the woman glaring at me from across to table.

"Are you serious? Aunt Charlotte is an empath. She'd lose her mind sitting through a Circle meeting."

How had I not known that? "An empath? Why hadn't anyone ever told me?" All those times I'd gone crying to her with my adolescent problems, and I had no idea she was absorbing all my angst and suffering right alongside me. "Jesus, I feel like shit now."

The housekeeper pushed a cart of food into the dining room and placed a platter of carved roast chicken on the table. My grandfather got up to help her and placed a second serving platter at the other end. After they finished loading the table with sides and bottles of wine, Rita pushed the cart back to the kitchen and returned with one more dish. This one was covered by a silver dome and placed between Mr. Miller and me.

"Bon appétit," my grandmother said, shaking out her napkin before placing it in her lap. She served me a few slices of chicken, signaling for everyone to help themselves.

Never one to ignore my curiosity, I reached for the covered platter. "What's this?"

"That's not for you," my grandfather said, grabbing my hand before I could lift it.

He left it at that, and I filled my plate with glazed carrots and mashed potatoes, eyeing the platter with an urge to rip the cover off. Maybe Mr. Miller had special dietary requirements and I'd just rudely reached for his dinner. He never touched it though. In fact, his plate was empty.

"Not hungry, Mr. Miller?" I couldn't resist asking.

Cabot cleared his throat. "Unless anyone has a particularly strong aversion to discussing business while we eat, I suggest we begin."

"No objection here," James said. "I have another meeting after this."

Olivia raised a carrot to her lips. "What's the poor girl's name?"

James had a "meeting" every night. He was ruthless in his pursuit of human females who could satisfy his monstrous libido, which had only grown stronger after his transition. Unfortunately, a mortal woman was no match for him, so he left an endless trail of happy victims while he searched for his Aphrodite.

Cabot continued. "We have a crisis in the city. The Night Walkers are multiplying like flies."

"How do you know that?" Ethan asked.

"The clan's connections at the NYPD have confirmed that the number of missing-person cases has gone up tenfold over the past six months. A small percentage of them have turned up as runaways or estranged family members. And of course there will always be a good amount of mundane murders in a city the size of New York. But the bottom line is there's a ninety percent rise of missing citizens that the police can't explain."

I decided to speak up, if for no other reason than to feel

useful. "That's a pretty suspicious increase, but what makes you think it's due to vampires and not some other supernatural threat?"

"Perhaps Mr. Miller can answer that question." We all looked at my grandmother as she spoke and then turned our attention to the mystery guest at the table. "Are you hungry, Tom?"

He looked at her, and for the first time since I'd noticed him sitting across from James, he seemed capable of holding a conversation. He nodded, his Adam's apple bulging as he swallowed and stared at the covered platter.

"Good." She stood up and slowly pushed the platter toward him. "A man like you needs to eat." She lifted the lid, revealing a lump of something dark and red that looked like raw meat. It smelled of iron.

Tom Miller couldn't take his eyes off it. His breathing grew rapid as he salivated and visibly forced himself to sit still. A tiny whimper slipped from his mouth, and he looked at my grandmother with desperate eyes.

"It's all right, Tom. Dig in."

He lunged for the plate, digging his teeth into what I suspected was organ meat. He ripped at it and swallowed whole chunks, his fingers covered in blood. Everyone watched with repulsion as he devoured it. Everyone accept Rebecca, who seemed to be enjoying the sight. She really was a cold bitch.

He wheezed as he took a breath, his body finally coming up for air. Then he looked down at his bloody hands and shirt and started to cry.

My grandmother grabbed a cloth napkin from the sideboard and handed it to him. "You did good, Tom. Remember, it will all be over with very soon and your family will be well taken care of."

As I watched the poor man cry, I reached my breaking point. "What is this?"

"This?" Cabot said, standing up and heading for one of the bedrooms. A horrible sound came from the hallway as he returned, dragging something behind him. He tossed another man across the dining room, where he landed next to Tom. The man's eyes were blood red, and he hissed like a cat as he struggled against something invisible that seemed to bind his arms to his torso and restrict his legs. "That thing on the floor is a Night Walker, and Tom here is about to become one."

Ethan barked out a laugh and then grimaced. "We interrupted him while he was dining on Tom the other night." He walked around the table and hovered over our guest, reaching for the front of Tom's buttoned shirt to rip it open. There was a gaping hole in the center of his chest where his heart had been removed. "We just fed Tom his own heart."

"You ripped his heart out?" My legs went weak as I fought faintness.

Ethan scoffed. "No. That thing over there ripped it out." He nodded to the struggling vampire on the floor, who was clearly bound by some kind of magic.

As I fought the nausea roiling up from my stomach, Ethan coaxed Tom out of his chair and started to lower him to the floor next to the bound vampire. "Remember what you're supposed to do now."

Tom started to backpedal, but Cabot came up behind him and blocked his escape. "It's the only way out, Tom." He bent down and rested his hand on Tom's shoulder and whispered something in his ear.

Tom took a few gasping breaths and then threw himself at the Walker. The vampire sank his teeth into Tom's neck and made a series of desperate sucking sounds that were only muffled by Tom's screams.

I turned away, unable to watch. A few seconds later, Tom's wails ceased and the vampire let out a sound that defied anything

I'd ever heard before, something between a hissing scream and a gasp for air that pierced my ears and forced me to look. The vampire was on fire. The flames reached the twelve-foot-high ceiling as the creature flailed back and forth and began to roll across the floor. A few seconds later, the fire became a flicker and the vampire was reduced to a pile of ashes on the dining room rug.

My grandmother sighed and shook her head. "Shame about that rug. I'll never find another one like it." She walked over to Tom's still body and gently closed his eyes. "You did good. We'll make sure your children are taken care of." She straightened back up and looked at me. "Mr. Miller was a victim. Once that Night Walker drained him and ripped his heart out, it was only a matter of time before he turned. We gave him a choice of how he wanted to end it. He could help us kill the thing, or we'd have to kill him once he became one of them. He chose to help us in exchange for financial security for his family."

Cabot bent down to examine the body. "I'll have the funds deposited into his widow's account by morning."

My grandfather patted me on the back. "I'm sorry we didn't warn you, sweetheart, but some things have to be seen with your own two eyes. This is what it means to be a Winterborne. It's what we do."

I looked back at Tom. "What killed the vampire?"

"We starved him for a couple of days so we knew he'd go after what little blood was left in Tom's body. His hunger was uncontrollable. Then we laced Tom's heart with a little banshee blood. Hard to come by, but it's one of the few things that will kill a Walker. Once Tom ate it, so did that vampire."

"That was an awful lot of work to kill a single Night Walker," I said, still staring at the mound of ashes on the rug. "No wonder their numbers are growing."

Her forehead scrunched. "Darling, this little show was for

you. There are much easier ways to kill a Walker, decapitation being one. But I prefer to ruin a single rug than to spend the entire evening scrubbing the walls."

"What will we do with Tom's body?" I asked, morbidly curious about how they planned to get rid of it.

"We'll have someone weight it down and dump it in the ocean," my grandfather said. "I know it sounds disrespectful, but it'll be much kinder to his family to think he's missing than to find out some monster ripped his heart out."

We all sat back down, and everyone finished their dinner, not the slightest bit put off by the dead body and the pile of vampire ashes at their feet.

CHAPTER 12

Were we as bad as the monsters we were hunting? Or were we just hardened or numb from all the killing? I was beginning to wonder what I'd be like a year from now, after I got a good taste of blood. A queen was expected to make sacrifices. Do whatever it took to serve her people, and this clan was my kingdom. But I couldn't get that man's face out of my mind. I had to force myself to remember that he wasn't a man anymore—he was about to turn into a monster. He might have even gone home and killed his own family if we hadn't stopped him.

As I headed for my bedroom to get the journal, I caught something moving past the window from the corner of my eye. It was just a flicker, but the hair on the back of my neck stood up. When I looked outside, I noticed the conservatory door was ajar. The wind had picked up and must have blown it open again. It was also starting to rain.

"I've got to get that door fixed," I muttered as I headed outside, my power hand itching from the heat building in my palm.

The door slammed shut behind me as I ran inside the steamy

conservatory. The glass fogged up quickly, and the scent of jasmine filled the air as the orchids released their night scent.

I headed deeper until I reached the waterfall, but Monoclaude wasn't in his usual spot on top of the boulder. "Where are you, frog? Why didn't you warn me about the Circle?" He had to have known about what I'd witness at the meeting, so could have at least prepared me for it.

"You know exactly what your people do."

I looked to my left and spotted him at the edge of the pond. "Yes, but I didn't expect to see my grandmother feed a man his own heart. I thought we just—"

"Killed them nicely? Politely drove stakes through their hearts quickly and cleanly?"

"Yes," I said. "There are kinder and more humane ways of killing vermin."

"Wake up, Morgan. The Winterbornes have been ridding the world of vampires for centuries. Develop a heart of stone, or you'll find yourself on the receiving end of a very sharp set of fangs. Bring it out for the kill but learn to shove it back inside when the deed is done. Now that's the sign of a queen."

I got a disturbing image of my mother in a pink Chanel suit, standing over a man with his bloody heart resting in the palm of her hand. Then I thought about all the times she'd come home late at night after a hunt with bloodstains on her clothes and debris in her hair. She'd head straight for the shower and come out half an hour later, looking good as new. My mother was a killer.

"Make no mistake, Morgan. It's us or them. They die, or all of New York dies."

A long breath shuddered out of me. "I just wish I had my mother's stomach for it."

He cocked his head and stared at me with his gold-speckled eyes. "You stayed to watch, didn't you?"

"Did I have a choice?"

"You're the queen. You have more choices than any of us. Do you think your mother did what she did because she had no choice? Don't be naive. Katherine Winterborne chose to be a hunter."

The revelation hit me hard. Maybe there was a killer inside me, inherited from my mother.

Monoclaude hopped on top of the boulder, his green skin fading to gray. "Choose, Morgan. A hunter or a safe queen in her castle. Now leave me to rest, and go find that crow."

"Wait! What about the crow?"

He hardened to stone faster than I could get him to answer me, but I had a feeling I knew what he meant. God, I hoped not.

The wind began to batter the sides of the conservatory as I made my way out. As I approached the door, I noticed a shadow standing perfectly still outside in the storm. The door flew open and I ran to shut it, not knowing who or what was out there and too wary to find out.

As I tried to pull it shut, someone reached inside and grabbed me around my waist, dragging me out into the pelting rain. I tried to raise my hand to release the magic building in the center of my palm, but my arm was trapped between us. I struggled harder and flew back against the conservatory glass.

"You!" I growled when I regained my balance and blinked the water away from my eyes. Hawk was standing a few yards away.

I raised my hand and hurled a ball of light at him, but he ducked and let it sail into the storm.

"*Stop!*" he said with a force that got my attention as I raised my arm for a second attack.

For reasons I couldn't fathom, I dropped my hand and looked around. The storm continued to rage, rain pelting the terrace like shards of glass spit from the sky and lightning cracking across the horizon. It was all around us, but the space we occupied was dry, calm and quiet as if the storm were outside a thick wall of soundproof glass.

"We're in the eye," he said. "As long as you stay close to me, the storm won't touch you."

"Just tell me what you want from me, Hawk. While you're at it, why don't you tell me what you are." I stared at his face for a moment, trying to figure him out. "Why do you keep coming here? I'm still alive, so you're not trying to kill me."

His face twisted up. "Why would I kill you?" He seemed almost annoyed by the question.

"Answer me," I said, pumping my fist to keep the fading energy stoked.

His eyes flashed red, eventually turning dark as his mouth parted. I felt my heart speed up when the tip of a fang peeked out from under his top lip. He came closer and grabbed my hand, pressing it firmly against the glass, glancing at the bright glow at its center. "I pegged you for a fire witch, but you prefer to play with light."

"And you're a vampire," I replied, the heat from his body traveling into mine. I thought he'd be cold, but he was warm and gave off an interesting scent, like pine needles and musk.

His head dropped to the crook between my neck and shoulder, and his lips grazed my skin, traveling back up the side of my cheek. "You can trust me," he whispered against my ear.

I opened my clenched hand to release the heat from my palm. Anything to cool myself down.

He abruptly let go of me and stepped back, and I shuddered from the cold that suddenly washed over me as the gap between us widened.

Before I knew what was happening, he pulled me against him and pressed his mouth to mine, the tips of his fangs grazing my lower lip. The kiss deepened, and the burning in my throat intensified. And then the taste of copper filled my mouth as he nicked me.

With my power hand, I shoved him, sending him stumbling back. The onslaught of the storm hit me as I ran out of the eye and headed for the terrace door. As I shut it behind me and looked back, the crow swooped down from the sky, gunning for Hawk with its talons spread wide. Hawk hit the conservatory wall, shattering one of the glass panes before disappearing into thin air.

The crow shot into the sky, circling the building once before descending again. It flew toward the door as if it intended to sail straight through it, but it suddenly stopped and hovered on the other side with its onyx eyes trained on mine. It stared at me for a few more seconds before dropping something from one of its talons at the foot of the door. Then it let out a loud caw and disappear back into the night sky.

Convinced it was gone, I opened the door and picked up the silver chain. Dangling from it was an alchemy symbol, and Monoclaude's words from the day before filled my head.

I've found you something better than an old frog.

∾

Katherine Winterborne
November 26, 1994

I can list on one hand the days that have profoundly changed my life. My wedding day, the days my children were born, and the night I just spent with Ryker. I never thought I could completely give myself to someone. Open myself up and lose all control to a man I barely know. Not even with Phillip. Especially not with Phillip. The passion I feel with Ryker is raw, dark, and frightening.

We made love last night on the rug in his living room, inches away from the flames in the fireplace. We couldn't get enough of each other or the heat. We kept inching closer to the fire until I thought my skin would burn. Afterward he got up and went to the desk on the other side of the room. He returned with a small box containing the most beautiful ruby earrings. He said he'd had them made for me in Paris, but we've known each other less than a week. How is that possible?

Ryker wasn't happy when I refused the gift. I told him they were too expensive. Everything about this affair is too expensive. I started to panic and wondered what I was doing there, but when I tried to get up to find my clothes, he kissed me and sent that drug racing through me again.

I'm beginning to wonder who I am, because something is happening to me. I can feel the magic in my bones turning dark and my blood thickening like honey when he says my name. He calls for me every time I close my eyes. He's my drug.

Ryker Caspian is dangerous.

CHAPTER 13

The light coming through my bedroom window startled me as I tried to remember what day it was. Realizing it was Sunday and I hadn't overslept, I relaxed back into the pillows and tried to clear my foggy head. When I sat up, the journal slipped off my stomach and fell to the floor. I'd fallen asleep while reading it.

I glanced at the nightstand and saw the alchemy pendant next to the lamp. What are the odds that it was the same one Monoclaude gave me twenty years ago? I climbed out of bed to see. My jewelry box was full of old necklaces and earrings I hadn't worn in years, and when I dug through the tangled mess of chains, I realized it was gone. The pendant on the nightstand had to be the same one. That crow was Monoclaude's replacement. My new familiar.

"Great," I muttered. "A familiar with talons." Wearing it didn't mean I was agreeing to the partnership, but I wasn't letting the pendant out of my sight. Not until I had a little talk with that frog.

Before I did anything, I was making myself something to eat. After heading into the kitchen and starting the coffee, I glanced at the ceiling over the table, dreading the thought of contractors tromping around my apartment for days. It was completely clean. The walls were pristine too, not a scorch in sight.

I went into the living room to find my phone. "Did you let a contractor into my apartment last night while I was at the meeting?" I asked Jakob when he answered. It was nearly impossible, but we were Winterbornes. We could buy anything, including a construction miracle.

"You'll have to be a little more specific, Mora."

I stuck my head back in the kitchen to make sure I wasn't losing my mind. "The burnt ceiling. It's been repaired, and I certainly didn't do it."

He went quiet on the other end for a moment. "Are you sure?"

"Of course I'm sure. I'm staring right at it."

"Interesting," he mused. "Subconscious magic. I'll be right up."

I looked back at the ceiling and shook my head. "What are you talking about?" He'd already hung up. "Subconscious magic? What the hell is going on around here?"

While I waited for Jakob, I glanced outside and remembered Hawk hitting the glass wall of the conservatory. How would I explain that without telling the entire clan about the vampire who'd shown up on my terrace and crashed through it? Surely someone would notice giant panes of glass being hauled up to the penthouse through the service elevator.

I went outside to get a look at the damage and come up with a story to explain it. Jakob walked out a minute later and found me staring at the glass. There wasn't a crack in sight. "Mora? Are you all right?"

"I'm fine," I said, still looking at it and wondering if Hawk had been here at all. Could I have dreamed it all up?

He glanced down at my bare feet and took me by the arm.

"It's cold out here. Let's go back inside and have a look at the ceiling."

We walked into the kitchen and Jakob looked up at the unmarred ceiling. "Nice work. I'm impressed."

"You're not suggesting *I* did that?"

"Well who else could have done it?" he said. "It wasn't me." He poured us both a cup of coffee and leaned against the counter next to me. "Your magic is getting stronger. In fact, it's getting so strong you can do it in your sleep—literally."

"You're saying I fixed the ceiling in my sleep?" A short laugh burst out of my mouth. "I couldn't fix it if I was awake."

"That's exactly what I'm saying. Subconscious magic is exceptionally rare. Your mother would be proud."

Maybe he was right. Even if a contractor miraculously slipped in here yesterday evening and fixed my kitchen, which I rationally knew was impossible, that conservatory glass hadn't fixed itself overnight. And since that alchemy pendant was lying on my nightstand, I knew Hawk and that crow had been here in the flesh.

"Not even the great Katherine Winterborne could master that form of magic. I couldn't be prouder of you myself."

Otto's voice announced a visitor. "Cabot is on his way up, mistress."

I glanced at Jakob and rolled my eyes.

"Keep this between us," he said. "Magic like yours makes you an even bigger threat to those who don't approve of their new leader."

We heard Cabot get off the elevator and walk into the living room.

"We're in here," I said.

He walked into the kitchen and eyed the two of us. "Morning, Jakob. What brings you up to the penthouse this early?"

"Just having a cup of coffee and debating where we should eat this afternoon." He glanced at me and winked. "I'm taking Mora out to lunch today."

"Oh really?" I said. "I'd like that."

Cabot laid his jacket over one of the kitchen chairs and headed over to pour himself a cup. "I'm afraid she already has a lunch date."

"I do?"

"With me." He took a sip of his coffee and dumped the rest into the sink. "How can you drink this stuff?"

Jakob must have noticed the surprised look on my face. "Does Mora know she's having lunch with you?"

"She does now." He locked eyes with Jakob for a second before grabbing his jacket. "Noon at my apartment. We have a lot to discuss before tonight."

"Tonight?" I said, trying to recall some forgotten event. "What's going on tonight?"

He stopped and turned around before leaving, suppressing a faint smile. "Your first hunt."

My legs went a little weak, and I suddenly felt like the wind had been knocked out of me. Sooner or later I'd have to take part in the hunt, but I'd thought I'd be warned in advance and have time to prepare for it.

Don't take the bait, Mora.

I glanced at Jakob as he pushed the warning into my mind, something he hadn't done in years. I didn't think he still could.

"Make it one o'clock," I said, using every ounce of my will to appear calm and unaffected by his attempt to shake me.

"Twelve thirty," he countered.

I agreed on the time, allowing him to win. After hearing the elevator door shut, I looked at Jakob. "You can still get inside my head?"

"We will always share a connection, but boundaries are to be respected. I crossed that boundary just now because I couldn't bear to see him provoke you. Not when you're about to face the enemy for the first time." His brow cocked. "And just so we're clear, you *let* me inside your head just now."

"Can I still get inside yours?"

He shrugged. "If I care to listen, as you just did."

I gave him a smile over the rim of my cup. "I'll always listen to you, Jakob."

~

REBECCA OPENED the door when I knocked at exactly twelve thirty, not a minute earlier than I had to.

She studied me for a few seconds before turning on her charm. "Punctual as usual. Come in."

I walked inside and inhaled the smell of peonies in a vase on the foyer table. They had one of the nicest units in the building, a corner apartment with views of the park and a clear shot up Central Park West toward the museum.

"Cute shoes," she said as we walked into the living room.

I glanced down at my feet. "Feel free to borrow them if you'd like."

"I think they're a little big for me. But thanks for the offer," she quickly said over her shoulder.

You would have a hard time filling them, I wanted to say.

"Are you joining us for lunch?" I asked.

She turned around and gave me a lukewarm smile. "Is that a problem?"

"Of course not. The more the merrier for a chat about hunting."

I heard something tromping down the hallway, like a small herd of cattle approaching. A young girl I'd never seen before came tearing around the corner with Georgia trailing behind. The girls sprinted across the living room toward the balcony door.

"Stop!" Rebecca yelled.

Georgia turned around when she heard her mother's voice, but her legs were still moving, sending her straight into a table against the wall. An antique Asian vase tipped over and fell to the hardwood floor. I thought Rebecca was going to have a heart attack when it shattered to pieces.

"Georgia!" she growled. "Fix it! Now!"

The anger in her voice made me jump, and Georgia got a look of fear in her eyes that broke my heart.

Rebecca glared at her daughter's accomplice. "Shouldn't your mother be here to pick you up by now?"

"I'm sorry, Mrs. Winterborne." The child's voice bordered on a whimper. "She'll be here soon."

Rebecca called down to Jakob and instructed him to look after Wendy until her mother arrived. Then she escorted the child to the door and gave her a pat on the shoulder. "Jakob has a surprise for you downstairs while you wait for your mother." After sending the girl on her way, she shut the door and inhaled deeply, shuddering dramatically as she turned around. "Children."

Still standing next to the broken vase, Georgia flinched when Rebecca gave her a look.

"Fix it."

Georgia raised her hands and focused on the broken pieces, her face visibly frustrated when nothing happened. She glanced at her mother and then focused harder, this time swaying her arms like a conductor. The shards of porcelain started to move, rising up and floating a few inches off the ground. They rose higher and started to circle, spinning faster as she continued to move her arms. The pieces sped up until all I could see was a blur of white streaks with hints of color.

When I glanced at Rebecca from the corner of my eye, I saw her watching me, gauging my reaction. The porcelain began to slow down, spinning into the recognizable shape of a vase that eventually floated to the floor, perfectly repaired.

"Bravo!" Cabot walked into the room and clapped his hands. "That's my girl."

"Did you see how easily she fixed it?" Rebecca said to him, a glowing smile on her face. "She'll be the most powerful one someday."

"Most powerful what?" I asked.

She looked at me like I was stupid. "The most powerful witch in this clan."

Georgia had never been officially designated as a witch. Her powers were undeniable, and she did appear to be one, but the test for a true witch comes at the age of thirteen. Georgia was only nine, still too young to tell. All children, especially the children of immortals, are born with magic. It's systematically stolen from them as they mature, an unfortunate consequence of the human race brimming with nonbelievers. Unless a child is sequestered on a deserted island with only her clan, there's no escaping it. Four years from now, Georgia would be put through a series of tests to confirm that her abilities were true and not just the lingerings of childhood magic.

"The source of Georgia's power hasn't been established yet," I said, correcting Rebecca as the queen should. "She's very talented, but she's not officially a witch yet." I met her condescending eyes, tired of being disrespected by a woman who didn't have a drop of Winterborne blood in her veins.

Her forced smile faded, and I recognized the face of a foe. She would never release her animosity for me because I was standing in the way of her vicarious dream. Her daughter would never rule the clan. Not while I drew breath.

"That's enough," Cabot said, feeling the growing tension between us. "Georgia, go play in your room while Mommy and Daddy have lunch with Cousin Morgan."

"Why can't I have lunch too?" she asked.

Rebecca shooed her along. "You've already eaten, and we have grown-up things to discuss."

She walked down the hallway toward her bedroom while the three of us headed for the dining room to discuss the hunt. Millie, their housekeeper and cook, served us salmon with roasted vegetables.

Rebecca shook out her napkin and placed it in her lap. "It's organic. Imported from Scotland." She fiddled with her necklace and noticed me staring at it. "It's a black opal," she said as if I'd asked. "My father had it custom made for me. The stone is very rare."

I'd never seen a dark opal before. The colors sparkling from it seemed to cover the full spectrum. "It's beautiful, and this lunch looks delicious. But you didn't have to go to so much trouble. A sandwich would have been fine."

She huffed. "Nonsense. Sandwiches are for children."

Cabot popped a roasted brussels sprout in his mouth and got down to business. "How much do you know about what the Circle does?"

I knew the clan tracked vampires and killed the ones who descended from an ancient line called the Night Walkers. While it was hard to justify the activities of any vampire, the Night Walkers were the ones who wreaked havoc on every major city across the world. They were the ultimate threat.

"We track and kill Night Walkers. You'll have to fill me in on the specifics."

"Oh dear," Rebecca said. "You'll be a sitting duck out there."

I swear she looked gleeful. As a Winterborne by marriage, she wasn't expected to participate in the hunt, but she chose to. For a woman who never deigned to cook a meal for her family or iron her own clothes, she had no problem slaughtering vampires in her spare time.

I ignored her callous remark. "I guess you can start by telling me how we find them."

Cabot put his fork down and wiped his mouth with his napkin. "We don't. The Flyers do it for us."

"What are Flyers?" My mother had never mentioned Flyers.

He got up and walked over to the window in the living room, beckoning for me to follow him. He nodded toward the park. "What do you see out there?"

"Trees. People."

"We rely on what lives in those trees to find Walkers."

A flock of blackbirds flew out from one of them as if on cue. "You mean the birds?"

"Exactly. Those birds become something very different at night. So do the falcons and owls, and most of the other animals that live in the park. Enough to form a small army of feathered vigilantes. And they can cover the entire city in a single night."

I looked out over the park and thought about *my* crow, wondering if it was possible that my new familiar was one of these Flyers he spoke of. What were the odds that the bird I'd rescued in that restaurant was one of them? If it was, God only knew what Jakob's blood had done to it. An immortal Flyer?

"The clan formed an alliance with them a century ago," he said before I could delve deeper. "They're a race of evolved creatures that scout the city at night and provide us with information. In return, we keep the Night Walkers under control for them."

"Walkers are a threat to a bunch of birds?"

He grinned slyly and headed back to the table. "Not directly, but if the Walkers don't get enough human blood, they start to feed off the wildlife. The birds have a symbiotic relationship with other species in the city. If the vampires kill the beasts, the birds suffer for it. The food chain is disrupted. It's basic biology."

I glanced back at the park that would never look the same to me again. "When is the next hunt?"

"As soon as the sun goes down."

"You mean tonight?" He had to be kidding.

He nodded and headed back to the table. "Finish your lunch. Hunting takes a lot of energy, so you need to eat well."

Heeding his advice, I sat down and tried to enjoy my meal, but my appetite had quickly gone south as my nerves grew. Until last night, the hunt had been sanitized in my mind. Staring down at my fish, it was like I could suddenly see the brutal reality of how that creature ended up on my plate, and the ugliness of killing filled my mind and made me put my fork down.

Cabot chewed his last bite of salmon thoughtfully. "Normally I'd advise you to eat a good dinner too, but since this is your first hunt, I'd suggest you go easy on food for the rest of the day."

I stood up, suddenly feeling like I hadn't slept in a week. "Thanks for lunch, but I think I need to relax for a few hours to prepare myself for tonight."

Rebecca smiled as she nibbled on a sliced radish she'd picked out of her salad. "By all means, rest up. Can't have you half-asleep with a vampire at your throat."

"Wait," Cabot said before I could leave. He headed down the hallway and returned with something in his hands. "You'll need to wear these tonight." He handed me a bundle of clothes: black shirt, black pants, and a leather jacket to match.

"We have a uniform?" I stopped myself from snickering. "We'll look like a bunch of ninjas."

"Exactly. There'll be a lot of commotion tonight, and those clothes you find so amusing will keep us from killing each other." There was no humor in his expression, only a dead-serious stare. "You'll receive your seal tonight."

I'd seen my mother's seal. It was a bright green stone similar to an emerald that she wore around her neck every time she left for a hunt.

With my new attire in hand, I walked out the door and headed for the elevator, desperate to lie down for a few hours. If I wasn't sharp as a tack for the hunt, I had a dreadful feeling I'd be dead before morning.

CHAPTER 14

"You've been summoned to council chambers, mistress."

I sat up on the sofa. "Council chambers?" Then I remembered the hunt. "Thank you, Otto."

My phone wasn't handy to check the time, but judging by the glow of city lights illuminating the penthouse, it was late. I'd curled up on the sofa after lunch and slept the entire afternoon away.

"Otto, what time is it?"

"Nine o'clock, mistress."

"Nine o'clock!" I jumped up and headed for the bedroom to change into the clothes Cabot had given me as quickly as possible because queen or not, the Elders didn't like to be kept waiting. The shirt and pants were a little snug, but the jacket fit me perfectly. Keeping in line with the whole ninja theme, I chose a pair of black combat boots. I felt ridiculous when I looked in the mirror. All of us dressed like this would stand out like a bunch of marauding thugs. We'd be lucky if the cops didn't stop and question us.

"Morgan!" I heard Cabot bark from the living room. "Where are you?"

I walked out of the bedroom and furrowed my brow as he stalked toward me wearing his matching uniform. "I was on my way."

He stopped and stared at me with a look of contempt on his face. "If we can't count on you to follow orders before the hunt even begins, you'll put us all at risk."

"What are you talking about, Cabot? I fell asleep. The next thing I know I'm being summoned. You should have called me an hour ago so I had time to squeeze into these ridiculous pants." I dropped down on my haunches to try to stretch them out a little. "Jesus, you could have just handed me a can of spray paint."

He glanced at my outfit when I straightened back up and then looked around the room. When he spotted my phone on the table against the wall, he grabbed it and shoved it in my face. "I did. About ten times to be exact." There were several messages on my phone. I must have been so tired I slept right through the ringing. "Get it together, Morgan. This isn't a game."

"I'm sorry. It won't happen again." I couldn't believe I'd slept through all those phone calls. I must have been more sleep deprived than I'd thought.

We stepped into the elevator without saying another word to each other, with Cabot staring at my reflection in the metal door.

"It's about time," Ramsey said when we stepped out of the elevator a minute later. The other Elders muttered and threw glances at me as I headed for my seat.

I started to apologize but changed my mind. I'd done nothing wrong, and it was time those sanctimonious old men started to treat me like their leader. I'd been patient with their patronizing, but they would never respect me if I let them treat me like a doormat. "Since we're running late, I suggest we get down to business," I said, motioning to Cabot. "The floor is yours."

He glanced around the table. Rebecca was sitting at the other end, tapping her fingernails against the oak surface. Ethan was sitting next to her, and James and Olivia were across from him. "Is this it?"

Ethan looked at him impatiently. "Well, we can hardly expect your parents to join us, seeing as how they've aged about forty years due to their little trip to the Winterlands."

"Where's Avery?" I asked.

Rebecca stifled a laugh. "You're joking."

My sister had done all but publicly announce her intention to formally leave the Circle, but to my knowledge she was still an active member.

"Avery is no longer a part of the Circle," Cabot said. "She's relinquished her seal."

That must be why she met with Cabot before coming up to the penthouse yesterday morning. Avery was distancing herself from the clan more and more every day, to lead the normal life she craved. I wondered if she planned to leave her cushy job at Winterborne Holdings eventually, securing her freedom from a life she'd always resented.

"Why wasn't I told?" I asked, realizing I should have been the one having that conversation with my sister. Avery wouldn't have dared go to Cabot if our mother were alive, and Cabot wouldn't have dared take the meeting.

Cabot didn't bother to sugarcoat it. "Avery didn't feel comfortable discussing her decision with you."

"And you didn't think it was important to tell me after the fact?" I stood up and decided to put an end to all the condescension. I might have been green, but I wasn't stupid. The more isolated I was from the smallest clan decisions, the harder it would be to hold on to my authority. Cabot was formidable, but he still answered to me. "I appreciate your concern for my sister's predicament, but from this moment forward, I expect to be directly involved in all clan business."

Ramsey opened his mouth to say something.

"*All* clan business," I repeated.

The look on Rebecca's face was chilling.

"Of course." Cabot motioned to the group. "Would you like to lead the charge tonight?"

"I think you're the best person for that task," I said. "So please begin."

He carried on with the plan. "There's an old warehouse at the north end of the park. It's been empty for a while, but the Flyers have witnessed the Night Walkers going in and out. They believe a cell has moved in, and we're going to clean it up tonight." He looked at James. "You and Olivia will go in first to check the place out. The rest of us wait for your signal."

James and Olivia were a team. Immortal twins were unheard of, and as such, they had a telepathic bond that made them exceptionally lethal. Having never participated before, I hadn't actually seen them in action, but their hunting skills were legendary. So was their ability to levitate and their mastery of mind over matter, gifts usually attributed to the rare witch born to the clan, such as myself. I could only hope to discover a fraction of those same talents in myself someday.

Before continuing, Cabot looked at me. "Let's get the formalities out of the way." He handed me a necklace. The chain was made of silver and had a brilliant green stone in the center of the pendant that hung from it. "By wearing this seal, you accept an oath to hunt the Night Walkers and serve as a clan guard while wearing it. It bonds you to the Circle and is to be worn only during the hunt."

The others around the table pulled their seals out from under their shirts. I was surprised to see that the others were blue. "I thought they were all the same?"

"All but one," Ramsey said. "This was Katherine's seal. As head of the clan, her seal goes to you."

I almost choked up when I ran my fingers over it, and I swear I felt her when I put it around my neck.

Something came sliding across the table at me when I looked back up. A dagger. It stopped an inch away from the edge. "What's this for?"

Cabot grinned. "How did you think you were going to kill them? With your bare hands?"

A burst of laughter filled the room but abruptly stopped when I looked around the table. "I don't know. Poison or banshee blood."

"Last night was a performance," he said. "To make sure you understood the brutal reality of what the Winterbornes do." He put it to me in a simpler way. "Here's a scenario. Let's say a vampire is gunning for you. Then a few more show up. Will you take a moment to think of a way to slip poison apples down their throats? Or will you slice their heads clean off their necks before they have a chance to rip your throat out?" He glanced around the table. "We'd all be dead by now if we ignored the most efficient method of execution."

"Take it," Ethan said as I stared at the knife. "You're of no use to us if we have to worry about protecting you all night. You might as well relinquish your seal right now."

I reluctantly picked it up. It felt heavy, and I knew the blade was lethal by the way the edges tapered to razor-thin steel. "Do you have something I can carry it in so I don't amputate my hand before we even get there?"

Cabot handed me a leather scabbard. "The knife was also your mother's."

I stood up and secured it to my belt and slid the knife into it. "Let's go."

"A few ground rules first," Cabot said. "Number one—don't kill your team. It's going to get crowded in that warehouse tonight, so take a good look at the *uniforms*. You see a ninja, back off. And if the black clothing is too much for you to remember, look for the seals around our necks."

I looked around the table and noticed that the stones in all the necklaces were glowing like neon signs. All but mine. "How do you get them to do that?"

"We don't *get* them to do anything. They light up on their own."

"Mine hasn't."

"That's because the seal doesn't know you yet." I must have looked a little scared, because he tried to put me at ease. "Don't worry. We know you, so we probably won't kill you tonight while that seal gets familiar with its new master."

"What's rule number two?" I asked.

"If you cut a vampire's throat, you better make sure its head rolls. Clean off, Morgan. Understood?"

I nodded, a queasy feeling in my stomach.

"I have an ominous feeling about this night," Ramsey said as he stood up and walked toward the back of the room with the other Elders in tow. "Be safe, my friends." They disappeared through the wall, signaling that it was time for us to leave.

As we headed for the elevator, Cabot muttered to me, "Just stay out of the way tonight. Stay close to me but keep back. Watch and learn."

We exited the building using the service entrance that led to the back alley. When we were almost to the side street, Cabot took me by the arm and pulled me straight through the wall of another building. The six of us stepped out the other side and found ourselves in a different neighborhood, eerily quiet and abandoned, with row houses full of broken windows and only the moonlight to guide our way. Across the street was the warehouse.

James grinned at me when he saw the look on my face. "First time traveling?"

The Winterbornes were supposed to blend in and live in the

mundane world, so traveling was discouraged. It was too easy to become lazy and rely on it, which was the reason it wasn't taught. It *was* my first time, although I had memories of my mother getting us from point *A* to point *B* in unusual ways on a few occasions when my siblings and I were children.

"It was interesting," I said. "I could get used to it."

Cabot jogged across the street with Rebecca and Olivia behind him. He signaled, and James lost his grin.

"See you on the other side, cousin. And remember, don't try to be a hero tonight. You can do that next time." He flashed his spectacular blue eyes at me before heading across the street.

"Nervous?" Ethan asked. He was standing behind me, jittery and clearly suffering from a case of his own nerves.

"Would you believe me if I said no?" Of course I was nervous. I'd been thinking about this moment for years, but nothing could truly prepare you like being thrown into the fire.

He put his arm around my shoulders and took a deep breath. "I remember my first hunt not too long ago. Nearly got myself skewered by a wooden table leg when a Walker tore it off and threw it at me. But you know what was interesting? I knew exactly what to do. I snatched it a second before it speared my chest and sent it right back at the fucker."

"You never told me that story."

"I never had a reason to until now." He let go of me and pulled on a pair of gloves. "Ever wonder why they throw us into the fire without any actual training and we always manage to come back in one piece?"

I laughed nervously. "The thought has crossed my mind."

"Because we're Winterbornes, Morgan. Killing is in our blood. I recommend you lie low tonight, but if you find yourself at the business end of a broken table leg, you'd be wise to remember that."

Cabot whistled to us. By the time we made it across the

street, James and Olivia were already heading inside. He pointed to an alley on the left side of the building and nodded to Ethan. When I tried to go with my brother, he grabbed my arm and shook his head. Rebecca followed Ethan down the dark and narrow space while I went with Cabot toward the alley on the other side.

The streets were empty, but on a Sunday night in a neighborhood filled with derelict and abandoned buildings, that didn't surprise me. I doubted anyone would last very long in a place like this, after dark and with a cell of vampires living in the neighborhood.

Cabot hopped on top of a dumpster and looked through one of the windows. He jumped back down and leaned against the building, placing a cigarette between his lips without lighting it. He gripped it with his teeth and spoke around it in a whisper. "Now we wait."

"For what?" I whispered back.

Before he could answer, a painful sound pierced my ears.

"That," he said, yanking me by the arm as he took off toward the back, dragging me along until I got my legs and could keep up with him.

We rounded the warehouse and came to a back door. Before reaching for the handle, he grabbed my jaw roughly and turned my face to his. "Do not leave my side." He glanced at the dagger secured to my waist. "Use it if you have to, but you better have a Walker breathing down your neck before you engage. Do you understand?"

I nodded.

"Say it!" he hissed.

"I understand."

Something flew overhead. The silhouette of a large bird sailed over the building, blocking out the light for a few seconds as its wings passed between us and the moon.

We entered the warehouse and crept along the wall, the light from the sky streaming through the windows and casting eerie shadows over the abandoned space. My heartbeat was out of control, and I thought I'd pass out from the pounding. But as quickly as the panic had set in, it started to fade. My nerves were still out of control, but I suddenly felt energized.

With his head flattened against the wall, Cabot turned to look at me, a smile edging up one side of his face as he seemed to sense my fear evaporating.

We are Winterborne, a voice whispered in my head.

Something moved at the front of the warehouse, and Cabot clamped his hand over my mouth before I could gasp. The sound came again, but this time it was closer. It sounded like someone was deliberately leaving a trail of noise to get our attention.

A distraction.

Cabot shoved me, and I flew sideways and hit the floor. A dark figure dropped from the ceiling, landing in the spot where I'd just been standing. I backpedaled as the figure turned to look at me. It walked toward me, but its boots made no sound as they hit the wooden planks. It stopped and hovered, bending down to get a closer look at my face, its eyes lighting up like red flares as it got a whiff of me.

A whooshing sound filled my ears as a glint of steel flashed above me. A machete slashed through the air and came within inches of my face, sending something black and oily spraying all over me as the Walker's head tipped sideways and hit the floor with a dull thud.

I nearly screamed when the head rolled and came to a stop beside me, but Cabot had already muffled me and yanked me out of the way before the body crashed down on top of me.

My fear returned, and adrenaline raced through me. Then I started to panic when I realized I was covered in the vampire's blood. Cabot spun me around and put his index finger to his lips.

He pulled a handkerchief from his pocket and handed it to me, giving me a moment to wipe the sticky substance from my face and eyes.

I followed him when he picked up the machete, stepped over the body, and headed for the light coming from a doorway on the other side of the room. As we silently moved along the wall, my eyes darted around, looking for the others.

The light grew brighter as we approached. Cabot put his hand up to stop me from following him any further. With his finger, he pushed the door open a few inches. Through the gap I could see Ethan backed against a wall. I breathed a sigh of relief that he was alive. But then all hell broke loose.

Cabot shoved the door open the moment a vampire lunged at Ethan. They rolled on the floor like two cats engaged in a blur of fur and claws, moving so fast I could barely make out who was who.

"Do something!" I growled at Cabot, who was transfixed by something else. I tried to run inside, but he stopped me. On the other side of the room was Rebecca, caught in the grip of a Night Walker, its fangs poised to pierce the skin between her neck and shoulder. A few other vampires were plastered against the wall by James and Olivia, who were mentally holding them in place.

Rebecca managed to shove the Walker away, and Cabot refocused on Ethan. He headed for the scuffle and shoved his machete in the center of it. My lungs filled painfully when I saw blood spray everywhere. The vampire flew back against the wall, a deep cut oozing from his abdomen. Ethan was in no better shape with a large gash over his shoulder and rib cage.

Cabot dragged Ethan out of the room and dropped him just outside the door. "Stay with him," he ordered before stalking back inside and heading for the wall. With a swift blow, the vampire's head was sliced down the center and began to split apart. The two halves toppled to the floor as the machete sliced across its neck a second later.

I dropped to my knees and propped Ethan up. "What can I do?"

He let out a weak laugh. "I was going to ask you to kill the fucker for me, but it looks like Cabot took care of that." Wincing, he looked at the deep gash on his rib cage. "I've suffered worse, but *fuck* that hurts!"

One of the windows shattered in the room where the battle was taking place. I got up and looked inside to see what was happening. A set of large wings careened across the room, getting everyone's attention, including the Walker's. Cabot took advantage of the distraction and started swinging. Rebecca ducked and her attacker's head went sailing through the air. With the twin's concentration disrupted, the vampires trapped against the wall managed to escape and fly out the broken window. James and Olivia headed out the side door after them.

When I looked back down at Ethan, his eyes grew wide and his mouth opened. But before he could get out a warning, I lifted into the air and started to fly backward. Ethan struggled to climb to his feet as the vampire dropped me on the other side of the room, next to the one Cabot had killed earlier.

It straddled me and pressed its face to mine, taking in my scent with a deep sniff. "I think I'll keep you, little sister." With the exception of its ghostly color, its face looked shockingly human, but the icy feel of its skin and its descending fangs said otherwise.

I tried to shove it off me, but it was too strong.

Use your light, Morgan!

I swung my head from left to right, trying to find the source of the voice, but Ethan was still stumbling around halfway across the room and Cabot was nowhere in sight. It was just me and the Walker. I raised my power hand and screamed, smashing a ball of energy into the vampire's face. It howled and fell backward, rolling on its side before shaking off the blast and climbing to its feet. I jumped up and conjured the light again, but the vampire anticipated my move and easily dodged it.

It lunged forward and slammed me against the wall, pinning my hand in a tight grip as its fangs grazed my shoulder and traveled toward my neck. I looked at Ethan's horrified face as he continued to struggle, losing his balance every time he stood up. Then I spotted Rebecca standing in the doorway behind him, her eyes fixed on mine.

Do it now, Morgan! Now! The familiar voice kept screaming in my head.

A few seconds passed, and the tips of the Walker's fangs pulled away from my skin. It reared back slightly, but its eyes were fixed on something to my right when I looked at its face. I followed its blank stare and thought I caught a glimpse of golden eyes disappearing into the darkness just beyond the open door where we'd entered the warehouse.

Cabot rushed from the back room and reached me seconds after the vampire's head fell to the floor, his gaze taking in the dagger gripped tightly between my fingers. "Give it to me," he said, holding out his hand.

I looked down at the bloody blade and felt a current of electricity run through me. There was no fear, just a feeling of surprise—and satisfaction. I'd actually done it. I'd made my first kill.

"Give me the knife," Cabot repeated.

I glanced at the door again and shook my head, wiping the blade against my pants before sticking it back in the scabbard. "No. I've earned it."

Ethan finally lumbered his way across the room and looked down at the body. "Well, *fuck* me," he said with a wide grin. "Welcome to the Circle, little sister."

CHAPTER 15

I was exhausted but exhilarated by the time I got home. Something had happened to me back in that warehouse, and I knew in my bones that I'd been changed. I also knew I'd had help, and not from Rebecca, but at least I knew who my enemies were now.

After sitting in the dark for a few minutes to let the memory of that head rolling at my feet sink in, I walked out on the terrace and scanned the stars. I'd seen those golden eyes peering back at me in the warehouse, but I'd also seen that bird crash through the window.

"Where are you, crow!" I yelled at the sky, gripping the alchemy pendant tucked under my shirt. "You answer to me, so show yourself!"

The sound of footsteps came from behind me, and I knew without turning around who it was.

"Don't call him yet," Hawk said. "He doesn't trust me."

"Should *I*?" I asked, still staring at the sky. "And how do you know the crow is a he?" I'd recognized Hawk's voice in my head back at the warehouse, right before I made my kill. Thanks to him, I'd had the sense to use that knife before I ended up dead.

But why was he here again? Hawk had not hidden the fact that he was a vampire. In fact, he'd been very willing to show me. So why would he keep coming back here, knowing we killed his kind? The bigger question was why had he helped me tonight?

His breath brushed the back of my neck. "I told you the night we met I wouldn't hurt you, and I never lie."

I finally turned around and looked up at his face, my heart beating so fast I wondered if he could sense it. "I saw you tonight. You're one of them."

"Do I look like a Night Walker?"

Hawk didn't look anything like them. The vampires I'd seen tonight had seemed dead and shallow with their cold, pale skin and eyes so evil there was no mistaking what they were. Hawk was different. His eyes were alive and his skin was warm. He was nothing like the Walkers in that warehouse.

"Then tell me what you were doing there."

He looked away, a hard edge to his face I hadn't noticed before. He took a steady breath through his nose, something else that distinguished him from the creatures we'd hunted tonight. He was alive. "I followed you."

"You did what?"

He laughed quietly. "I almost lost you when you disappeared into the travel portal, but I managed to find you on the other side with the help of a few friends."

I walked away and shook my head, confused and a little angry that he'd invaded my privacy. And what did he mean *with the help of a few friends*? "Help me understand what's going on here," I said, turning back around to face him. "Why would you follow me?"

A sly grin appeared on his face. "Aren't you glad I did?"

Exasperated, I headed for the door. "You can leave the way you came. And don't bother to come back until you're ready to tell me the truth." As I reached for the handle, I felt a gust of wind at my back. A pair of wings spread behind me, making me look like an angel in my reflection in the glass. "Crow?" I said, turning around. But what I saw hovering behind me didn't have the glossy black feathers and onyx eyes of my AWOL familiar. It was a hawk, with sable wings and golden eyes.

"Dear God," I muttered, taking a seat on the garden bench outside the door when I felt my legs begin to buckle.

The bird landed, and suddenly Hawk was standing in front of me. "I was afraid to tell you," he said. "A vampire is strange enough. I thought I'd wait until we knew each other a little better before showing you the rest of me."

"You're a vampire *and* a shifter?" I shrugged as a nervous laugh escaped me. "And I'm a witch. I guess we're both a little strange."

I moved over and patted the seat next to me. His thigh brushed mine when he sat down, sending a rush of warmth through me. Instead of giving me some space, he spread his legs wider so he was pressed against me, and I didn't try to move away. I didn't want to.

"Tell me your story?"

He inhaled sharply and raked his hand over the top of his head. "Well, let's see. Where should I begin? My father is a vampire, which explains the fangs." He glanced at me to gauge my reaction. When I raised my brow, he continued. "But my mother was something very different. She was a falconer. A priestess for a coven of raptor goddesses. I got my wings from her."

"I guess that explains that stunt the other night when you caught me." *After you threw me off the building!* "You refer to her in the past tense. Is she gone?"

"Dead? Yes. She died a while back. I never met my father though. I assume he's still out there somewhere, ravishing innocent women."

I looked at him, horrified. "Did he force himself on your mother?"

"No," he said, shaking his head. "It's a bad joke. I just meant he's probably out there feeding from them. My mother mentioned his preference for female blood. It was her way of putting me in my place when I got a little too cocky with women. She used to tell me the apple didn't fall too far from the tree." He quickly added, "But those days are over. I'm a one-woman man now."

"Don't get any ideas," I said when he gazed at me suggestively. I stood up to put a little distance between us. "I am curious though. Why me? I'm sure there are plenty of women in New York who would be thrilled to have you show up on their terrace." I left out the part about his smoldering eyes and handsome face because I didn't want to encourage him. As much as I wanted to take him inside, he was still a vampire, and the clan would invade the penthouse with pitchforks and machetes if they got wind of him up here.

He lost his playful demeanor and pinned me with another intense gaze. "I don't know what it is, Morgan. You have this…" He hesitated like he was trying to choose his words carefully. "I don't want to creep you out, but you have this scent that triggers something in me. It's like a memory."

Nothing disturbing about a guy you barely know mentioning how you smell.

"It's time for you to leave," I said, fearing Cabot and the rest of the Circle would come barging in at any second.

He stood up and started to walk toward me but stopped when I raised my power hand in warning. "You must think I'm some kind of psycho." He sat back down and dropped his head, showing no sign that he intended to leave, and to be honest, I didn't want him to.

"I think you got the wrong impression from that kiss last night," I said. "That was my fault. I should have stopped it."

He looked back up at me, the gold in his eyes turning to amber. "You wanted that kiss as much as I did."

Irrational or not, I couldn't deny it. But my clan kills vampires; we don't sleep with them.

I sat back down and touched his arm. "Why are you so warm? Vampires are cold."

He huffed a laugh. "Because I'm not dead. My mother was half hawk and half human, which makes me even more of a mongrel. Her genes are dominant."

I broached my next question as tactfully as possible. "I don't know an easy way to ask this, but—"

"Do I drink blood?" he said, anticipating my question. "I eat whatever I want. Pizza, ice cream, rabbits."

"Rabbits?"

He shrugged and turned to look me in my eyes. "I'm a hawk, Morgan. And yes, I do need blood, but I get it from prey. It all works out in a strange reciprocal way. I'm thankful that I don't need human blood to survive."

I was relieved. I think that would have ended whatever relationship we were building. What a strange life he was living.

We sat there for a few minutes without saying another word, and I resisted the urge to invite him in. That would have been too dangerous. Not for me—for him.

The heat between us suddenly grew from a spark into an ember. Then it flamed as he leaned closer and barely touched his lips to mine, teasing my mouth before attacking me with a kiss that made my body arch against his. He pulled me onto his lap, and I straddled him against the bench, kissing him deeper as I threw all common sense out the window.

The wind picked up behind us, and the sound of flapping

wings interrupted what might have been the most spectacular kiss of my life.

"No!" I growled, scrambling from Hawk's lap to face the crow that was hindering my love life. "Get out of here!"

The crow let out a loud caw that rattled my ears and sent Hawk flying into the air with his wings stretch wide. He flew above the crow and headed toward the park, disappearing into the trees. The crow's eyes followed him, but it stayed put, hovering in front of me with its shiny eyes fixed on mine.

"I know what you are," I said, pulling the pendant out from under my shirt. "You're my new familiar."

The crow hovered closer. After getting a good look at the alchemy symbol hanging around my neck, it flew to the terrace wall and landed.

"You're supposed to be my advisor, not my babysitter." The bird perched motionless like a statue, refusing to leave. "Jesus, Monoclaude sent me this?" I said to no one in particular before turning around to go inside.

No. You brought me here.

I whipped around to face him. "What did you say?"

But instead of letting me die, you chose my fate. I'm indebted to you whether I like it or not.

There were no words coming out of the crow's mouth, but I was hearing them clear as day in my head. "Let me make this easier for you. I release you from the debt. You're free as a bird."

And where am I supposed to go, looking like this?

My eyes ran up and down his unusually large form. Eventually he'd probably be hunted down by some idiot thinking he was the Mothman or some other urban legend. Then I glanced at the conservatory. "You can stay in there until I figure something out." I owed him that much. "But let me make something very clear—Hawk is off-limits. When he's here, you're gone. Understood?"

The crow didn't respond. His wings caught the breeze, and he flew into the sky and headed toward the Hudson River. *I'll take my chances*, I heard fade into the wind as he disappeared from view.

I needed to have a talk with Monoclaude about that bird, but my exhilaration had quickly turned to exhaustion. Even my mother's journal would have to wait. Looking out over the park, I suddenly wondered where Hawk lived. I doubted he slept in the trees. I just prayed that damn crow hadn't scared him off for good.

"Good night, Hawk," I whispered as I turned toward the door, the memory of his lips igniting that flame inside me again.

Sweet dreams, Morgan, I thought I heard him whisper back.

CHAPTER 16

What the hell are you doing, Morgan? Michael stared at me like he wanted to ream me out for something.

"I was hungry," I said, looking at his disgusted face.

He grabbed the plate and pulled it out from under my bloody hands, shaking his head. "There is something seriously wrong with you."

My hunger was so strong it gnawed at my bones. "I know."

A BEAM of morning light streamed through the window, making me wince when I opened my eyes, but I was thankful to wake from the horrible dream. I considered rolling over and going back to sleep for a few more minutes, but with new commissions coming in and a mountain of follow-up tasks associated with weekend auctions, Monday mornings were too busy for anyone to stroll in late. Especially important international auctions like the one we'd held on Saturday. I also intended to find out what I could about Ryker Caspian. You didn't just hand an auctioneer two hundred thousand dollars in cash and leave with your goods, so there had to be a paper trail of information on his financial records.

I quickly showered and got dressed. My appetite was nil, but I grabbed a muffin for later and headed out.

Jakob gave me a once-over when I stepped off the elevator and entered the lobby. "How did it go last night? You don't look worse for wear, so I take it your newly discovered skill came in handy."

"You could say that. I would have bitten the dust last night if it weren't for you helping me get my power back."

He chuckled. "I doubt that. I'm sure it would have found its way to the surface given the circumstances, which I assume were eventful."

I stared down at my shoes and relived the moment again. "I didn't think I could do it, Jakob. That thing had me pinned against a wall with its fangs pressed to my skin, and I sliced my dagger right through its neck. I kind of enjoyed it too." My eyes came back up to his. "Does that make me a monster?"

"It makes you a Winterborne," he replied with a faint smile.

Edward pulled the car up to the front door.

"I better get going. It's going to be a busy day and I'm already late."

"Any sign of the crow?" he asked as I headed out.

I laughed quietly, but I felt sorry for the bird that seemed to be lost between two worlds thanks to me. "I don't think it's coming back." With no time to explain, I headed for the car.

"Good morning, Morgan." Edward gave me his usual charming smile and held the door open. As I climbed in, my phone rang.

"How'd your meeting go Saturday night?" Jules asked. "And by the way, why the hell haven't you called me?"

"Good morning to you too," I said. I'd told her about the invitation to the Circle meeting when she stopped by Saturday afternoon to drop off Ryker's gift, but I hadn't talked to her since because I'd been a little busy. She was going to blow a gasket when I told her about the hunt.

"I thought you got arrested or something."

I glanced at Edward in the mirror and lowered my voice. "We went hunting last night."

The phone went silent for a few seconds. "Are you shittin' me?"

"Would I shit about something like that, Jules?"

"Jesus, woman. I can't believe you haven't called me."

I understood her reaction. Jules had known about the Circle almost as long as I had. I'd relayed every detail my mother had given me over the years, and my best friend had yearned to be adopted by my family so she too could wield a weapon against the Night Walkers. But she'd come to her senses and lost her desire to hunt vampires years ago.

"Meet me for lunch and I'll tell you all about it."

We pulled up to the auction house as I hung up. I let myself out and headed for the door, determined to be productive for the first time since I took leave to deal with my mother's death. We had a shipment of rare artifacts coming in from a client in Chicago, and each one needed to be appraised and cataloged for an upcoming sale. I couldn't wait to get back to work doing what I loved, putting my hands on rare objects full of history and mystique.

"Morning, Kerry," I said as I passed her desk and opened my office door. When I walked inside, there were a bunch of boxes stacked high on the table near the window. The new shipment I assumed. "Are these from Chicago?" I yelled through the door.

She came in and handed me an itemized list. "It's the first shipment. The rest should be here tomorrow."

I tossed my jacket on the chair and noticed a small box on the desk. "What's that?"

She shrugged. "I have no idea. The guard at the front desk handed it to me when I came in this morning. He said it was for you." On her way out, she stopped. "It was left by Mr. Caspian, the bidder who bought the Gurdjieff letters on Saturday."

I stared at it in disbelief. Ryker Caspian had left me another box, and the thought of opening it unnerved me. "Did he leave a note or say anything to the guard?"

"I don't know, but do you want me to go down and ask?"

"No, of course not. I can go down myself."

"You sure? I don't mind."

I waved her off. "It's fine."

It was anything but fine. After she left, I closed the door and sat down at my desk to see what kind of game Ryker Caspian was playing with me now. The box was long and narrow, but it was the same signature green of Van Cleef & Arpels. After lifting the lid, I sat back in my chair, relieved to see a bracelet that looked similar to the ring and earrings, not something more sinister like someone's snipped-off finger or an ear. Caspian was showering me with jewels. But why?

Eyeing the bracelet for a moment, I finally took it out of the box to get a better look at it. It had a string of rubies on each side of an intricately carved medallion in the center, and it appeared to match the other pieces as if they were all part of a set.

"What do you want from me, Ryker Caspian?" I whispered as I put it back in the box and shoved it in a drawer.

A few minutes later, I went out to Kerry's desk. "Can you do me a favor? Find out what address Mr. Caspian has on file." Bidders often took their merchandise with them the day of auction, but a lot as valuable as the Gurdjieff letters would require at least one business day to settle the funds before he could take possession. Either he was coming back to pick them up or we were shipping them to a listed address.

When I returned to my office, the bracelet was back on top of the desk. I pulled the empty box out of the drawer, positive I'd put it back inside. With my index finger, I nudged it, expecting it to move or do something else ridiculous. Then for some reason I wrapped it around my wrist and watched as the clasp hooked itself. I let out a small gasp as the stones began to sparkle and glow. It was beautiful. Felt electric against my skin.

Kerry stuck her head through the door, startling me. "That's beautiful." When she noticed the open box on the desk, her brow tightened. "Is it a gift from Mr. Caspian?" I'd be curious too if a client gave her such an elaborate gift.

"No," I said, stuffing the box back in the drawer and covering the bracelet with my other hand, feeling like I'd done something inappropriate. "It was my mother's." I don't know why I'd said that. The only thing I knew for sure was that the earrings were hers. "Did you find an address?"

She handed me a piece of paper. "This is the one from his file."

It was an address on Riverside Drive. I planned to check it out later, if for no other reason than to make sure it was real and not some fake address just to satisfy the paperwork.

"Where are the letters now?" I asked, wondering if he intended to pick them up in person, which would reinforce my suspicions about that address.

"They're gone. Mr. Caspian had them picked up just before you got in."

I glanced at the time. "The banks are barely open yet."

"The banks in London are five hours ahead. The funds were already transferred to our account when our bank opened this morning."

"Damn it!"

Kerry looked surprised. "Is something wrong?"

"No. I'm sorry." I felt like an idiot for snapping. Cabot would have had a field day if he'd seen me lose my cool in front of staff.

If I'd used my head and anticipated this, I could have had Caspian's messenger followed. Then I'd know exactly where to find him when I figured out what he was up to.

I headed for the boxes piled on my table, the bracelet still wrapped around my wrist. "Where did those come from?" I nodded to a couple of paintings propped against the wall. They were covered in padded blankets, and as far as I knew there were no paintings in the Chicago shipment.

Kerry glanced at them and shook her head. "I don't know. They must have been delivered by mistake when they dropped off the boxes."

I reached for one of them and carefully lifted the protective blanket to check the tag on the back. The frame was unremarkable, black with slight undertones of gold, but the scene was anything but plain. A tingling sensation ran across my arms and down my spine as I looked at the man slumped over a chaise with his head to the side. Blood was coming from a vicious wound in his neck, and three female vampires were ravaging his body.

"Good God!" Kerry said, grimacing. "They were definitely delivered to the wrong office."

My eyes followed one of the female figures, noting the thick blood covering her fingers as she gripped her victim's arm and suckled from his wrist. The other two were staged in similar poses depicting bloodlust. It was almost erotic the way they draped over the man, their gowns twisted and torn, revealing their blood-stained breasts.

"I'll call downstairs and get someone to pick them up." As she turned to go back to her desk, she glanced at me with a peculiar look on her face. "Are you okay?"

"I'm fine," I said, pulling my eyes away from the painting while I ran my fingers around the chain of rubies on my wrist. "It's mesmerizing, isn't it?"

An uncomfortable smile formed on her face. "Are you sure you're okay? Your cheeks are bright red."

I reached for my face and felt the heat coming from my skin, and for a second I couldn't remember what I was doing. But the fog quickly cleared when I glanced back at the painting. "Yes. Call downstairs, please."

With the blanket pulled back over the canvas, I got to work on the boxes, trying to get the image of the painting out of my mind. I felt ashamed of the strange feeling of pleasure it brought me. It was normal, I told myself, knowing that perfectly decent people were affected by the taboo in unexpected ways. And since I'd killed my first vampire the night before, I'd probably had some kind of subconscious reaction to the painting.

The rest of the morning was spent opening boxes and examining a collection of Civil War artifacts. The sale would draw every serious collector in the country. These weren't your average artifacts. They were museum-quality relics that would spark bidding wars.

I glanced at the time when someone from the shipping department knocked on my door, realizing I was supposed to meet Jules downtown in twenty minutes.

"I'm sorry about the mix-up, Ms. Winterborne," he said as he went to grab the paintings. "It won't happen again."

"You need to be more careful, Miguel," I warned gently. "Make sure they get to the right office this time." A recent hire, Miguel was the son of one of our managers. Winterborne's was one of the most reputable auction houses in the world. Misplacing a pair of valuable paintings would leave a dark stain on the company's impeccable reputation. My mother would have given him a warning like I did, but Cabot would have had him fired.

On my way out, I locked my door and handed the list of

cataloged artifacts to Kerry so she could arrange to have them taken down to the vault. Then I called for my car.

Edward was leaning against the door with a magazine in his hand when I walked outside. Handsome with a million-dollar smile, how he'd ended up driving for the Winterbornes was a mystery. He'd been on the family payroll since as far back as I could remember.

"I have a lunch date in the Village," I said as I climbed in. "Sixth and Greenwich."

We arrived twenty minutes late, and I headed inside the small Italian eatery where Jules was seated in our usual booth near the back. A well-kept secret from tourists, it was unlike a lot of places in the area. This one was a no-frills family restaurant with some of the best pasta in town, but if you wanted a glass of water, you had to ask for it.

"It's about damn time," Jules said, popping an olive in her mouth. "I got hungry and ordered an appetizer."

I slid into the booth and grabbed a menu. "Sorry. Got sidetracked." I couldn't decide between a salad or pasta. Cabot could call at any time to summon me for a hunt, so food choices had suddenly become a critical decision at every meal. Since vampire hunting required a reasonably empty stomach, I decided to stick with a salad.

Jules was staring at me when I looked up. "So? How did it go?"

The waitress stopped at the table to take our order. As soon as she walked away, I began. "Do you want to hear about the guy or the hunting expedition?"

"What guy?"

"The one I met at the club Friday night."

Her mouth went still for a second as she stopped chewing her olives.

"Oh, that's right. You were too drunk to notice."

She leaned against the wall and lifted her foot on top of the bench, tossing her olive back into the bowl. "Now you're just starting to piss me off."

"I thought he was just some guy trying to pick me up," I continued. "He was gone when I came out of the bathroom, and you were so buzzed I didn't think you'd care to hear about it." I shrugged and got on with it, conscious of the time and not wanting to take a two-hour lunch. "Then he decided to show up on my terrace the other night." I omitted the fact that he'd shown up for the first time Friday night, because that would have sparked a whole new conversation about why I hadn't mentioned it to her when she dropped by Saturday.

"You live in the penthouse, Morgan. How the hell did he get up to your terrace?"

"With his wings, of course," I said with a lyrical lilt.

She looked at me like I was speaking a foreign language.

"He's a shifter, and his name is Hawk for a good reason."

"Jesus," she whispered, closing her eyes and sinking deeper into the booth.

"You know, like an actual... hawk."

She cringed and waved her hands back and forth in front of her face, stopping me before I could continue. "God, your family is fucking weird."

"Sorry. I know you didn't sign up for this shit when we met in high school."

She snickered and swung her foot off the seat. "Are you kidding me? I mean, I know you guys are... out there, but I love your family's *shit*. I just worry about you."

"You don't have to. I've seen him a couple of times since then, including last night right after the hunt. If he wanted to hurt me, he would have already tried." I exhaled and slowly shook my head. "I like him, Jules. A lot."

"Speaking of the hunt," she said with a cocky grin. "Did you kill one?"

"As a matter of fact, I did."

"Seriously?"

I stared at the table as I thought about the Night Walker pinning me to the wall with that blank look on his face. The knife felt like an extension of my own hand as I sliced his head off and watched it roll across the floor. The sensation it gave me felt so right and so wrong at the same time, kind of like how I felt when I was staring at that painting this morning.

"Yeah," I said, still looking down at the table. "And you know what? It felt good."

The waitress set my plate down, snapping me out of the memory of last night. When I looked back up at Jules, she was waiting for me to continue. "Does that make me evil?"

She took a bite of her pasta without taking her eyes off me. "I think it makes you human—and honest. Seriously, Morgan. You've been through a hell of a lot lately, what with your mom and everything. I think you've earned your right to a little depravity."

I picked at my salad and laughed. "Only you could find a legitimate way to defend depravity, Jules."

She glanced at the bracelet on my wrist. "That's nice." Then she did a double take and grabbed my arm. "It matches the ring."

Without thinking, I yanked my arm away and knocked her glass over in the process, splashing red wine all over her clothes. "Don't touch it!" I growled.

The look on her face was one of anger and surprise, letting me know I'd crossed a line. "What the hell, Morgan?"

Yeah, what the hell?

CHAPTER 17

Edward took me home at seven o'clock. My feet were on fire, and all I wanted to do was get out of my shoes and have a glass of wine before settling in with the journal.

After I'd apologized profusely to my best friend for snapping at her like a lunatic at lunch, we'd dropped her off at her shop and I'd gone back to work. I don't know why, but I wanted that bracelet off my wrist as soon as possible, and the clasp wouldn't budge. I thought I'd have to break it, but it mysteriously dropped from my wrist when I pulled a pair of pliers from my desk drawer, a handy tool in my profession.

"Michael is looking for you." Jakob said, glancing up from his book when I walked into the lobby.

"I know. He left me a couple of messages." He'd called me twice while I was in a meeting that afternoon. "I'll call him later."

The elevator door opened, and Michael was standing inside.

"Perfect timing," he said, grabbing my arm to pull me in. "You weren't ignoring me, were you?"

"I was in a meeting when you called." I stepped inside and reached for the penthouse button, but he beat me to it and pushed the button for his floor instead. "You're coming to my place for a little chat."

"Michael, please," I groaned, knowing we'd end up discussing his latest boyfriend problems for half the night.

"We need to talk, Morgan." By the look on his face, I could tell it wasn't his love life. Something was seriously wrong for him to sport such a grave expression. "And don't argue with me."

We got off the elevator and headed inside his apartment. As a bachelor, Michael had one of the smaller units in the building, without four extra bedrooms and all the unnecessary space. His walls were covered with overpriced contemporary art mingled with his own paintings, which often bordered on the bizarre, reminiscent of Salvador Dalí or Leonora Carrington. But as a former culinary student, he did have a large kitchen with all the tools any chef would die for—a professional range, an enormous refrigerator built into the wall, and stainless steel countertops. He even had a marble-slabbed work area for his obsession with confections that required quick cooling of chocolate and spun sugar creations.

I followed him into the kitchen and sat down at the island while he grabbed a box from the counter.

"Try this," he said, handing me a chocolate ball. "I've been experimenting with chipotle."

When I bit into it, the soft filling spread across my tongue like silk. The pepper ignited in my mouth in a burst of heat that quickly melded with the sweetness of the dark chocolate before I could run to the sink for water. "Wow," I said, licking my lips to capture every drop. "That was amazing."

"Good, isn't it? I was thinking of selling the recipe."

Not that he needed the money, but Michael had found a way to capitalize on his culinary training without having to set foot in a commercial kitchen. He sold his recipes to high-end restaurants, often getting paid by the hour to develop something specific.

"Well, you have a winner there."

"Yeah, it's brilliant," he said, handing me the box. "Take them. I made extra."

I set the box on the counter and got on with it. "So, what did you want to talk about?" I was eager to get this over with so I could go upstairs and unwind after my long day.

The intense way he was looking at me was making me uncomfortable. Michael was uncomplicated, rarely dampening my mood, but this evening was one of those occasions. Before I could press him to get to the reason he'd dragged me in here, he turned around and pulled a plate from the refrigerator. Another experimental recipe, I assumed.

"Hungry?" he asked.

"Not really."

He slid the plate toward me and handed me a fork. "Try it anyway."

I indulged him, hoping it would get me out of there quicker than arguing about it. "What is it? A salad?" Not his usual exotic fare, but still a work of art on a plate. I stuck my fork into a bright red medallion and held it up. "Pickled beets?"

"No," he said as I took a bite and began to chew. "It's my interpretation of beef ceviche."

The taste of raw meat filled my mouth, gagging me as I ran to the sink to spit it out. "You *asshole*!" I snapped at him after rinsing my mouth with water from the faucet. I'd sworn off red meat years ago, and he knew it. "Why did you do that to me?" I wiped my mouth with the dish towel before turning around to glare at him.

"I guess I just wanted to see if my sister was back."

I continued to stare at him like he was crazy. "What the hell is wrong with you, Michael?"

"I think a better question is what the hell is wrong with you?"

"Me?"

He ran his hand over his head and blurted out a humorless laugh. "You don't remember any of it, do you?"

"Jesus, Michael, what are you talking about? What am I supposed to remember?"

He grabbed the plate and walked over to the sink with that strange, concerned look on his face again. "I woke up in the middle of the night and thought I saw you sitting in the corner of my bedroom." While he shoved the food down the garbage disposal, my mind worked frantically to process what he was saying. "Of course I had to be dreaming, so I turned over and went back to sleep. I woke up a few minutes later and found you in here, eating that meat, only it hadn't been sliced and marinated yet."

"I don't know what you're talking about," I said, my defenses rising.

He turned around and pointed to the spot where he'd just fed me that vile salad. "You had a raw beef tenderloin in your hands, and you were gnawing on it like an animal. Jesus, Morgan, you were eating it with your bare hands! I cleaned you up and put you to bed in the spare room, but you were gone when I got up this morning."

What are you doing, Morgan?

I was hungry.

I almost fell over when my dream came rushing back. "I was dreaming," I whispered. "It was only a dream."

He took me by the shoulders and shook his head. "No, it wasn't. You scared the shit out of me."

My brow tightened as I frantically tried to reconcile what had happened the night before. "Maybe it was," I said, nodding. "I must have been walking in my sleep. You remember. I used to do it all the time when I was a kid."

When I was five or six, I used to sleepwalk and take the elevator down to the lobby in the middle of the night. I was tall enough to reach door handles and elevator buttons. If it hadn't been for the lock requiring a key on the front door of the building, I would have been strolling around Central Park in my nightgown. More than once, someone in the building had forgotten to lock their front door and had found me sleeping on their sofa in the morning.

Michael gave me a weak smile. "You had your first hunt last night. Maybe—"

"That's right!" I hadn't talked to him since, so he didn't know about my first kill. That could make anyone have bad dreams and do strange things. "I killed my first Walker last night. It probably messed with my head." I tried to convince myself, but I was anything but confident that my strange behavior was a fluke.

He studied me for a few seconds. "Maybe. You should sleep down here for a few days just in case. I'm a little worried about you."

I got up to leave. "I appreciate the offer, but I'll be fine."

After convincing him that I wasn't losing my mind, I went upstairs to the penthouse and headed straight for the conservatory, ignoring Otto's greeting as it echoed off the walls. Something was definitely wrong with me, and I prayed Monoclaude could help me figure it out before I ended up in Michael's kitchen again. Or worse, Cabot's. The whole clan would know about it if Rebecca caught me rummaging thought her refrigerator in the middle of the night.

The conservatory was hotter and muggier than usual, but the orchids loved it and rewarded me with a heady fragrance. I was barely inside when I heard a strange sound.

"Monoclaude?"

My shoes slipped on the wet floor as I headed toward the back where the conservatory ended and Monoclaude's world began. I took them off and continued in my bare feet as the sound of the waterfall grew louder. When I reached it, there was no sign of him anywhere.

"I know you're here," I said, trying to hide the feeling of dread getting stronger by the second. "The crow is gone, so you're all I have left."

It was too quiet. The birds and insects that usually made themselves known in the distance suddenly went silent, and the water cascading over the rocks began to trickle and come to a stop.

"Monoclaude!" I called louder. "Jesus, frog, you're scaring me!"

Something caught my eye near the edge of the pond. I crept closer, shaking my head as I recognized what it was.

"No," I whispered, dropping to my knees near a heap of shattered stone. I gathered the pieces into a pile, trying to fit Monoclaude back together. "We can fix this," I kept repeating.

A loud sound came from somewhere in the orchid room. Something had either fallen or gotten knocked over. "Who's there?" I yelled.

I let go of the pile of stone and stood up to head back toward the door, the energy in my hand growing hotter from my fear. Slowly I crept toward the thicket of ferns that separated the conservatory from Monoclaude's realm, each step making my heart beat faster. Then the lights went out.

"Show yourself, coward!" My fear dissolved as my rage took over.

A tall shadow raced across the conservatory wall, blocking out the snow-white blooms that glowed from the moonlight shining through the glass. The door swung open, and a fog filled the terrace as a cloud of moisture escaped.

When I reached the entrance, there was nothing there. The

terrace was empty, but I caught a glimpse of something trapped in the hinge of the door. It was a shiny black feather.

Filled with rage, I ran to the wall and searched the sky. "You want out?" I yelled. "You've got it." I reached inside my shirt and ripped the chain from my neck, hurling the alchemy pendant into the wind. "I'll hunt you down and kill you for this!"

I stood there for a few minutes, looking out over the park, catching my breath and letting my racing heartbeat settle. I didn't know what to do. Monoclaude was gone. If I'd come straight home instead of going to Michael's apartment, I might have prevented this.

My phone rang, distracting me from all my grief and guilt.

"Get dressed," Cabot said when I ran inside and answered it.

"For what?"

"We're going hunting tonight."

"Good," I said. "I need to kill something."

CHAPTER 18

When I got off the elevator and stepped into council chambers, everyone was already there, including Jakob.

"Why are you here?" I asked, surprised to see him.

In true control-freak fashion, Cabot answered before Jakob could even open his mouth. "Tonight's hunt will be challenging, so we'll need every hand we can get, and Jakob used to be one of the best."

"Used to be?" Once a master always a master. Cabot's comment was an insult.

"Cabot's right," Jakob said. "I laid down my seal a long time ago. I'm only here for you, Mora."

"Me?"

The snicker coming out of Cabot's mouth almost set me off, but I held my tongue for the sake of a smooth hunt. Nothing like a fallout with a teammate right before jumping into the arena.

Of course Cabot had to comment. "I think he's worried about his queen."

"As I should be. And so should you," he added, which wiped the sneer from Cabot's face. What was with these two? "Besides, it was either me or Michael."

Was Cabot insane? "Michael? You're kidding me."

There were only two mortals in the circle—me and Ethan. Michael had no obligation to serve yet, and he wasn't even close to reaching majority. He'd die out there without someone protecting him during the entire hunt. A hindrance more than a help. What was the point?

"You won't throw Michael to the wolves," I said to Cabot. "Not as long as I'm queen of this clan."

The room buzzed with murmurs. Not since my mother had someone spoken to him so bluntly, but Michael was more important than Cabot's bruised ego.

James hijacked the awkward conversation. "What did the Flyers say?"

Cabot backed down and pulled his eyes away from mine. "They found a hive."

I took a seat next to Jakob, the one person in the room I could trust more than all the rest, and glanced at all their stunned faces. Even Jakob seemed surprised. "What's a hive?"

"Just what it sounds like," James said with a satisfied grin. "The mother lode. The nest."

Cabot clarified it for me. "It's where they live. A large cell of them anyway. We've been looking for this particular one for some time now."

"And every time you find it, half of them escape and start a new hive," Jakob said.

Cabot gave him a look. Calm, measured, filled with contempt, it was hard to read. "Perhaps you can rejoin us permanently and grace us with your tracking skills."

Jakob bit his tongue, and I began to wonder why he'd really left the Circle. That was a conversation I planned to have with him very soon.

"Where is this hive?" I asked.

"An old theater in the South Bronx. It's been closed for

decades. The Flyers believe there's an underground room where they sleep."

"I think it's called a basement," Ethan said, slouching in his chair with his eyes glued to his phone.

I thought Cabot was going to wipe the smirk right off Ethan's face. "Since you've so wisely identified this *basement*, I'll let you go first when we get there so you can find it for us."

Ethan shoved his phone in his pocket and sat up. "I just meant—"

"We're entering a war zone tonight," Cabot continued. "The room is buried underground, and the Flyers haven't been able to figure out how the Walkers are getting in and out of it."

"No door?" Jakob asked, his brow raised.

Cabot shook his head. "They go in, but they don't come out. When the Flyers swoop in to investigate, the place is empty."

When no one asked the obvious question, I decided to. "How do they know the Walkers are underground?" I got chills envisioning sleeping vampires hanging upside-down from the rafters. "Is there an attic?"

"Don't forget what the Flyers are. They're animals. They can hear and smell them belowground, and that's all the confirmation we need."

Olivia stood up and nudged her brother. "Let's get moving. I have a date when we're done exterminating these fuckers tonight."

Exceptionally beautiful *and* intelligent, Olivia plowed through men with a vengeance. Mortal men were her favorites. They didn't stand a chance when she set her sights on one of them. After playing with tonight's conquest, she'd move on to a new one tomorrow, and the day after that. Her twin was just as ravenous with women. If my uncle Samuel were here, I was certain he'd put a stop to all the carnal carnage.

We headed out the same way we had the night before and

walked straight through the wall of a building on the other side of the back alley. As we stepped through the travel portal and exited at our destination, the East River was the first thing I saw, with Rikers Island in the distance. I kept looking overhead to see if Hawk was circling the sky—or that traitorous crow that had a dagger waiting for him if I found out he killed Monoclaude.

A few blocks west, we spotted the theater. Like the night before, Olivia and James headed inside first while the rest of us waited for Cabot to give us our orders.

"You were kidding about me going down into that hellhole first, right?" Ethan asked Cabot.

Cabot didn't bother to reply. Instead, he studied the building for a minute. "Head down the alley on the left but stay outside until someone gives you the all clear." As Ethan started to head across the street, Cabot grabbed his arm. "I mean it," he growled. "We can't afford anyone going commando tonight. Wait for a signal."

"I got it." Ethan yanked his arm away. "Take it easy, man."

My brother was smart, but smarts and wisdom are two different things, and Ethan could be impulsive. I was perfectly happy letting Cabot rein him in and call the shots during the hunt. At least for now.

Cabot motioned for me to go with Rebecca.

"Morgan can come with me," Jakob said, my given name sounding foreign coming out of his mouth, testament to the grave nature of tonight's hunt.

Cabot got that snide look on his face again, the same one from earlier. "You want to question me about my decisions for a hunt, do it back at the house. Besides, I need you with me." He reached out and shoved me toward his wife. "Move."

I hesitated and glanced at Jakob. He nodded for me to follow her, and I knew he'd have my back once we were inside.

When we reached the theater, Rebecca made a beeline for the

steel steps of the fire escape that led to the second floor. She took them silently two at a time, like the cat that she was, not bothering to look back to see if I was behind her.

When we reached the top, she pressed her back against the wall and craned her neck to look through the broken window. Then she nodded for me to climb through first. "Don't cut yourself," she whispered, motioning to the jagged glass protruding from the frame. It wasn't out of concern for me. Blood would bring the Walkers out like hungry wolves.

She followed me inside and headed across what looked like a concession area for the second-floor mezzanine. After all these years, there were still empty popcorn boxes and candy bar wrappers scattered around the floor.

I heard what sounded like a plastic cup being crushed under the weight of a shoe. Rebecca yanked me back against the wall and clamped her gloved hand over my mouth. A shadow appeared in the archway leading to the balcony, and Ethan stepped through it and charged us with his knife raised in the air. He stopped a few feet away when he realized it was us.

As she continued to muffle my mouth and use me as her human shield, I almost bit into her glove. When I finally broke free from her, I gave her a knowing glare that made her look away.

"Where's Cabot and Jakob?" I whispered to Ethan.

He pointed toward the roof. "The place is empty," he whispered back. "Start looking for a door."

After checking the mezzanine for visitors and finding none, Rebecca headed down the left staircase while I followed Ethan down the right. I didn't care what Cabot said, I was sticking with my brother.

The main floor was eerily quiet. Rebecca was already working her way across the wall at the other end of the theater, looking for a hidden door in the paneling. I started on our side while Ethan walked ahead and did the same halfway down. The old paneling was still in good shape. Filthy, but solid. It was a shame to waste such a beautiful old building to house Night Walkers.

They met up at the front row while I continued making my way down the wall toward the halfway point where Ethan had started. When I glanced over at them, they were on top of the stage and heading for the back.

"Shit," I hissed under my breath, suddenly feeling very vulnerable when they disappeared behind the old curtain that was literally hanging by threads. Cabot, Jakob, and the twins were nowhere in sight either.

Cabot eventually came through the archway and walked down the aisle toward me. "Don't waste your time," he said, his voice hushed as he placed an unlit cigarette between his lips. "It's not in the wall. It's got to be somewhere backstage."

"Why do you do that?" I asked. "With the unlit cigarette?"

His brow arched as he muttered around it. "So we don't get killed."

"I've just never seen you smoke before."

He took it out of his mouth and stuffed it in his pocket. "That's because I don't." Then he headed across a row of seats, barely fitting between the narrow gap, motioning for me to follow.

I headed down the next row, moving with more ease than he had. As I turned down the main aisle to catch up to him, I heard a sound above me. When I looked up, I almost shrieked but caught myself before blowing everything to hell. Olivia and James were hovering overhead, pressed against the high ceiling. Despite managing to keep my mouth shut, I stumbled and grabbed the edge of a seat, twisting my ankle as my foot crashed through a rotting floorboard.

James descended from the ceiling and landed next to me. "Can you move it?"

"I think so." I applied pressure to see if my ankle was injured. That's when I felt something soft move under my foot.

He looked at my shocked face, and without a word he yanked my foot out of the floor. A pale arm reached out from the splintered hole and grabbed at my leg. As I fell and backpedaled, James grabbed me around the waist and flew back up to the ceiling, giving us both a bird's-eye view of the horror below.

The hole in the floor began to widen, and all I could see was a soup of ghostly limbs squeezing through the small break until the floor burst into a cloud of splinters. The room filled with the sound of hisses as the Night Walkers began to wake up.

"Jakob!" I screamed, spotting him on the second-floor balcony. "They're in the floor!"

He jumped down, landing in the aisle about ten feet away from the hole. *"Fuck."*

Olivia flew across the room and disappeared behind the ragged curtain. A second later, Cabot, Ethan, and Rebecca appeared on the stage while the vampires continued to crawl through the floor. More appeared between the rows of seats. The "doors" were everywhere, nothing but loose planks. The Night Walkers were sleeping under the floor.

"We're going down," James said.

I glanced at the swarm of Walkers directly below us. "Down there?"

Without bothering to ease my concern, he flew across the room, over the sea of vampires, and set me down on the stage. "You do have your knife?"

Still stunned, I quickly recovered and pulled my dagger out. "How do we get out of this alive?"

He grunted a laugh. "We kill them all."

James flew into the swarm and started hacking away. Olivia descended next to him, releasing a primal cry as she sliced heads off like a banshee on fire. Cabot and Jakob were already in the thick of it too. They'd somehow maneuvered to the top of the theater and were working their way back down toward the stage like a well-oiled machine, working as a lethal team.

Jakob kept glancing at me with a look of fear in his eyes. Not for himself but for me.

While I stood there contemplating where to jump in, something came up behind me and knocked me to the ground. I rolled onto my back as a Walker landed on top of me, aiming for my jugular. Unable to reach the knife that had been knocked out of my hand, I shoved him back and prepared to hit him with a ball of energy. He laughed and grabbed my power hand, digging his teeth into my wrist before I could strike. I managed to reach the dagger with my other hand and jabbed it into his rib cage. He barely flinched.

As I felt myself start to fade from the pain, I pulled the blade from his ribs. The rest was a blur. All I could hear was his head hitting the floor next to mine, his face coming to a stop with his dead eyes fixed toward the ceiling.

I sat up and looked at my wrist. He'd torn it deep, the light glowing bright in the center of my palm a few inches up from the vicious bite. But the wound began to heal before my eyes, restoring my strength.

When I climbed to my feet, I spotted Ethan across the room with two Walkers trapping him against the wall. Rebecca was closer to me, her own fate in the hands of a couple of vampires. The choice was easy. I jumped off the stage and weaved my way through the carnage, dodging the corpses. With a savage swing, I let out a loud grunt and beheaded the female about to take a bite out of my brother's shoulder. Her male companion turned and caught my wrist, twisting my arm until I howled in pain and dropped the knife. He grabbed it and raised it into the air, bringing it down hard, but I turned, letting my shoulder take the brunt of the sharp blade.

As I started to fall, a familiar face came into view. Hawk caught me and lowered me to the ground. He straightened back up, and the Walker fell to the ground next to me, his head split in two and barely attached to his neck by a thin flap of flesh.

Hawk dropped to his knees and gently rolled me on my back. My eyes focused on his face just before I spotted the knife raised above him. Ethan's dagger reflected the light coming through the window as he prepared to bring it down on Hawk's head.

"We have to get out of here," Hawk said, slipping his arms under me. I shoved him away and swept Ethan's legs out from under him, sending his knife flying into the air. He jumped to his feet before I could and caught it as it came back down. Then he turned back to Hawk to finish him off.

"No, Ethan!" I held my right hand to his chest, sending him flying back against the wall, knocking him out instantly.

Cabot, Jakob, and James were preoccupied with the Walkers on the other side of the theater. "Go!" I said to Hawk. "If they see you, you're dead!"

He hesitated but changed his mind when he saw the fierce warning in my eyes. "Get out of here, Morgan."

As Hawk's wings sprouted, Jakob turned around. He spotted the hawk as it flew through the window and kept his eyes on it for a moment before looking at me. "Are you all right?" he yelled.

I glanced at Ethan. "I'm fine, but Ethan took a bad blow. He's out."

Cabot and James finished off the last few Walkers before heading over. They bent down to pick Ethan up and carry him to the stage. As I caught my breath and headed over to check on my brother, I spotted Olivia staring at me from the side door. Had she seen Hawk? More importantly, had she seen me save him?

Her eyes never left mine as I walked past her, and something told me I'd be facing the council by morning.

CHAPTER 19

Cabot was furious. The hunt had been brutal, and most of the Night Walkers had escaped due to our failed attempt to kill them while they slept. To make it worse, I think he blamed me for sticking my foot through the rotting floor and waking them up. To hell with him.

I had a faint scar on my wrist where the Night Walker had bitten me, but thanks to the power of my right hand, the bite was no worse than a scratch. My shoulder hadn't fared as well, but Jakob applied a few drops of his blood to the wound to speed up the healing, so at least it no longer hurt like hell.

We'd suffered a few casualties with Ethan having a minor concussion and Rebecca getting her arm broken. But being immortal, she would heal completely by morning. I couldn't say the same for my brother, but he was approaching his transition, which would speed up his healing considerably.

There was a knock on the terrace door when I got off the elevator and walked into the living room. My heart began to race when I saw Hawk standing outside with a relieved look on his face.

"Are you all right?" I asked him when I opened the door.

He looked at me with disbelief. "Am *I* all right? You could have been killed tonight." His voice was sharp.

"This is what we do, Hawk. My clan hunts vampires. If anyone could have been killed tonight, it was you."

Realizing it was silly to be having the conversation at the door, I held it open and waited for him to come inside, but he just stood there at the threshold staring at me. "Oh," I said, feeling a little awkward. "I guess I need to invite you in. I thought that was just fiction. Come in."

I stepped back to avoid his brooding vibe when he walked inside. "It is fiction. I was just being polite. Do you enter someone's house without an invitation?"

"Did I do something wrong?" I asked. "Because the way I remember it, you were the one about to get your head cut off right before I intervened."

He walked past me and looked around the room. "Nice place. You're richer than I thought."

I ignored his comment and glanced at the conservatory, thinking about Monoclaude broken and gathered into a pile of shattered rocks near the waterfall. My mother would have known what to do with him, but I had no clue. In the morning I'd talk to Jakob.

"You want something to eat or drink?" As I headed for the kitchen, he grabbed my arm and spun me around. My instincts kicked in, and I automatically shoved him away.

He stumbled back and caught himself on the edge of the sofa. "Wow. You really are vicious. Twice now I've watched you wield a knife and slice off the heads on those vampires like it was nothing. It's who you are, Morgan, isn't it?"

"When it's kill or be killed, yes. The Night Walkers are a threat to everyone in this city."

For good or bad, the Winterbornes were killers. Upstanding citizens by day and assassins by night. But for some reason, the truth coming out of his mouth hit me in the gut. It was probably the look in his eyes more than anything. Last night I was straddling his lap and kissing him, and now he was looking at me like I was a coldhearted killer.

"You don't understand what we are," I said, trying to justify the bloodlust that lived inside me. Here I was, a woman who couldn't step on a bug but found it second nature to cut off the heads of vampires, trying to convince the man who made my heart skip a beat every time I looked at him that I wasn't a monster.

He took a cautious step toward me. "Then make me understand."

"We're Winterbornes. Hunting is what we were sent here to do." I looked around the penthouse that the average person would never be able to afford in their lifetime. "My clan is very old. And yes, we're rich, but we make sacrifices for that. Our Elders struck a deal with the gods centuries ago. We rid the world of Night Walkers, and in return they give us…"

"Give you what?" he asked, pressing me for the truth.

I gazed out the door at the conservatory, unable to get Monoclaude out of my mind, wondering what he would think of my divulging the clan's secrets to a vampire. "Immortality."

Hawk stared at me for a few seconds as if he hadn't heard me correctly. "You're immortal? How could I have missed that?" he muttered under his breath, cocking his head and squinting at me. "You don't look like an immortal, and you don't smell like one either."

There he went with the *smell* thing again.

"You need to stop smelling me, Hawk."

He shrugged and stepped closer. "It's the hawk in me. My eyesight is superior too." By the way he was examining me, I doubted he was convinced. "If you're immortal, you shouldn't have needed me to catch you the other night when I tossed you over the building."

Way to go, Hawk. Keep reminding me.

"That's because I haven't reached majority yet. I'll transition on my thirtieth birthday. I'm a hunter because it's my duty as head of the clan." I headed toward the kitchen to get those drinks I'd offered him earlier. Even if he didn't want one, I did.

"So you're a witch and a future immortal?" he said, following me into the kitchen.

"That's right." I poured two glasses of wine and handed him one. "Congratulations. You know my deepest and darkest secrets."

"Then we're even."

I knew his, and he knew mine. If things went south for us, our leverage against each other would mutually cancel out.

He drank his wine in one shot and set his glass down, leaning closer to look into my eyes. I would have taken a step back, but I was already pressed against the counter. Instead, I lowered my eyes to his chest.

"I'm half vampire," he whispered as he lifted my chin to bring my eyes back up to his. "Will you eventually kill me too?"

My breath hitched when I saw the gold in his eyes shine. "I hope I don't have to."

He slid his hands around my waist and pulled me against him, barely touching his lips to mine until I couldn't stand it any longer. I deepened the kiss and forgot about all the things that could tear us apart. Half vampire, half hawk—it meant nothing in that moment.

I took his hand and led him to the bedroom, stripping off my clothes before he could come to his senses and change his mind. He didn't. We stood naked in the moonlight shining through the windows and gazed at each other, separated by just enough distance to consider the consequences of our union. Then we met in the middle and embraced, falling onto the bed without a doubt in our minds that the choice was no longer ours to make.

～

I ROLLED over and watched my vampire sleep, his thick eyelashes twitching as he dreamed.

Dear diary, what the fuck have I done?

It was six thirty, an hour before I had to get up. We were up half the night and had probably gotten less than two hours of sleep. By noon it would catch up with me.

Too distracted to go back to sleep for a few more minutes, I quietly pulled the journal out of the nightstand drawer and continued where I'd left off.

Katherine Winterborne
December 28, 1994

It's been weeks since I've written. I guess I've been a bit of a zombie lately, paralyzed with fear of what will happen next and unable to put down in words what I'm feeling right now. But I think what scares me most is documenting the truth for anyone to stumble across. What if I get hit by a bus tomorrow? My things will be picked through, and this journal will be all the evidence the clan needs.

Phillip has been calling me and trying to talk his way back into the house. After what I've done, that can never happen. He's a good man. I love him, but I've never been in love with him. Not the way a wife should love her husband. Our marriage was nothing more than a convenient solution for my unplanned pregnancy with Avery, and that's all it's ever been. And now I've felt real passion for the first time in my life, and I'll never settle again.

Unfortunately, there are consequences for this passion. Ryker is beginning to scare me. I tried to end the affair shortly after I discovered what he was. Well, discovered is a pleasant word. Ryker went out of his way to show me and to make it very clear that I would never leave him, and he holds something very precious as collateral. That and the power he's always had over me. If I had only known what he was before he seduced me, I would have died before taking the risk.

For now I'll play Ryker's game. But there will come a day when I'll be free. They say the truth will set you free, but this truth will be a death sentence for my unborn child. I'm pregnant with a girl. I know it in my heart, and the gods have shown me.

So, I write our history for you, Morgan, and I've made damn sure this journal will be well hidden until you're ready to know your legacy. The dark legacy of all Winterborne women.

I DROPPED the journal in my lap, stunned by what I'd just read. Then I picked it up and read it again twice to make sure I hadn't misinterpreted the part where she mentioned my name. Michael was right, at least about my being a product of our mother's affair. Avery and Ethan were both born years before they'd met, and based on her obvious regret when she found out what Ryker was, I doubted she'd made the same mistake twice. She must have gotten pregnant with Michael after Phillip moved back in.

"That must be why he's stalking me," I whispered to myself. "I'm his daughter."

Hawk woke up and pulled me toward him. "What's this?" he said when the journal slid from my lap and fell between us. He rolled onto his back, grinning as he opened it. "Are you writing about me in your diary?"

I snatched it out of his hand and hopped off the bed. "It's my mother's journal."

He must have read the shock on my face because he lost his playful smile and sat up. "Is everything all right?"

"Everything's fine." I grabbed my robe from the chair and quickly put it on. "I have to get ready for work, and you should probably get going before the sun comes up." I just assumed his vampire side was intolerant of sunlight.

By the look on his face, I'd given him the wrong idea. Made him feel convenient and used. "I guess I should leave." He found his pants and pulled them on but stopped to look at me before hunting for his shirt. "Did I do something wrong? Because I thought we were both enjoying ourselves last night."

I put the journal back in the nightstand and shut the drawer. "Last night was perfect. I just remembered an early meeting I have at the auction house this morning." It occurred to me that he knew nothing about my mundane life. "We own Winterborne's. It's an auction house."

"I know what Winterborne's is," he said, searching for his missing clothes.

He finally found his shirt, but before he could put it on, I wrapped my arms around his waist. "I'm sorry, Hawk. I'm not trying to get rid of you." His skin was soft against my cheek. "I wish I could keep you here all day."

"Good, because I'll be back tonight."

Otto's voice startled both of us. "You have a visitor, mistress."

Before I could think to hide Hawk in the closet, Avery came

barging into the bedroom. "Don't tell me you're still in bed." She stopped in her tracks when she saw Hawk standing next to me half-naked.

Hawk pulled his shirt on and extended his hand. "I'm Hawk."

Avery gave him a once-over before shaking it. "*Oookay*. It's nice to meet you, Hawk." She glanced at me and then back at him.

"Coffee?" I grabbed Hawk's hand and headed for the kitchen to make some.

"I have to go," he said as I dragged him halfway across the living room. "I'll see you tonight?"

I nodded, and he headed for the terrace without thinking.

Avery went to the door after he walked outside. "Where did he go?" she asked, stretching her neck to look past the conservatory.

"Uh… home?"

She followed me into the kitchen and grabbed my wrist to turn me around. "I was going to ask you who your new friend is, but I guess I should be asking you *what* he is. Unless you've had an elevator installed recently, there's only one way off the terrace, and don't tell me he's waiting for you in the conservatory."

I pulled my wrist away and started the coffee, hoping she'd drop it if I ignored her. Avery was smart, but she had the attention span of a two-year-old at a circus.

"Hawk," she said, cocking her head. "What an odd name. His parents must be new-age hippies."

"Something like that," I mumbled.

"Tell you what," she said. "I'll tell you about my new boyfriend if you tell me about yours."

Avery had been on the rebound for nearly two years. After her douchebag boyfriend, Royce, broke off their engagement a month before the wedding, she swore off relationships and hadn't started seeing anyone since. She said she was tired of men, but I thought she'd been pining for Royce all along.

"You first," I said.

"Well..." She got a ridiculous grin on her face as her eyes traveled up toward the ceiling like she was trying to find the words to describe him. "His name is Decker and he's rich, which doesn't really matter because, well, so am I. And he's very handsome." She went on for the next few minutes about this and that, boring me to tears.

The coffeepot mercifully filled, and I handed her a cup. "There's half-and-half in the fridge if you're drinking dairy again."

She sipped her black coffee and continued without missing a beat. "I've been exploring Buddhism."

I choked and nearly spit my coffee out. "Buddhism? You have got to be kidding me." Avery was a borderline atheist, which didn't sit well with the clan—or the gods. The only thing she seemed to believe in these days was herself.

"Well, I'm glad you find that funny. Do you want to hear this or not?"

"Please," I said. "Continue."

"I met him at a meet-and-greet at the temple. We hit it off immediately, and I decided to become one of his pupils."

Suddenly fascinated by the conversation, I asked, "What kind of pupil?"

"He's my spiritual advisor. Laugh all you want, Morgan, but he's helping me."

Avery never asked for help from anyone. She couldn't even conceive of the idea that someone knew better than her. The epitome of a know-it-all.

"He's helping me shed my immortality."

The cup went still at my lips. You didn't just *shed* immortality. You could go to the Winterlands like our grandparents had, but there was no guarantee of ever finding your way back out, especially without the help of the immortals she wished to distance herself from. And affronting the gods with such a request could get you killed. Make no mistake, Avery liked her life. But underneath it all, she just wanted to be a privileged mortal New Yorker with an Upper East Side address, a devoted mortal husband, and two perfect children enrolled in Dalton.

There was more to this story. I could feel it. And then she proved me right.

"We've been living together for a few weeks, but don't you dare tell Cabot or the Elders. They'll cut me off."

"No one's cutting you off, Avery. At least not as long as I'm head of the clan." Spiritual advisor? Please. I suspected he wasn't rich at all and was after her money.

She took another sip of her coffee and grimaced. After putting her cup in the sink, she folded her arms and gave me a pointed look. "It's your turn."

There was no time to beat around the bush, and I had leverage now. "Hawk? He's a shifter." I didn't dare mention the vampire part because that might have been enough for her to betray me, for my own good of course. "I'm sure he was already flying over the park before you made it to the terrace door."

"Really, Morgan? A shifter?"

"You're such a snob, Avery." I headed out of the kitchen. "I have to get to work, so let yourself out."

She headed for the elevator but stopped to check her face in the mirror. "We'll invite you and Hawk to dinner next week. You're going to love Decker."

"I look forward to it," I said as she got on the elevator.

As soon as she was gone, I went out to the conservatory to see if, by some miracle, those shattered pieces of stone had put themselves back together again. It wouldn't be the first time a witch's familiar had escaped death.

I made my way past the orchids and headed for the waterfall.

As I took a step through the giant ferns, I hit something hard. I stuck my hand beyond the leaves and felt a flat wall against my palm. My heart raced as I tore at the foliage and clawed at the wall until my fingers hurt.

A lump filled my throat as I stepped back and looked at the solid wall where the conservatory ended and Monoclaude's realm used to begin. He was gone.

CHAPTER 20

The entire world beyond the boundaries of the conservatory was gone, along with Monoclaude's stony remains. I touched the solid wall one more time and pulled myself together because I couldn't call my assistant at the auction house and tell her my old familiar had died and I needed to take the day off to mourn.

After putting on a pair of slacks and a white blouse, I sat in front of the mirror to do something with my face. The sight of my messy hair and the bed in the reflection conjured the memory of Hawk and me having sex the night before. Or making love. Whatever we were doing. Time would tell what last night really was. All I knew was that his skin had felt right against mine, and I couldn't wait to feel it again.

I glanced at the three green boxes on the dresser. I don't know why, but I put the bracelet on, and the moment it touched my skin, I felt a surge of energy run up my arm. Maybe it was because I thought it had belonged to my mother at one time, just like the earrings had. It practically glowed against my fair skin. I put the earrings on next, my smile growing as that same spark tingled through my ears and traveled down my neck.

Before I knew it, I'd taken the ring out and slipped it on my finger.

With my eyes closed, I felt warm energy weave through me, like I was touching a live wire with a mild current running through it. Even my mood began to shift, and the sadness of losing Monoclaude drifted away. But in its place, a heaviness began to fill my chest as hunger gnawed at my throat. I suddenly felt like I was going to be sick as I stared at the bright rubies twinkling back at me through the mirror.

I took the earrings and bracelet off and put them back in their boxes before shoving them in the drawer. But when I tried to remove the ring, it wouldn't budge. The harder I pulled, the more my finger swelled, making it impossible to wedge off. I went into the bathroom and covered my hand with liquid soap, frantically twisting the ring until a streak of blood appeared. It suddenly popped off and landed in the sink, the running water washing it down the drain. I thought about letting it go, but then I turned the water off and stuck my finger into the hole as far as I could. The ring was gone, possibly stuck in the elbow of the pipe, but it would have to wait until I got home that evening.

The cut was superficial and stopped bleeding almost immediately. I wiped my hand clean and walked back into the bedroom to put the ring box back in the drawer with the others. When I picked it up, I gasped and dropped it on the dresser. Nestled in the velvet interior was the ruby ring I'd just watched disappear down the drain.

I scooped the box into the drawer, careful not to get my fingers anywhere near that ring, and slammed it shut. As I stared at the dresser, I contemplated what to do. I knew one thing for sure—I wanted that jewelry gone, preferably packaged up and addressed to Ryker Caspian on Riverside Drive.

Pulling myself together, I slipped my shoes on and headed for the elevator. On the way down, I pressed the button for Michael's floor. I needed to talk to him, and it couldn't wait. If Ryker Caspian was my father, there was a slim but possible chance he was Michael's father too.

The elevator opened, and I walked down the hallway, trying to decide what to say. The last thing I wanted to do was blurt out what I'd read in the journal that morning, although Michael was the one who'd suggested we might be products of our mother's affair. The idea didn't seem to bother him one bit. But when you hadn't known the man you thought was your father, it probably didn't matter.

The door opened a few seconds after I knocked. A guy wearing jeans and Nikes was standing on the other side.

"Hi," he said, breezing past me as he pulled his sweatshirt on and headed for the elevator.

"Who was that?" I asked Michael when I walked inside.

He sat down on the sofa and propped his feet up on the coffee table, just as scantily dressed as his friend. "Just some guy I met."

By the looks of his bare chest and messy hair, I'd say my brother was up to his usual reckless behavior. "Please tell me you at least know his name."

He swung his legs off the table and sat up, resting his elbows on his thighs. "Of course I know his… first name. Jesus, Morgan, what do you think I am?"

"I think you're a reckless little man whore." I grinned at his mock look of indignation. "At least tell me you're being safe."

He laughed it off. "I'll be immortal in six years, so who gives a shit?"

"Not if you're dead before you reach majority. Seriously, Michael, he could have been a psycho."

Leaning back into the cushion, he rubbed his face and ran his hands over the top of his head, smoothing his disheveled hair. "Do me a favor and make me some coffee before I die."

When I walked into the kitchen and opened his refrigerator to grab some orange juice, I got a shocking flashback. I swear I could smell that raw meat like it was right in front of me. "Want some juice?" I yelled to him. "Helps me when I'm hungover."

"God no," he yelled back. "What are you doing here anyway? Shouldn't you be at work?"

"I thought I'd stop by on my way out."

When I pulled my head out of the fridge, he was sitting at the kitchen island, firing up his bullshit detector. I had about five seconds to decide if I really wanted to tell him. I trusted him as much as Jakob, and I knew he'd take whatever I told him to the grave. Besides, he had a right to know if there was a possibility that he was Ryker Caspian's son. It was the part about Ryker being a vampire that made me hesitate.

"Cut the shit, Morgan. What are you doing here?"

I decided to start with the basics and see where the conversation went from there. "You know the other day when I was telling you what I read in Mom's journal? About that guy she met at the library?"

His brow knitted together as he recollected the conversation. "You mean my comment about us being bastards?"

"Well, I wouldn't use *that* term."

"It was a joke, Morgan." He lost his grin when I stared at him silently. "You're serious?"

"Mom confirmed it in her journal. She was pregnant with me when she wrote it."

"Shit," he muttered, scratching the top of his head.

"The only reason I'm telling you is because…"

"You think I might be his kid too." He gave me a long look after finishing my sentence, like he was searching for similarities between us other than the obvious ones we'd gotten from our mother.

"I can't explain my red hair," I said. "I certainly didn't get it from him."

His thoughtful expression vanished as his eyes settled on mine. "How do you know that? Have you seen him?"

"Yeah. So have you. He's the guy who was watching me at the memorial service."

Michael was rarely lost for words, but as he gazed at me, the pieces came together. "Wait a minute. You said the guy from the memorial service was the same guy in the picture Ramsey showed you. Some vampire called the Reaper."

I nodded. "My biological father is a vampire. His name is Ryker Caspian."

"Jesus Christ," he whispered, his eyes growing wider. "We're half vampire?"

"*I'm* half vampire, Michael." I feared he might panic and do something stupid like tell Cabot. "If it makes you feel any better, I think it's a long shot that she got pregnant a second time with Ryker."

"Yeah, but you don't know that for sure."

It was a mistake to tell him. I could see that it terrified him, and that made him unpredictable. "I really don't think we have the same father, Michael. And you're right, I don't know for sure. But she said in the journal that if she'd known what he was, she would have never taken the risk."

"What does that mean? Risk of what?"

"Risk of sleeping with him, I guess. She mentioned some legacy of the Winterborne women. I don't think it was an accident that the journal ended up in my office in that box. She's trying to tell me something, and I have a feeling it's going to get much worse."

CHAPTER 21

"How's the shoulder?" Jakob asked when I walked into the lobby.

"Good as new." I put on a fake smile and tried to act as if I hadn't just told my darkest secret to my brother and wasn't worried that he'd have a breakdown and tell Cabot. "Your blood seemed to do the trick."

"You would have been right as rain on your own. I just sped up the healing a little bit." He smiled and followed me as I walked. "Is everything all right?"

"Sure. Why wouldn't it be?"

He studied me for a few seconds. "You seem a little jumpy this morning. Are you sure everything's fine?"

Everything is perfect. Monoclaude is dead and my father is a vampire. What could be better?

He grabbed my arm as I headed for the door. "Where did you get that?"

I glanced at the ruby bracelet circling my wrist. I thought I'd taken it off with the rest of the jewelry. In fact, I knew I had.

Before I could answer, Edward pulled up to the curb and got

out. He walked around to the rear passenger side and leaned against the car to wait for me.

"It was my mother's." I had no time to explain it, and as soon as I got in the car, I planned to rip it off my wrist and shove it in my purse. That jewelry definitely had to go. "I'm really late for work, but we'll talk tonight." I needed to tell someone about Monoclaude because I had no idea how to properly deal with the death of a familiar. Some kind of death rite had to be performed, and I was sure Jakob would know what to do.

"I know who it belonged to," he said, letting go of my arm.

Before he could drag the conversation out any longer, I pushed the door open and walked toward the car.

Edward straightened up and buttoned his jacket before reaching for the door handle.

"Morgan!" someone called out before I could climb in.

I looked back at the doorway and saw Cabot standing next to Jakob. "I'm late, so make it quick."

"Come with me."

"Come with you where? I told you I'm late. Can it wait until tonight?" The look on his face made me nervous, and his voice had an edge to it.

When I didn't comply fast enough, he walked up to the car and took me by the arm. "Now please."

Edward glanced at Cabot's hand tightly clenched around my forearm, and his sunny expression faded. Cabot gave him a warning look and then ushered me back toward the building.

Jakob was watching from the doorway and nodded discreetly for me to cooperate with my uncle.

I pulled my arm out of his grip and glanced back at the car. "Wait for me, Edward. This shouldn't take very long." When we were back inside, I glared at Cabot. "Don't ever grab me like that again."

My warning didn't seem to faze him as he headed for the

elevator, glancing back to make sure I was following him. Jakob grabbed my forearm as I walked past him, slipping the bracelet off my wrist like a magician performing sleight of hand. He shoved it in his pocket, and I didn't question it.

When I stepped into the elevator, Cabot pushed the button for council chambers but didn't say another word as we ascended. My heart began to race as my imagination went wild. Had Michael panicked and called Cabot the second I left his apartment? My mouth went dry when the door opened and the entire clan was seated at the table. Everyone but Avery, who had all but relinquished her family ties.

I locked eyes with Michael as I walked past him, but his expression was impossible to read.

As I took a seat, Ramsey came through the wall with the rest of the Elders behind him. "Morgan Winterborne," he bellowed dramatically as he approached the table. "You have been accused of a high crime."

My mind raced so fast I felt dizzy. I had no idea what was going on, but it didn't seem like they were about to slice my head off for being the daughter of the notorious Reaper. I shot Michael another look, this one filled with fear. He must have suddenly realized I thought he'd betrayed me, because he suddenly looked horrified and discreetly shook his head.

As my eyes wandered around the table, Ramsey's voice muting in my ears, I caught Rebecca's accusatory glare. Then I realized why I was there. I knew Olivia had seen me with Hawk in the theater, but Rebecca must have seen us too. I'd rushed right past her to save my brother, leaving her to fend for herself with those vampires cornering her against the wall, and I bet she couldn't wait to pay me back. Which one had betrayed me?

Ramsey continued. "You are accused of consorting with the enemy. Do you deny attacking a fellow Circle member last night in order to prevent him from killing a Night Walker?"

"Yes," I said, denying it. Hawk wasn't a Night Walker, so the accusation was technically false. But they must have sensed his vampire blood and assumed he was.

The room filled with whispers when I replied, but Ramsey kept going as if he hadn't heard me. "The same Walker who attacked Rebecca Winterborne this morning."

Rebecca pushed her chair back and stood up, unbuttoning her blouse just enough to pull it away from her left shoulder to reveal a vicious bite mark. "I went for an early run this morning around five a.m., but I didn't get very far."

Since when did Rebecca run?

"He's not a Night Walker," I said. "And there's no way he did this." I'd helped Hawk in the theater, and I was about to pay the price for that, but I knew he couldn't have attacked Rebecca because he was with me until dawn. But if I was stupid enough to provide his alibi, they'd sentence me to a worse crime and kill him anyway. One way or another, Hawk was damned.

Cabot, who had held his tongue so far, stood up to retrieve a laptop from the deck. He set it on the table in front of me and hit the Play button on a security video. It showed Rebecca dressed in leggings and running shoes leaving the building before dawn. But before she even made it to the end of the block, something jumped her and dragged her around the corner to the side street. It was too dark to make out the face of her attacker. A minute later, her assailant came back into view, shifted into a large bird, and flew into the park. It could have been a hawk, but it also could have been another large bird, like a falcon or a crow.

Cabot shut the laptop. "Security footage doesn't lie."

Rebecca looked at Cabot and sighed. "If it hadn't been for the knife I jammed into his side, he probably would have finished me off. All I could think about was Georgia growing up without a mother."

I had news for her. Every time she participated in a hunt, she was taking the risk of her daughter growing up motherless.

"What do you have to say for yourself, Morgan?" Ramsey demanded. "We have two witnesses, so be very careful with your reply."

So they'd both betrayed me. "His name is Hawk. And yes, I helped him because he was helping me! A Walker was about to rip my throat out, but Hawk stopped him. When Ethan tried to kill Hawk, all I did was put my hand up to stop him." I looked at my older brother, who seemed shocked and hurt by my confession. "I wasn't trying to hurt you, Ethan. Believe me, I was horrified when you hit that wall. You're my brother, for God's sake. I love you!"

"How do you know this vampire?" Cabot asked.

"Vampire *and* shifter," Rebecca said, fueling the fire. "I saw him shift and escape through the window."

I took the Fifth, because I wasn't about to tell them I'd been seeing him for days. God forbid they found out he was in bed with me when Rebecca was attacked.

"Since you refuse to defend yourself, the council has no choice but to assume your guilt in the charges against you."

There was more chatter filling my ears as Cabot stood up and held out his hand. "Relinquish your seal, Morgan."

"My seal?"

"You've committed a high crime against your clan. You've been banished from the Circle."

I pulled the green stone out from under my shirt and lifted the chain from around my neck. Before I could hand it over, Cabot snatched it from me.

"Is that it?" I said, knowing damn well the gavel hadn't swung yet. "Because I have to get to work."

"No, you don't," he said. "You no longer work for Winterborne Holdings."

"What?" I felt like I'd been punched in the gut. Like I'd lost everything. My mother, Monoclaude, and now my job. What next? My home? "Are you planning to strip me of my title and kick me out too?"

"If only we could," Rebecca said with a smug grin.

The urge to fly across the table at her was overwhelming, but that would definitely render me homeless and penniless.

"For now, you'll retain your title," Ramsey said. "You'll be sequestered in the penthouse until we hunt down this vampire and deliver justice. Once he's dead, we'll have a formal trial to address the charges and determine your fate."

Dead? Even after everything I'd said, they still intended to kill Hawk?

I laughed nervously. "You can't lock me up! I'm the head of this clan!"

"Yes, we can," Cabot said. "A high crime against the clan is sufficient to strip you of your power until the trial is completed." He stood up and headed for the elevator. "I'll escort you up."

"This is ridiculous." Not wanting to test my magic against all of theirs—especially the twins—I got up and followed him.

When we arrived at the penthouse, Cabot walked me into the living room, Otto's calm voice greeted us as we passed through the foyer. It was humiliating to be treated like a criminal in my own home. I was still head of Clan Winterborne, but what good was it if it was in title only? No one would listen to me. I was officially a pariah. A traitor.

He held his hand out when I dropped my bag on the coffee table. "Give me your phone."

"My phone? I'm not giving you my phone. Jesus, it's the only thing I have left. You might as well lock me up in solitary confinement."

His brow arched. "That can be arranged."

I groaned and handed him my only link to the outside world, feeling completely isolated as it slipped from my fingers.

"This is for your own good, Morgan. That vampire is playing you for a fool." He glanced at my bedroom door and sighed. "If it makes you feel any better, most of us have been fooled by the heart at one time or another." He stuffed the phone in his pocket and gave me a weak smile. "I know it's difficult to see that right now, but you will. In time I'm sure the clan will forgive you. We might even let you go back to work at the auction house."

As he headed toward the elevator to leave, I stopped him. "I guess you've won."

"Won?" He looked back at me with a twisted brow. "I didn't know we were at war."

"Right," I scoffed, heading for the kitchen, hoping I had a full supply of alcohol to keep me from losing my mind while I was caged up like an animal. "Your wife is a liar." I stopped and looked at him as a thought struck me. "Did you put her up to it?"

I must have pushed his buttons because his voice dropped to a growl. "That security tape didn't lie, Morgan. You're in denial."

"You can get out now."

Without another word, he left, and I went to work thinking about what to do next. Hawk was on their kill list, and I had no way to warn him. He'd show up on my terrace eventually, and they'd be waiting.

"The terrace!" I ran to the door and reached for the handle, but my hand stopped a few inches away from it, hitting an invisible wall. When my second attempt failed, I stepped back and raised my power hand to build a ball of magic in my palm, but the light I hurled at it bounced off the mysterious wall and nearly hit me when it ricocheted back.

"It won't work," someone said. "James and I sealed the place pretty tight."

I turned around and saw Olivia standing at the other end of the living room, wisely keeping her distance.

"Aren't you brave," I said, resisting the urge to unleash my anger on her because she could put me in my place in a heartbeat. "Why did you do it? I thought you were better than that."

My cousin had always been fair. She usually kept her nose out of other people's business, so I couldn't understand why she'd betrayed me. She had to have seen Hawk save me from that Walker's blow, and it was obvious I hadn't intended to hurt Ethan. She was also intelligent enough to recognize that he wasn't a Night Walker. So why hadn't she come to me before opening her mouth to the council?

"I wouldn't have said anything if he hadn't jumped Rebecca," she said. "You know she saw the whole thing last night too." She snorted a laugh. "Hell, I thought he was just trying to save his girlfriend. By the way, you've got some king-size balls."

"Meaning?"

"Hooking up with a vampire when your job is to kill them."

"Come on, Olivia. You know as well as I do he's not a Night Walker. And I'd bet my life he didn't attack Rebecca either."

"Then how do you explain that video?" She sat down and crossed her boot over her knee. "Don't be a fucking cliché, Morgan. I hate when women do that shit."

"It wasn't him in the video. You saw how dark and grainy it was. I think our dear uncle hired one of his Flyer buddies to frame Hawk."

"Why would he do that?"

I hesitated to say it because I wasn't sure I could ever trust her again. "He has his reasons." I left it at that and decided to get rid of her. The damage was done, and I had more important things to worry about than trying to convince her that Cabot was out to get me. "I don't think there's much more to say, so I think you should leave."

"I'm sorry," she said as she stood up. "I did this to protect you. I hope you see that someday."

It wasn't worth a reply. I believed she thought she was protecting me, but I couldn't forgive her for not coming to me first.

As soon as the elevator door closed, the wheels in my head started to turn. I waited a few minutes to make sure Olivia had gotten off, and then I tried to call the elevator, but I couldn't reach the button. I kept hitting an invisible barrier just like the one around the terrace door.

"Otto, get the elevator for me please." It was worth a shot, but I doubted I'd be able to step into it anyway.

"I'm sorry, mistress. I'm not authorized for that."

They must have reprogrammed Otto.

Knowing my magic was no match for the spell the twins had thrown up, I looked around for something to write on and found an empty cardboard box. It wasn't likely that Hawk would show up on my terrace while the sun was up, but I was going to make damn sure I could warn him if he did.

I tore a side off the box and grabbed a black marker. Then I dragged one of my comfy chairs over to the terrace door and sat down. I'd sleep in the damn thing if I had to. In my hand was a cardboard sign that said RUN!

CHAPTER 22

"You have visitors, mistress."

Otto's voice startled me. After sitting in that chair for hours, I'd dozed off and let the sign slip from my hand and fall to the floor. I grabbed it and stuffed it under the cushion after standing up to see who it was.

"Mora," Jakob said, looking at me with pity in his eyes. Michael was standing behind him.

"Did you come to see the outcast?" I asked them, glancing at the open elevator door. Jakob gave me a sympathetic smile, which I hated. Sympathy was the last thing I needed. "How'd you get up here?"

"We can come and go as we please," Jakob said. "It's you who can't."

"I thought the place was sealed tight?"

Michael headed for the sofa and sat down. "The twins used a binding spell on you."

"A binding spell?" My face knotted up. "That's pretty damn dirty."

"Yeah, but effective as hell. You're not going anywhere, so you might as well settle in for a while."

They'd used a spell to bind me to my own home. It wouldn't let me leave the boundaries of the penthouse.

Jakob was staring at me when I looked back at him. "It was that hawk in the theater last night," he said. "I thought I saw his true face when he flew out the window."

"By true face, you mean…"

"Vampire." His eyes roamed over my face for a few seconds. "What have you gotten yourself into, Mora?"

Unable to stand his intense stare any longer, I looked away. "He isn't what you think he is."

"Oh? Then educate me."

"His father is a vampire, but his mother was a half-breed."

"Half-breed of what?" Michael asked, suddenly curious.

Jakob filled him in before I could. "I think your sister is telling us she's in love with a tri-breed."

"I'm not in love with anyone, but I am pretty damn fond of him." But I was falling for Hawk. I think I was plummeting. "His name is Hawk, by the way. And what's a tri-breed?"

"Exactly what it sounds like. Three species in one. His mother was half human and half raptor. Correct?" He slowly shook his head and squeezed his eyes shut. "For the love of God, Mora. What were you thinking?"

I took a step back and looked him in the eye. "What was I thinking? I met a man who is kind and doesn't judge me for what *I* am. Not to mention that he saved my life last night. That's what I was thinking."

"What *you* are?" Jakob tilted his head and looked at me from the corner of his eye. "What do you mean by that?"

I hadn't told anyone but Michael about my biological father, but Hawk had to sense the vampire blood in me, even if he didn't fully recognize what it was.

"Come on, Morgan," Michael said. "It's Jakob. Just tell him."

I opened my mouth but hesitated, scared that I'd alienate the only father figure I'd ever known.

"You read the journal," Jakob said before I could continue. "You know the truth." He glanced at Michael and got a wary look in his eyes. "And you told Michael."

"You knew about Ryker?" To say I was shocked was an understatement. But then I remembered Jakob's comment to me the day I showed him what was in the mystery box.

Promise me you won't show it to Cabot until you've read it. All of it.

He got a distant look in his eyes and seemed to gaze right through me. Then he abruptly snapped out of it. "As I've told you before, you're not the only child in this clan I practically raised."

Michael stood up and met him eye to eye. "What about me?"

"Phillip was your father. Your mother was a woman who learned from her mistakes."

The comment stung. I was a mistake. She even said so in her journal.

"Don't do that, Mora," Jakob said when he saw the look on my face. "Katherine loved you. Her actions were mistakes, not you. Do you think she would have named you as her successor if she thought you were a mistake?"

She loved me, all right. But a mother's love is unconditional, even for the worst little monsters they create. If anything, she'd shown me too much love and attention. Avery used to call me our mother's little shadow because she took me everywhere with her. It was like she was afraid she'd lose me if she let me out of her sight for more than a minute.

"I have to warn Hawk," I said, changing the subject. "They'll hunt him down and kill him."

Jakob nodded, agreeing with my grim prediction. "Tell me where to find him."

I would have laughed if it wasn't so tragic. "I don't have a clue. He just shows up."

Michael snorted. "And you called me a whore?"

It was an innocent joke between us, but the look Jakob gave him was brutal.

"Come on, Jakob," Michael said, glancing at me to save him. "I didn't mean it like that. She's my sister."

Trying to cool Jakob's temper, I stepped in. "It's just a bad joke between us. Believe me, I've called him worse."

Jakob furrowed his brow and shook his head. "My father would have given me a hundred lashes for calling a woman a whore. A thousand for saying it to my sister."

"When's the next hunt?" I asked, defusing the tension between them.

Jakob finally let up on Michael and looked at me. "I'm not sure. Why?"

"Hawk follows me when we hunt. That's how he knew where I was last night."

He thought about it for a moment and then turned to leave. "Sit tight. I'll figure something out." On his way to the elevator, he glanced back at Michael. "Are you coming, boy?"

Michael hopped up and followed him, just like he had when we were children.

"Jakob," I said before they stepped into the elevator. "Don't let them hurt him."

He smiled briefly and gave me a nod, but I knew he'd be powerless against the entire clan if they got their hands on Hawk. The best I could hope for was to get to him before they did.

⁓

THE DAY DRAGGED ON. Hawk would appear on the terrace as soon as the sun went down and fall right into a trap. Cabot hadn't actually said they were watching the building, but any fool knew they were. Especially since Cabot suspected Hawk and I were intimately involved.

I left the chair a few times to try to break through the binding spell that had me trapped in my own home. But every time I tried to reach for the elevator button or slam a ball of light through the glass door, that damn wall would stop me. The spell was too powerful.

"You have a visitor, mistress."

If I survived this and still had a home when it was over, I swore I'd end that open-door policy of people just showing up whenever they pleased. I'd put my own ward on that elevator.

When I turned around to see who it was, Jakob was standing behind me. Nestled in his palm was the ruby bracelet he'd maneuvered off my wrist that morning before I followed Cabot to council chambers.

"I forgot about that," I said.

He handed it to me. "I was afraid someone would recognize it, and I figured you had enough to deal with this morning."

"I remember the earrings from her portrait in the living room," I said. "But I never saw her wear them. Or the bracelet or ring."

His face went stone cold. "You have the ring?"

"The earrings, bracelet, and the ring," I replied, looking at his puzzled eyes. "How do you know about the jewelry?"

He motioned for me to take a seat on the sofa next to him. Then he took my hand and opened it, the rubies sparkling in my palm. "Where did you get it, Mora?"

"From Ryker." I watched his eyes closely to catch his reaction. He obviously knew who Ryker Caspian was. "He left it in my office at the auction house. The earrings too."

"And the ring?"

"He walked into Jules's shop the other day and left it for me."

He dropped my hand and sighed. "Christ, he's getting bold."

"I don't have time for this, Jakob. Tell me what's going on."

The concerned look on his face turned angry. "Ryker Caspian is a vampire!" he blurted out.

"I know."

I must have shocked him, because he went silent and just gazed at me for a few seconds. "Then you know about the gene."

"The what?"

He switched gears and stood up. "Ryker nearly destroyed your mother with those rubies. If it hadn't been for Phillip coming back into her life, he would have succeeded."

I was more confused than ever. "I don't know what you're talking about. All I know is he's been following me since the memorial service, and he keeps leaving me these gifts. Jewelry that used to belong to my mother. What does he want?"

"He wants you, Mora! Why do you think your mother never let you out of her sight when you were a child? You have no idea of the power brewing in your blood, but he does and so did your mother. That light in the palm of your hand, your subconscious magic, it's nothing compared to what's sleeping inside you, and Ryker Caspian wants it."

It took a minute for my brain to figure out what he was saying, but even then I was still in the dark. I was just a witch with a few impressive abilities, nothing like the twins. But he was talking as if I was some force of nature, which I wasn't. Believe me, I'd know. I couldn't even break through a binding spell.

"Those rubies are the Caspian jewels. They're laced with power. Katherine would have lost her free will entirely if Phillip hadn't been so persistent about reconciling their marriage. He saw what happened to her every time she put those earrings on, and it got worse with the bracelet and ring. But it was the damn necklace that nearly sent her over the edge."

"Necklace?"

He gave me a curious look. "You don't have it?"

"No."

"Thank God for that," he said. "Phillip took the jewels while she was sleeping one night. She was about to leave him again, and he knew it was those rubies. The reason you never saw her wearing them was because Phillip flung them into the Hudson River that night. That's the last we've seen of them. Until now."

I felt sick to my stomach, but I had to ask. "Does Cabot know about Ryker?" All I could think about was my uncle holding the secret of my paternity as ammunition. His ace in the hole if he couldn't find an easier way to oust me while keeping me for my usefulness to the clan.

Jakob stared out the window with a somber look on his face. "No one knows. Phillip claimed you as his daughter, and life went on as if nothing had happened. Ryker finally lost his control over Katherine."

"No one knows except you, Jakob. Why is that?"

Laughing softy, he glanced at me over his shoulder. "Who do you think covered for her all those times when she disappeared to see Ryker? Your mother was like a daughter to me. I would have done anything for her. Just like you, Mora."

I'd never doubted Jakob's loyalty. I knew in my heart he'd take a bullet for me.

"Jakob?" When he turned around and looked me, I said, "You mentioned a gene. What did you mean by that?"

He clammed up and stared at me for a few seconds. "We can talk about that later. Right now I need to get you out of here so you can find Hawk, just like I used to do for your mother."

"Well, unless the twins decide to let me go, I don't think I'm going anywhere."

He grinned slyly. "Someday the twins will look like amateurs next to you. In the meantime, I have an idea. Let's go get the rest of those jewels."

We headed for the bedroom, and I took the boxes out of the dresser drawer.

"That ring isn't normal," I said, remembering the little stunt it carried out that morning. Neither was the bracelet. But if those jewels could be tossed into the Hudson River and end up on my dresser years later, surviving a bathroom drain was a pretty small feat.

"Put them on," he said.

I hesitated when I remembered the way I felt when I'd worn the set that morning.

"Don't worry," he said. "Without the necklace, you'll be fine. A little foggy but still in control for the most part. Just promise me you'll call me if you get a box with a large ruby pendant inside."

I wanted to trust his plan unconditionally, but I was a little wary about putting that ring on my finger again. "What exactly are we doing, Jakob?"

"Olivia and James put a binding spell on Morgan Winterborne. But once you put those jewels on, you'll start to become someone else. You'll lose some of your free will and start to give in to the Caspian spell."

"That's what I'm afraid of."

"I've got you, Mora. You'll be fine. Individually the jewels have little power, but the more of the set you wear, the stronger their hold on you. It's the pendant you should be afraid of. It can render the wearer completely helpless, especially when worn with the other pieces. Hence my warning to call me if it shows up on your desk."

Trusting him, I put the earrings on and then the bracelet, saving the obnoxious ring for last. The current of energy I'd felt that morning started to flow through me again. "Feels like I have my finger stuck in a low-voltage socket. I also feel a little woozy."

"Good. Let's see if we can get you out of here. Don't say a

word once we leave the bedroom. We don't want that spell picking up on your voice."

"I still don't understand how this is going to work."

He let out a heavy sigh and tried to explain it again. "Think of that spell as a blind assassin. If it can't detect your essence or hear your voice, it can't find its target. Wearing those jewels alters your essence, which basically makes you invisible to it. Understand?"

"Okay," I said, nodding. "It'll work."

"I hope," he muttered. "One other thing. We're going out through the terrace door."

I looked at him like he was crazy. "And then what? We fly?"

"Trust me."

We walked into the living room and headed for the terrace. When we approached the door, he put his hand up to stop me. After opening it, he motioned for me to walk outside.

I tried to step through the door, but my foot slowed down as it passed over the threshold, like I was walking into a wall of gel that wouldn't quite let me through. At least it wasn't a solid wall anymore. I tried again with my other foot but got the same result. Even my arm couldn't penetrate the soft wall that seemed to stretch as I pushed against it. Maybe my "essence" wasn't as altered as Jakob had anticipated.

He motioned for me to step back and gave it some thought. Then he snugged me tightly against his side and led me forward, pulling me along with him side by side as if we were one person. The resistance was still there, but it was very faint, and we slipped past it with a little effort.

"It worked!" I cringed and threw my hand over my mouth, fearing the spell had heard me and was about to suck me back in.

"It's all right," Jakob said. "You can speak now. Without a target, a binding spell is useless. It was already weakened the moment you put that jewelry on. And now that you're out of the penthouse, it's dead."

My elation suddenly went south as I looked over the edge of the building. "What are we supposed to do now?"

"Well, I guess now would be a good time for that second lesson."

"Lesson in what? Flying?"

"It's time you learned how to travel on your own." He pointed to the park across the street. "You should be able to end up over there by using this," he said, tapping his temple. "You've always had the power, you just didn't know it. It's no different than when we walk through walls and come out on the other side when we hunt."

"Yeah, but I'm just hitching a ride with the others." I suddenly questioned that logic when he grinned at me. "Aren't I?"

"It's so natural for you that you don't even know you're doing it. Your problem is you don't know how to travel at will." He nodded to the wall. "It's like teaching a baby bird to fly. The fledgling has to follow its instincts and just leap from the nest."

He couldn't be suggesting what I thought he was. "You don't really expect me to jump off the building to test that theory, do you?"

"I promise you, Mora, if you jump over that wall, you won't hit the sidewalk. Your natural abilities will kick in before that happens."

As I recalled, the last time I went over that wall, Hawk had to catch me before I splattered all over the sidewalk.

He was starting to say something else to convince me when we heard Otto's faint voice announcing visitors. "Fuck! Wrap your arms around me!"

"I forgot the journal!"

"It's too late now." He grabbed me and headed for the edge,

but instead of leaping over the wall, he walked straight through it, with me pressed tightly to his chest. I thought he was going to let go, but it was just like all the other times. A second passed and I was somewhere else, in the park across the street. This time though, I felt a rush of adrenaline that made me a little queasy. Jakob was standing a dozen yards away from me with a smile on his face.

"You did let go!" I said in disbelief. "You dropped me!"

"Calm down, Mora. You're still in one piece."

As my peripheral vision went fuzzy and the sounds of the city were replaced by a high-pitched ringing in my ears, my legs turned to jelly. "I think I need to sit down for a second." I hit the ground, and the darkness behind my closed eyes exploded in a shower of lights. It was like fireworks filling my head. A moment later, my eyes popped back open and I sat straight up. "What the hell just happened?"

Jakob walked up to me and chuckled. "You just got your passport stamped. Welcome to the wonderful world of travel."

"Yeah, but how do I do it again without jumping off a building?"

He helped me up and steadied me. "You'll get the hang of it. You'll be walking through walls before you know it."

I hoped he was right, but for now I was taking the subway or walking if I didn't get some cash.

"Give me the jewels," he said, holding out his hand.

I took everything off and gladly handed them over. "What are you going to do with them?"

"I'll try burning them this time. We'll see how useful they are after that." He glanced up at the top of the Winterborne Building and lost his smile. "But right now we need to find you a place to hide."

"I know where to go," I said, feeling for spare change in my pockets. "Got any cash?"

CHAPTER 23

"Jules is meeting me downtown," I said, handing the phone back to Jakob.

He fished a few bills out of his pocket and handed them to me. "Forty will get you there, but it won't buy much else."

"Thanks. I'll borrow some money from Jules until I can figure out what to do next." I gave him a hug and took a deep breath, feeling naked and vulnerable for the first time in my life. "What would I do without you, Jakob?"

His eyes softened as he prepared to send me out into the streets of New York without a parachute. "I'll always be here for you. I just wish your mother could be here too. She'd put those self-righteous immortals in their place." His concern for me was hard to hide. "Don't do anything stupid like try to call me or come back here before this is all over with."

I stuffed the money in my pocket and looked at the Winterborne Building across the street. "You're assuming it *will* be over with. I swear, Jakob. If they kill Hawk, I'll burn that building to the ground."

"No, you won't," he said with a weary smile. "That building is your home, and those are your people. No man is worth destroying your family over. Now go find him so you don't have to make that choice."

My heart ached when I thought about what they'd do to Jakob if they knew he'd helped me escape. "You better get back in there before they come down to the lobby. You'll be one of the first people they interrogate."

"Right." He headed back toward the street but looked back before crossing over. "Don't bother with the subway, Mora. Take a cab."

Wasting most of the money in my pocket was probably foolish, but a cab ride was tempting. I hadn't been on the subway in years, and I didn't have time to figure out which train would get me where I needed to go.

I jogged a few blocks down before exiting the park to hail a cab. On the ride down to the Village, I thought about everything that had happened over the past twenty-four hours. I'd gone from being the queen of my clan to being a fugitive, and the only thing that would make it worse was if Jakob got caught helping me. He'd be banished—or worse.

"Miss." The driver snapped me out of my dark thoughts when we pulled up to the curb.

I handed him my scarce cash and climbed out, paranoia following me all the way to the door. We were meeting at a dive bar I'd never been to before because I didn't want to risk the clan tracking me to one of our usual places.

The bar was half-empty when I walked inside, giving me a good view of the exits. And judging by the sawdust on the floor and the help-your-fucking-self decor, there was no need to wait for a nonexistent hostess to seat me. I headed for a booth in the back and waited for Jules to show up.

A skinny guy wearing a ratty T-shirt came over to take my order. When I told him to come back in a few minutes, he stuck his pencil behind his ear and let out a weird little sigh before shuffling over to the bar. Jules was never late, and I was starting to worry. Not having a phone to call her with—or to receive her call if something was wrong—was frustrating, but Jakob had pointed out the obvious reason why giving me his was a bad idea. Phones were trackable.

I was about to beg a complete stranger to let me use their phone when she walked through the front door.

"Sorry I'm late. I almost kicked some guy's ass for trying to steal a pair of boots from the shop." She slipped into the booth and plopped her bag on the table. "The son of a bitch tried to walk out wearing a pair of vintage Ferragamos. You know how much those things cost?"

When I didn't comment on her plight, her irritation turned to concern. "What's going on?" she asked, glancing down at the sawdust on the floor. "And what the hell are we doing in this dive?"

"You suggested it."

"Well, you said some place where no one would think to look for you, and I think this place qualifies. Now tell me what the hell is going on."

The waiter shuffled back to the table, so we ordered some drinks to get rid of him.

"I'm in trouble, Jules. Cabot's wife was attacked this morning. She went out for a run before sunrise—which is real interesting since I've never seen the woman so much as break a sweat before—and someone came out of nowhere and jumped her."

"That sucks, but what does that have to do with you?"

I sat back against the hard booth and exhaled. "We hunted again last night. A vampire attacked me, and Hawk showed up and killed it. Ethan saw him and thought he was a Walker. When he tried to kill Hawk with a knife, I panicked and slammed him against the wall." I showed her my palm. "Remember when I stopped that car on Park Avenue years ago when it almost hit me?"

"Please don't tell me you killed your brother."

"No, but I gave him a pretty serious concussion, and Cabot's wife, Rebecca, saw it all. Then all of a sudden, I get pulled into council chambers this morning and they show me this video and try to pin the attack on Hawk. Rebecca opened her damn mouth and told them everything."

"Why did Ethan think Hawk was a Walker?"

I'd never hear the end of it for not telling her about Hawk's *other* side. "There's something I didn't tell you about Hawk. I told you he's a shifter, but I didn't mention his other half." She prompted me to spit it out, so I did. "He's also half… vampire."

She cocked her head. "I'm sorry, what?"

"You heard me. But he's not a Night Walker," I quickly added in his defense.

"Okay," she said, throwing her hands up when I tried to continue. "You need to stop before I lose my mind."

The waiter delivered our drinks and a bowl of peanuts, which seemed to give her just enough time to settle down. She took a sip of her beer and cleared her throat. "I think you've outdone yourself this time with that little bit of news."

"Not really," I said, stuffing a few nuts in my mouth and chewing them thoroughly before giving her the next news that would put our friendship to the ultimate test. "I think I know why Hawk can't stay away from me. We're a lot alike."

"Oh yeah? How's that?" She snorted a half-baked laugh and popped a handful of peanuts in her mouth.

"Because I'm half vampire too."

ON MY WAY into the apartment building on the Upper East Side, I was accosted by an elderly woman who seemed to think she was the building police. I showed her my key and assured her I had permission to be there. After she continued through the lobby and out the entrance, I took the elevator to the eighth floor and stuck the key into the lock of apartment 821. I was so relieved to be safely inside, I slid to the floor and just sat there for a few minutes, letting the sun bathe me through the windows as it began to set.

Jules had taken the news better than I expected. But then again, she knew me better than anyone, and we'd gone through some crazy shit for each other over the years. I came from a clan of immortals, for God's sake. What was a little vampire blood running through her best friend's veins?

Eventually I climbed to my feet and headed for the kitchen to check for supplies. If Margo Wells had coffee in the cabinet, I'd be fine. Food would be nice too, but caffeine was a necessity. I was in luck and found an unopened bag of French roast.

I toured the apartment, taking an inventory of the philodendrons I'd be looking after until this was all over with or Mrs. Wells came back from vacation. Jules had given me her mother's apartment key, telling me I was doing her a favor by sparing her a trip uptown twice a week to water the plants. Her mother and current stepfather spent a month in Europe every year. This time it was Italy.

My stomach growled when I walked back into the living room. I hadn't bothered with breakfast that morning, so a handful of peanuts back at the bar was all I'd eaten since yesterday.

The refrigerator was empty except for condiments, half a dozen eggs, and a few plastic containers of something Mrs. Wells would regret not throwing out before she left for her lengthy trip. I took a whiff of the contents of one container and shuddered before tossing the whole thing into the trash. She'd thank me for it. I finally decided to open a can of baked beans I found in the cabinet and ate them cold right out of the can, a favorite meal back in college.

As the sun started to set, I knew Hawk would come looking for me soon, escalating my fear and need to find him. But how was I supposed to do that? I didn't have the vaguest idea where to look for him, which prompted me to make a mental note to ask him where he lived if he survived the Winterborne lynch mob trying to hunt him down.

After practically licking the can clean, I tossed it in the trash and headed for the windows. The apartment had a spectacular view of the East River but no balcony. I feared what I had to do next, and part of me wanted to use the money Jules had given me and take a cab back to the West Side to wait in the shadows until I saw him sailing over the Winterborne Building. But what was I going to do then? Yell at him from the street nine stories below?

I drank a glass of water before heading out of the apartment to look for the stairwell. I spotted an exit sign at the end of the hallway and pushed the door open to climb the steps to the roof, my heart practically beating out of my chest as I reached the top. I found myself looking over the edge of the building before I had a chance to talk myself out of my plan and head down to the street to hail that cab I'd considered a few minutes earlier.

"Damn you, Hawk," I muttered, angry at myself for never asking him where he lived. It was a reasonable question to ask a man you were sleeping with.

I spotted a table and some chairs on the other side of the rooftop. Gathering my nerve, I grabbed one of the chairs and carried it to the wall, my hands shaking as I raised my foot to climb on the seat. "I hope you're right, Jakob."

With my eyes closed, I took several deep breaths and tried to steady my trembling body. All I could think about was hitting the sidewalk fourteen stories below, my bones shattering into splinters and my head splitting open like a ripe melon.

"I can't," I whispered. Defeated by fear, I turned to climb off the chair.

"Morgan!"

The sound of Hawk's voice startled me. I twisted around, losing my balance. For a second, I thought I'd tumbled down onto the rooftop, but when the city lights began to whirl around me and the building flew past me in a blur, I knew I'd gone over the edge. As I plummeted toward the sidewalk, I looked back up just as the wide wings of a hawk sailed off the roof. It took a few seconds for him to catch me, but I slipped away from him as if his feathers were an illusion. Then suddenly I was standing back on the roof, looking over the edge as he flew back and forth several stories below.

Hawk dived toward the sidewalk and then shot back into the sky. He circled the rooftop and spotted me, then landed several feet away. As he shifted back, I began to shake from all the adrenaline coursing through me. Jakob was right. My powers had kicked in, and I'd just traveled for the first time on my own.

"Is there something you want to tell me, Morgan?"

I planned to tell him everything, but first I had a question of my own. "How did you find me?"

As he approached, his eyes lingered on mine. "After last night, I'll always know where to find you. I can sense you." He leaned in and kissed my cheek, continuing up to my ear. "You're inside me, Morgan, and I'm inside you."

"I don't know if I like being found so easily," I whispered, heady from the feel of his warm breath against my skin.

He pulled back to look into my eyes. "No?"

I smiled slowly and took him by the hand. I was so thankful that he *had* found me. "You can find me anytime you like."

I'd had enough talking for one day. I led him back down the

stairs to Mrs. Wells's apartment, past the master bedroom, to the guest room down the hall.

"We can talk in the morning," I said, slipping my hands under his shirt and around his waist, his skin soft and smooth against mine.

We took our clothes off and climbed into bed, the lights from the city and moon casting a warm glow over us, my back to his chest with his arm wrapped around me. My mind and heart were finally at peace from having him safe and sound next to me, and I turned around to press my lips to his, my heart melting as his golden eyes looked into mine.

"I think I know why you're so attracted to me," I whispered against his mouth, wondering how much of my vampire blood be could sense.

He placed his finger against my lips, quelling a conversation that could wait until morning. Then we gave in to the desire binding us together and satisfied ourselves to sleep.

CHAPTER 24

It was just before dawn when I woke up. Hawk was sound asleep next to me, his breathing heavy and labored like he was dreaming of running or flying. I decided to let him sleep while I threw on my clothes and headed for the bare kitchen to scrounge for something to eat.

With the coffee brewing, I found a loaf of bread that had expired two days earlier and stuck a few slices in the toaster oven. The eggs in the refrigerator where a godsend, and I even found some powdered coffee creamer in the cabinet.

I cracked four eggs into a skillet and let them cook for a minute or two before turning the burner off and placing a lid over it. When I turned around to check the toast, I jumped. Hawk was leaning against the wall, watching me.

"You shouldn't sneak up on a woman with an unpredictable power hand."

He walked into the kitchen and gave me that look that seemed to reach all the way down to my soul. "I like watching you when you think no one's looking. I can see you better that way. Who you really are."

"Ah," I said. "Well, you're seeing me, all right. I need a shower and a toothbrush."

As I combed my messy hair with my fingers, he reached for my hand and turned it over to kiss my palm. "I like you this way," he said, glancing over my shoulder at the smoke billowing from the toaster oven. "But I prefer my toast on the lighter side."

"Damn it!" I grabbed the door and swung it open, praying the fire alarm wasn't about to go off. The last thing we needed was for the neighbors to show up and call the police on the intruders in Margo Wells's apartment.

Hawk stuck his hand inside and pulled the blackened toast out, barely flinching from the heat. When he lifted the cover off the skillet and looked at the eggs, he nodded a couple of times. "I've never been much of a toast eater anyway, but those eggs look delicious."

"Good, because that's all we have unless you like moldy leftover takeout."

I plated the eggs while he poured the coffee. It was time to have a talk.

"I have to tell you something," I said after he sat down at the counter next to me.

His brow arched. "Like how you managed to slip through my hands last night and then miraculously reappeared on the roof?"

"Among other things. But first you need to know why I'm staying in a stranger's apartment."

He took a bite of his food and chewed it thoughtfully for a few seconds. "I was wondering about that, but I figured you'd eventually get around to telling me whose apartment we're in."

"It's a friend's place. She's out of town for a while."

"And you're staying here because…"

"Because my aunt and cousin saw you at the theater the other night. Then they saw me give my brother Ethan a concussion when he tried to filet you with a knife."

He swallowed his mouthful of food and set his fork down. "I take it they're not too happy about their queen sleeping with a vampire?"

"Well," I said, chuckling, "they don't know about that part. You'll have an even bigger bounty on your head if they find out you've *defiled* me."

"Bounty? What are you talking about?"

Suddenly losing my appetite, I pushed my plate away and took a fortifying sip of coffee. "I think my uncle and his wife are trying to frame you. Rebecca went out for a run yesterday morning and got attacked before she even made it past the block."

By the look on his face, he seemed to be getting the gist of what I was saying. "What did they say?"

"The attack was caught on the building's security camera. It was obviously a shifter, but it was too dark to make out her attacker's face. He pulled her around the corner, out of the camera's view, and sank his teeth into her shoulder. Then he came back around and shifted into a bird before disappearing into the park."

"Do you know how many bird shifters live in Central Park?" He laughed bitterly and shook his head. "Talk about being railroaded."

"I know about the Flyers, but Rebecca swore it was you. You were with me at the time, so she's clearly lying. And even if you weren't, I wouldn't believe her for a second."

His ran his hand over the small of my back. "And you obviously can't provide my alibi because that would make it worse. But why would they frame me? I'm a stranger to them."

"I think my uncle Cabot put her up to it. He's been trying to undermine me since my mother died and named me as her successor, and anything that will get Rebecca closer to the Winterborne throne is all the motivation she needs to lie. You're nothing but a convenient pawn to them. They've already accused me of the crime of attacking Ethan to protect you. Now that you're a fugitive, imagine how much more they can accuse me of for helping you."

"Man," he said, shaking his head. "Nothing personal, but your family is brutal."

"They stripped me of my hunting duties and fired me from the auction house. Then they confined me to the penthouse so I couldn't warn you."

"How did you get out?"

"My friend Jakob helped me. He showed me how to travel, although I'm still trying to master that little skill so I can do it at will."

"Travel?"

I stood up and walked over to the window, getting that same queasy feeling as I looked eight stories down. "It's what you've seen us do when we leave for a hunt." I nodded to the living room wall. "We just walk from one place right into another, usually through a wall."

"You mean teleportation," he said matter-of-factly.

"I guess. We call it traveling."

"I'm not surprised. It's an immortal talent." He shrugged. "It probably just kicked in a little early for you, being the daughter of an immortal, I mean."

"Jakob has known me since I was born. He said I've had the talent to travel all along." I pressed my hand against the wall and willed it to pass straight through, but it didn't. "Last night when I fell over the building was the first time I've done it on my own, but I still can't figure out how to do it whenever I want."

"I'd like to meet this Jakob someday," he said. "It sounds like he's a good friend."

I smiled at the thought of Jakob giving Hawk the third degree when they finally met. Never mind that I was a grown woman. A father never loses his protective instincts for his daughter, and Jakob was more a father to me than Ryker Caspian would ever be. "When this is all over with and we find the real attacker, I'll make dinner for the two of you."

"It's a date."

I walked back to the kitchen and leaned across the counter. "Remember when I mentioned last night why I thought you're so attracted to me? It's because we're a lot more alike than you know."

He froze and got a wary look in his eyes. "Don't tell me you're an owl? I knew there was something familiar about you." A smile inched up the side of his face.

"My father is a vampire too," I blurted out.

For a second I wasn't sure if he'd heard me. He didn't say a word and barely blinked. But then he stood up and leaned over the counter, coming within a few inches of my face. He breathed in through his nose and examined my green eyes intently. "You're telling me the truth. I can smell it. And your eyes have that flicker at the core of your pupils. It's unmistakable."

"What?" I ran to the mirror hanging in the living room and looked at my reflection. I got as close as possible and stared at my eyes until I spotted it. The tiniest flash of red flickered and then quickly disappeared. I was shocked—and a little horrified.

"Don't be afraid of it, Morgan." Hawk appeared behind me in the reflection and ran his hands gently up and down my arms. "It's almost impossible to detect unless you know to look for it. Why didn't you tell me sooner?"

I turned around and gazed at his surprised face. "It was in my mother's journal. I just read it yesterday morning."

He took a step back. "The one you were reading when we were in bed?"

"Yes. I was too shocked to tell you. I didn't even believe it right away."

"Well, it's true. The only difference between you and me is a pair of wings and that wicked power hand of yours." He pulled me closer and whispered against my mouth, "It makes me want you even more."

That bedroom was only a few steps down the hallway, but when I took his hand and tried to coax him back there, he resisted. "What's wrong?"

"As much as I'd love to spend the morning in bed with you, I have to leave."

"Leave?" I let go of his hand and cocked my head. "You can't leave. The clan is looking for you. They're skilled hunters, Hawk. Finding vampires is what they do best." With the mood killed, I shook my head and walked back to the kitchen to clean up. "You're staying right here with me."

He got an uncomfortable look on his face.

"Just say it, Hawk. I'm a big girl." I started washing the plates. "Just tell me why you want to leave so *desperately*."

With a deep sigh, he explained. "I can't take the sun when it gets too bright. It makes me weak, and I'm already exhausted."

I put the plate down, feeling awful. I'd just assumed he was more like his mother since he ate food and didn't need human blood to survive. The sun didn't bother me, and I was just as much a vampire as he was.

"The hawk can take the sun all day, but when I'm like this," he said, motioning to himself, "it's difficult." He must have read my mind or the perplexed look on my face. "You're lucky, Morgan. Your immortal blood saved you from this… curse."

"Don't say that. You're not cursed."

He let out a bitter laugh. "Right. You deserve someone who can take you to lunch or walk through the park with you in the afternoon. That's not me, Morgan. It'll never be me."

I took his hands and made him look at me. "Then shift into a hawk and stay. It doesn't matter to me. And lunch is overrated, by the way."

He pulled back and got that uneasy look on his face again. "I've been a hawk more than a vampire for the past week, and I'm ready to drop. I need to sleep in my own bed."

"Where is that exactly?"

He pulled me into his arms again and tried to distract me. "We'll talk about that later. You wore me out last night, so now you have to trust me and let me get some rest. I'll be back as soon as the sun goes down."

"All right. But you have to make me a promise."

"Anything."

"Promise me you won't go anywhere near the Winterborne Building."

He peppered my neck with soft kisses all the way up to my ear. "I promise."

I followed him into the bedroom and watched him dress.

"I have to talk to them," I said as he pulled his shirt on.

"Talk to whom?"

"The Flyers. You know as well as I do that it was one of them who attacked Rebecca."

He sat on the bed and rubbed his face, probably out of frustration with me. "They won't talk to you, Morgan. They won't even show themselves to you. You're an outsider."

"I'll take my chances. The clan has had a long relationship with the Flyers, and it's time I introduced myself. The council may have stripped me of everything else, but I'm still the queen of the clan."

He finished getting dressed, grumbling under his breath as he put his shoes on. "Wait for me. We'll go together tonight."

We headed for the roof after I agreed. The sun was barely rising over the buildings, and Hawk seemed okay with the bright orange light hitting his face.

"Does it hurt?" I asked, wondering if he was putting on a tough act for me. If this relationship was going to work, we had to show each other the ugliest and most vulnerable sides of ourselves. Put it all out there.

"No," he said, rubbing the back of his neck. "But it will as soon as the sun gets a little higher." I think he thought I was afraid he'd self-combust if he took a direct ray of sun to his face. "Look, Morgan. I'm not going to incinerate in the afternoon sun if that's what you're worried about. It just drains me of all my energy and makes me feel sick. I'm useless until it goes back down, and then I spend half the night recovering. Trust me, it's no way to live. I'm better off as a night owl."

I gave him a faint smile and pointed to the sky with my thumb. "Then get out of here so I have you nice and energized for tonight."

As he shifted before my eyes and flew into the sky, I made a silent promise to clear his name even if it meant a fight to the end with my own flesh and blood.

CHAPTER 25

Jules showed up around eight p.m. to bring me some clothes and enough food to hold me over for a few days. "I got you some olives and cheese just in case you feel like entertaining while you're here," she said as she went into the kitchen to unpack the bags.

I snickered and followed her into the kitchen. "Yeah, right."

"Hey, you never know." She shrugged and handed me a phone. "Got you a prepaid burner."

"God, I love you, woman." I'd been starting to get itchy without a connection to the outside world. "I promise I'll be out of here as soon as I can."

She stopped unpacking and looked at me. "You'll stay as long as you fucking want. Mom won't be back for weeks, and if she decides to fly back early—which she won't—you can stay with me."

"You know I can't do that," I said. "I guarantee you Cabot has someone watching your place." I got a bad feeling as I said it and headed for the front door to make sure it was locked. Not that a mere lock would stop an immortal from getting in, but it made me feel better.

"Stop worrying," she yelled across the room. "No one followed me."

"You sure about that?"

She scoffed and tore open a bag of potato chips. "You think I'm stupid? I had Ralph close the shop while I slipped out the back door. Even wore a disguise."

Owning a vintage clothing store, there were any number of ways she could have slipped past someone without being recognized. The shop had a plethora of clothing, jewelry, wigs, and eyewear that attracted everyone from your average New Yorker to drag queens and set designers for film crews.

She reached into the bag and pulled out a lavender wig and tossed it at me. "I knew this thing would come in handy someday. Took two cabs and a subway ride just in case." She shook her head and sat on a stool at the counter. "If Cabot was able to follow me, he deserves to find you."

I sat down across from her and grabbed a handful of chips. I'd earned a little junk food. "You want to meet Hawk?"

"You found him?" She glanced down the hallway and lowered her voice. "Is he here?"

"Actually, he found me. He left this morning, but he'll be back any minute now. We're taking a little trip to Central Park later tonight."

She gave me a look like I had a few screws loose, which was a perfectly normal response to anyone saying they were taking a late-night stroll through the park.

"Don't look at me like that," I said. "I can't go home until I find out who attacked Rebecca. They'll crucify me for helping Hawk if I don't clear his name. You know, he isn't the only shifter in New York City. There's a whole world of them right down the street in Central Park, and I'm pretty sure one of them was hired to jump Rebecca."

Why wasn't I surprised that she didn't even blink at what I'd just said? Jules was getting far too comfortable with the strange and unusual.

She tilted her head. "I don't recall ever seeing you act like this over a guy. Got it pretty bad, don't you?"

"Yeah, I think I do."

A faint knock on the door got our attention. The sun had gone down, so it was probably Hawk. Just in case, I crept up to the door and looked through the peephole before opening it.

Hawk stepped inside, his height barely clearing the doorframe, and gave me a quick kiss before turning his eyes to Jules.

"Jules, this is Hawk."

"Well, shit," she said, staring at his golden eyes unabashedly. "I get it now."

He walked up to her and held out his hand, but she hugged him instead. After releasing him, she stepped back but continued to stare at him like she was mesmerized by his eyes. I knew exactly how she felt.

"So," I said, breaking up the gazing contest.

Jules finally snapped out of it and headed back into the kitchen to grab her keys from the counter. "I guess I should be heading out. Traffic's a bitch this time of night. I'll be lucky to get a cab."

I would have tried to talk her into staying longer, but Hawk and I had to plan for the evening. When I walked her to the door, she turned around and looked back at him.

"It was really nice to finally meet you, Hawk," she said with a pleasant smile. "Take care of my girl tonight. If you don't, I'll hunt you down and castrate you. Got it?" She kept her eyes on his for a moment before disappearing down the hall.

When I shut the door and turned around, Hawk was still staring at the spot where she'd been standing, his face apprehensive.

"She comes off a lot tougher than she is," I said. "She's just a little protective of me."

He finally looked at me. "Protective? She's a rottweiler, and I'll be feeling her teeth if anything happens to you tonight."

"But since nothing will, you have nothing to worry about," I said with a chipper smile before heading back into the kitchen. "Jules brought food. You hungry?" I reached into the paper bag and felt the neck of a wine bottle. "Bless you, Jules."

Hawk took it away from me when I grabbed a corkscrew from the drawer. "No alcohol tonight."

"Just a glass. It'll barely take the edge off."

He shook his head and went back into the living room, taking the bottle with him.

"I'm not a child, Hawk. You don't have to ration my alcohol."

"We need to talk about tonight." There was heaviness in his tone, like a doctor delivering a grave prognosis. "You don't know what we're walking into."

I sat down next to him and rested my hand on his thigh. He was tense in a way I hadn't seen before. "So tell me what I need to know."

He set the bottle on the coffee table and raked his fingers through his hair. "The Flyers aren't what you think they are."

I shrugged. "Birds? Animal?"

He laughed quietly. "Something like that. But if you think we're going to find a bunch of nightingales in the park tonight, you're in for a surprise." He looked out the window and seemed to contemplate his words before continuing. "They can be dangerous when threatened, and strangers are threats."

"But they know you, right?"

"Yeah, but I'm not one of them. And just because you're with me doesn't give you a free pass to enter their territory. There's a good reason the park is closed at night."

He was starting to sound cryptic. "What are you saying,

Hawk? Don't you want to find the Flyer who framed you? You'll be a target for the rest of your life if you don't. And when the clan finally gets their hands on you—and eventually they will—they'll kill you. All they'll see is a vampire, and vampires equate to Walkers in their eyes."

"We'll go," he said. "But you have to do exactly as I say when we get there. These aren't cute little furry creatures like sparrows or squirrels."

"Then what are they?"

Instead of telling me, he looked me in the eye and held my gaze. "It'll be easier to show you. Just promise me you'll let me do the talking when we find the queen."

"The queen?" It sounded silly, but it was no sillier than me being labeled the queen of the Winterborne clan.

"Understand?" he asked. When I stared at him blankly, he asked me again. "Do you understand, Morgan?"

"Yes, I understand!"

We sat on the sofa in awkward silence for a few minutes with me wondering why he was so nervous and agitated about paying a visit to a bunch of shifters who seemed to have a lot in common with him.

"What do we do now?" I finally asked when I couldn't take the quiet any longer.

He sank back into the cushions and pulled me against him. "We wait."

"Why don't we walk up a block and go in the entrance like normal people?" I asked.

It was one a.m. and we were standing on the sidewalk along Fifth Avenue, staring at the wall that bordered Central Park. When I asked him why we had to wait so long to leave the apartment and head over, he said the Flyers only came out after midnight when the park officially closed.

"Because that's not where we'll find them."

Instead of arguing that we could go in at Seventy-Sixth Street and make our way back down to where we were now, I followed him as he scaled the wall and landed in the park on the other side, nearly skewering myself on a bush.

"Remember," he said. "Do exactly what I say and don't speak unless I tell you to."

"I heard you the first ten times you told me."

He ignored me and headed through a thicket of bushes, glancing back every now and then to make sure I was still behind him. There wasn't a pedestrian in sight, which made sense since the park was officially closed, but where were all the paths? It was like we were in the middle of the woods.

He led me to a small clearing with a stone circle in the center. It was ten to twelve feet in diameter, and the glow coming from the streetlights in the distance illuminated symbols carved into the individual stones it comprised.

"What is this place?" I asked.

He held his hand up to keep me quiet while he surveyed our surroundings. Then he signaled for me to head toward a patch of trees on the other side. I stepped on one of the stones, not realizing he meant for me to walked around the circle, and he grabbed my arm to pull me back.

The streetlights went out the second my foot lifted off the stone, and we were left with nothing to see but the silhouettes of the trees against a dark blue sky.

Something flew past me, creating a gust of wind that nearly knocked me over.

"Morgan!" Hawk yelled.

I looked up and saw him floating in the sky, held up by two creatures on either side of him. They flew in the opposite direction, carrying him away so fast it was like he evaporated into thin air.

"Hawk!" I tried to orient myself in the darkness, to see where they'd taken him. "*Hawk!*" I yelled louder as panic set in. Then my hand started to burn as a blue light glowed under my skin in the center of my palm.

A fluttering sound broke the silence.

I whipped around to see what it was, my heart feeling like it would burst in my chest. Hovering in the center of the circle was a tiny bird. In looked like a wren or a sparrow, its details obscured by the darkness. I just stood there frozen as it suspended itself, its wings flapping as fast as a hummingbird's.

Its wings began to slow, and it appeared to split down the middle, the halves becoming two separate birds. Then those began to split until the stone circle was filled with a flock of tiny flying creatures with their shapes defined only by their shadows in the darkness.

A few minutes passed and I took a step back, gauging the distance between the circle and the wall we'd scaled to get in. They were just birds. I could make it out.

The moment I turned to leave, their eyes lit up like tiny red flares, and they flew out of the circle and swarmed me in a riot of feathers. I covered my eyes when I felt their claws sink into my skin and lift me up. They carried me to the circle and hovered over it as the center stone began to glow and shift to the right, revealing a black hole. When they let go, I tumbled into the dark abyss, eventually hitting bottom.

I lay on the ground, squeezing my eyes shut from the pain of the fall and the burning gashes they'd left on my skin. When I reopened them, I was back where I'd started, staring at the stone circle under a dark sky. But this time it wasn't filled with tiny birds. Standing in the center was a strange figure with a set of wings that opened and closed with the rhythm of its breath.

Crouched behind it was a smaller creature, dark and submissive, the tips of its wings dragging across the stones as it moved.

The light around us grew brighter, allowing me a better look at them. The larger one was no more than three feet tall, and its head was covered with long feathers that trailed down its back and reached the stones, mimicking a mane of hair. Its eyes were difficult to look at. They were almost clear with a faint hint of blue, without pupils. I was staring into pits of ice. The only thing human about its face was its pale skin and its thin lips, which were curled into a mocking smile.

"Who are you?" I asked, even though I had a good idea.

The trees filled with the sound of a thousand blackbirds congregating above us.

"Silence!" The creature's voice was female, confirming that it was the queen. Who else could it have been? She looked me up and down and lost her smile. "Who the hell are *you*?"

"Morgan Winterborne," I replied, trying to steady my shaking hands. "Queen of Clan Winterborne."

The park went completely quiet. The trees no longer buzzed with chatter, and the Flyer queen herself seemed a little lost for words.

"She's lying!" One of the birds swooped down from the trees and grazed my cheek with its talons.

I hit the ground and felt the spot as it burned, my fingers bloody when I pulled my hand away.

She looked unconvinced. "There is no queen of the House of Winterborne anymore. Only a king."

So my uncle had lied to the Flyers. Made them believe he was in charge of the clan now.

"He's been lying to you," I said. "Katherine Winterborne was my mother, and she named me her successor, not my uncle Cabot."

Her thin lips formed into a wicked smile. "Then I guess all you have to do is prove it."

"Or what?" I asked, my fear skyrocketing as I wondered what they'd done to Hawk and what they planned to do to me.

Her eyes flashed black, and for a second I got a glimpse of something just beneath the surface of her skin that chilled me to the bone. It was the moment I realized she had no intention of letting me leave.

My palm began to tingle as the magic started to build into a glow. She caught a glimpse of it and her mocking turned to anger.

"Or this!" She raised her arm and commanded the army of creatures to descend from the trees.

The sky filled with a flurry of wings and talons until they formed a death squad over my head and blocked out the moonlight. The energy in my hand was so hot it burned. There were too many of them, but if it came down to it I'd fight them, setting as many ablaze as I could until they plucked my eyes out or ripped me apart.

"Hawk will tell you who I am!" I blurted out, praying she'd trust a shifter who, for all I knew, lived among them. "Your army took him right after we entered the park."

She got a curious look in her eyes when I mentioned his name. "I was wondering what that hawk was doing with you." After giving it some thought, she gave a command to the cowering creature behind her. "Spatza! Fetch the hawk."

The creature disappeared into the trees. A few seconds later, Hawk fell from the sky. I thought he was going to hit the ground, but he shifted just in time, spreading his wings and flying back up toward the death squad. Eventually he landed next to me and shifted back. He shot a menacing look at the queen, but he was smart enough to hold his tongue.

"Is it true?" she asked him. "Is this woman the daughter of Katherine Winterborne?"

He glanced at me while he replied. "Yes, she is. She's the queen of Winterborne House."

With a wave of her hand, the birds vanished from the sky. "I should kill Cabot Winterborne for lying to me. But that would trigger a war and ruin a beneficial alliance."

I took the opportunity to get what we came for. "I know a way for you to get a little revenge without ruining your relationship with the clan." She was intrigued—I could see it in the way her strange eyes flashed with light.

Hawk gave me a warning look, but I was through backing down. She didn't dare threaten me now.

"Go on," she said.

"Cabot's wife was attacked yesterday morning in front of the Winterborne Building. It happened just before dawn, and it was all caught on the security camera. The video shows her being jumped and dragged to the side of the building. Her attacker got away by shifting into a bird, and she swore it was Hawk. We believe the attack was staged, that they paid a shifter to frame him."

The queen's curious look turned suspicious. "What does this have to do with us?"

"It's the reason we came here tonight." I glanced at Hawk with complete trust in him. "Hawk is innocent."

"Are you suggesting it was one of us?"

"Possibly," Hawk said, sparing me from insulting the queen.

Her eyes filled with anger, but Hawk tempered the situation. "We're not here to point fingers, but I swear on my mother's grave that I didn't do this. All we're asking you to do is rule out your people. Then we can move on to the next suspect. And once we find him, we can prove that Cabot and his wife staged the attack."

She gave it some thought and reluctantly agreed. "Just to clear our name."

"That's all we ask," he said.

I glanced at Hawk, relieved that we'd accomplished what had begun to feel like the impossible. When I looked back at the circle, the queen was gone.

After finding our way out of the park, we headed back toward the apartment. "Do you really think there's another suspect out there?"

His face went stone cold. "Hell no. One of those bastards did it. Let's just hope the queen can ferret him out."

CHAPTER 26

I woke to the sound of faint tapping. Hawk was sound asleep next to me when I rolled over and noticed a shadow cast across the bedroom wall. It floated back and forth as the tapping grew louder, and it was coming from the window.

Climbing out of bed quietly so I wouldn't wake Hawk, I crept across the room, nearly yelping when I saw the winged creature hovering on the other side of the window, eight stories above the street. It was the queen's cowering servant. Spatza, she'd called it.

Fiddling with the window lock, I finally managed to get it partially open. But instead of entering the room, the creature stuck its hand inside and dropped something on the floor that landed at my feet.

"You were right," she said in a raspy voice that was barely above a whisper and clearly female. "The traitor has been found and punished." She nodded to whatever she'd dropped on the floor. "That was his payment, and now it has been paid back."

I pushed the window open a little more and stepped aside. "Come in." I wasn't keen on inviting the strange creature into the apartment, but I was hoping to get more information out of her.

Spatza let out a bitter laugh before expanding her wings and disappearing into the night sky.

"Morgan? What are you doing?" Hawk climbed out of bed and walked up to me. He grabbed my shoulders and shook me gently when I just stared at the glass without speaking. "Are you awake?" he asked as he shut the window.

"She was just there." I pointed to the spot where the creature had been hovering.

He glanced out the window and scrunched his forehead. "Who?"

Slipping out of his grip, I stepped up to the window and looked in the direction where she'd flown. "The queen's servant. The one who dropped you from the sky."

"What's this?" He lifted his foot and bent down to see what he'd stepped on.

When I saw the necklace in his hand, I stopped breathing for a moment. "It's a black opal. The queen's revenge."

I took it from his hand and headed for the kitchen to get something to drink. My throat had gone completely dry.

Hawk was right behind me. "Morgan?"

"Have a seat, Hawk. This is your lucky day."

With a glass of water in my hand, I sat down and dropped the necklace on the counter. "That's not just a black opal. Rebecca's father had it custom made for her. She said the stone is rare." He still seemed confused, so I clarified it for him. "I wasn't dreaming. Spatza, the queen's minion, just hand-delivered it to me. She was tapping on the window. Scared the shit out of me when I saw her hovering on the other side of it."

"Tell me exactly what she said."

"She said we were right and that the traitor had been punished."

"Killed," he said. "That's how they deal with traitors."

I continued with the incriminating part. "Then she dropped

that necklace on the floor. She said it was his payment and now it was being paid back."

"That makes sense. Flyers have no use for money, but something like this is worth a fortune." He picked it up and dangled it against the light. "I bet it was a crow or a raven who did it. Shiny little objects are their obsession. In fact, they're notorious for stealing jewelry."

"The necklace is the equivalent to paying off a hit man with a bag of cash."

"That's right!"

As excited as I was about the new evidence, we still had a very big problem. We needed the queen to testify that she recovered the necklace from the guilty Flyer. Without that, it was our word against Rebecca's. She'd probably accuse me of stealing it from her to save Hawk, and since my integrity was already in question, I had a good idea who they'd believe.

"How likely is it that the queen will come forward and testify in your defense?"

He groaned and scratched the side of his neck. "About as likely as a cold day in hell."

I'd had a feeling he'd say that. Unfortunately, it meant I couldn't go home until I found a way to convince her to come forward.

Hawk got up and headed down the hallway. "Come back to bed. There's nothing we can do about it at five a.m."

For once I was glad he'd be leaving in an hour or two. As soon as he was gone, I was going back to the penthouse to get the journal because sooner or later they'd tear the place apart looking for clues of where I'd gone. I could have kicked myself for forgetting it, and if Cabot got his hands on it, I was as good as dead.

As Hawk sailed into the sky, I vowed that this would be the last morning I said goodbye to him without knowing where he was going. He liked to change the subject when I brought it up, but if he was sleeping with me and hanging around for breakfast, it was time he told me where he lived.

Now that he was gone, the first thing I planned to do was retrieve the journal. If I'd told him I was going back to the penthouse, he would have tried to stop me. Or worse, he would have insisted on going with me. But I would never let him go anywhere near the Winterborne Building before this was settled.

The first thing I had to do was figure out how to get in without being seen. I considered calling Jakob with the burner phone Jules had given me, but the deeper I dragged him into this mess, the greater the danger he was in. If the clan caught him helping me, he'd be gone. I would die before doing that to him.

I headed for the edge of the roof and looked over the wall, considering my options. I had to practice if I wanted to learn how to travel at will, but diving off a building in broad daylight with a sidewalk full of people below would have my fellow New Yorkers calling 911 in droves. I'd find myself in Bellevue for evaluation if the NYPD showed up.

After heading back down to the apartment, I walked over to the living room wall and flattened my palm against it for the hundredth time. As usual, it did nothing but stop when it came into contact with the solid surface.

"What am I doing wrong?" I muttered, pushing harder.

Glaring at the wall, I tried to remember exactly what we'd done the other times when we left for a hunt. Was I missing something? Maybe I was supposed to walk right through it without hesitating. To get a good start, I stepped back to the center of the room. "Have a little faith, Morgan." I walked straight toward the wall this time, not slowing down a bit, but all I did was slam into it.

"Ow!" I winced, letting the sting subside. "What the hell am I doing wrong?"

Stop trying to walk through a wall.

The familiar voice filled my head. I sat down and went completely still to see if I could hear it again, but my mind went quiet.

You have to let the wall disappear. Visualize your destination before you step.

I jumped up and nearly cried as Monoclaude's words filled my head again. Had he been there all along? I got a sudden recollection of what he'd said to me the day I found him in the conservatory after all those years of thinking he was dead: *I feel dead sometimes. But I'm always here, Morgan.*

"Thank you," I whispered, looking at the wall with a completely different set of eyes. It took a while, sort of like learning how to properly meditate for the first time, trying to find your still point, that point when everything falls away except for that exact moment in time. All the mind clutter disappears and you're left with the here and now.

Focusing on a spot in the center of the wall, I let the living room fall away and visualized the conservatory full of beautiful blooms. I reached out toward the bright pink flower on the top shelf and had almost touched it when the sound of the ice maker in the kitchen broke my concentration and brought the living room rushing back.

"Damn it," I groaned, waiting for the sound of falling ice to cease.

When the room went quiet, I tried again. This time it worked. At first it was like walking into a thick fog that resisted me as I tried to go deeper and enter the conservatory, but then I took another step and I was inside.

It felt like I was dreaming. But when I closed my eyes for a few seconds and reopened them, I was still there. I was actually in the conservatory, staring at the wall that used to lead to Monoclaude's realm.

"I owe you, my friend. I'll make it right." I intended to keep that promise when this was all over and I hunted down that murderous crow.

The awe of finally traveling at will was suddenly replaced by anxiety. I had no idea what or who I'd find inside the penthouse. I could be walking into a trap.

My hand began to clench as I stoked my power. If Cabot or one of his spies was in there, I was prepared to use it and get myself declared a traitor. I just prayed I didn't run into the twins.

I headed out of the conservatory and crept toward the terrace door. The living room was vacant, and I was thankful that the door was open so I wouldn't have to practice my traveling skills again. I needed to save that for getting out of there as soon as I had the journal.

After slipping inside, I checked the kitchen and found it empty. The coffeepot was still half-full, just as I'd left it, which meant they probably hadn't invaded the place yet. After a quick look in the other rooms, I headed for my bedroom to get the journal.

As I approached the door, I heard Otto's voice. "You have a visitor, mistress."

Already hopped up on adrenaline, my heart started to pump faster, the flow of my blood roaring in my ears. I ran into the bedroom and pressed my back to the wall behind the door, peering through the small gap at the hinges. No one entered the living room.

I muffled a scream when I turned around and saw a figure sitting in the wing chair in the corner of the room. It was Ryker Caspian, and the journal was lying in his lap.

He glanced at his watch and looked up at me. "I was beginning to wonder if I was in the right apartment." His voice was deep, and he took his time with his words. Then he patted the journal. "But then I found this and realized I hadn't forgotten the address at all. Where have you been, Morgan?"

"What do you want?" I asked, nervous about someone walking in on us. If they found him here with me, I wouldn't have a leg to stand on, especially with the evidence right in his lap.

He laid the journal on the table next to the chair. "I'm here for you. I would have come sooner, but your mother made that very difficult. She was quite a force of nature, wasn't she?"

"Give it to me," I demanded.

He glanced at the journal and cocked his brow. "The journal?"

Trying to hide my nerves, I inched closer and held my hand out. All I wanted was to take the journal and disappear the way I came.

"If you want it so badly, take it."

I gave him a wide berth as I reached toward the table, his eyes trained on me like a snake poised to strike. But I knew he wasn't about to let me leave with it, so I opened my hand to give him a good look at the blue light getting brighter as my fear surged.

A smile appeared on his face when he saw it. "Are you planning to use that on your own father?"

"If I have to."

He threw his head back and laughed, and I used the moment to snatch the journal and run for the terrace. I yanked the door open and ran to the edge, hesitating as I looked nine stories down at the sidewalk below.

"Fuck!" I hissed, cursing my fear.

"There's no one here to catch you this time," he said, standing in the doorway.

Had he been watching me and Hawk?

My eyes darted to the conservatory as I tried to focus and

shut everything out but the image of Mrs. Wells's apartment across town. It was impossible. All that mind clutter was back.

He laughed again. "There's no one in there to save you either. I'm afraid your familiar is gone."

My lungs filled painfully as I gasped. "It was you? You killed him?"

The world around me started to crumble, and my vision grew spotty as darkness bled into my peripheral vision. With the journal held tight against my chest, I took a step back and leaned against the waist-high wall. My last memory was of the blue sky filled with billowy clouds as I tumbled backward over the edge.

CHAPTER 27

I rolled over and hugged the soft pillow wedged between my cheek and neck, breathing in the delightful scent of lavender. Everything about that pillow seemed wrong, and the memory of falling jolted me fully awake. I sat straight up, my fingers still gripping it.

The sheets made a soft rustling noise from my limbs shivering. When I looked down at my clothes, they were soaked in sweat. So was the comforter. That's when I remembered seeing Ryker Caspian's face just before I saw the sky. I'd thrown myself over the edge of the terrace and tried to travel, but I definitely wasn't in Mrs. Wells's apartment. He must have caught me before I disappeared.

The ruby bracelet around my wrist caught my eye, and then I saw the ring on my finger. I reached for my ears and felt the earrings too.

"What the hell is going on?" I whispered. Jakob had said he was going to burn them, but after what he told me about Phillip throwing them into the river years ago, nothing about the rubies surprised me anymore. I yanked at the ring, but it just got tighter around my finger, and the earrings seemed to be welded to my lobes.

I glanced around the strange room. It was furnished with antiques, and the floor was covered with a fine Persian rug. Ryker's apartment, I assumed. The one on Riverside Drive.

I climbed off the bed and checked the door. It was locked. Then I went to the window, relieved to see the river and New Jersey on the other side, confirming that I was still in New York. There were no bars on the outside of the glass. He must have thought I wouldn't risk jumping from six or seven stories, but he obviously didn't know about my newly discovered traveling skills. All I had to do was take a dive, but first I had to smash the window.

My hand felt weak. I tried clenching it several times, but the light in the center of my palm had gone out. It was like my power had been unplugged. The son of a bitch was controlling it with the rubies.

With a firm yank, I tried to rip the bracelet off, but it was like steel welded to my wrist, the same as the earrings and ring. The delicate filigree wouldn't even bend.

I looked around the sparsely furnished room and spotted a couple of small wooden chairs in the corner. But as I picked one of them up and headed for the window, I heard the lock on the door disengage. I quickly put it down.

The door swung open and Ryker walked inside, carrying a tray. "I thought you might be awake by now. Hungry?"

"Hungry?" I stared at him in disbelief.

He set the tray on the dresser and glanced at the chair next to me. "Go ahead."

"Go ahead and what?"

"Break the window," he replied in a cavalier tone as he offered me a cup of coffee.

The bastard was pissing me off, so I grabbed the chair and

swung like Babe Ruth. The wooden legs came within an inch of the glass and abruptly stopped, jolting me.

He walked over to the window and pick up the chair, sliding it toward me. "Have a seat, Morgan. We have things to discuss."

Realizing my options were limited and this would probably go a lot easier if I cooperated, I sat down.

"Now, do you want coffee or not?"

"Sure." Maybe a little caffeine would help me think.

As he handed me a cup, he bent down to look in my eyes, and I felt something slip over my head.

"There now," he said, adjusting the pendant to lie perfectly centered against my chest. "The set is complete."

The cup slipped from my hand and hit the floor, shattering to pieces. I grabbed the ruby necklace he'd so easily slipped around my neck, instinctively trying to rip it off. But I couldn't.

"I would have put in on you while you slept, but I wanted to see your eyes when I captured your will." The satisfaction on his face was revolting. "Now I have all of you. Just like I had Katherine."

"What do you want from me?"

He pulled the other chair up to mine and took a seat. "I want your power."

"If it would get me away from you, I'd gladly hand it over."

He stared at me blankly for a moment and then began to chuckle as if I'd told a lukewarm joke. "You're definitely your mother's daughter. I remember the first time I met Katherine. We were at the university library and she was pretending not to notice me." His lips rose into a faint smile as he seemed to gaze right through me. A moment later, he snapped out of it and focused on me again instead of her memory. "But you know that, don't you? You've read the journal, which means you know who I am."

"You're an assassin." I refused to acknowledge him as my father. "The Elders call you the Reaper."

He lost his smile and suddenly looked like he wanted to strike me, but instead of flinching, I glared at him defiantly. Regardless of the ruby hanging around my neck, he would never control me completely.

"They're nothing but a bunch of old fools." He stood up to look out the window. "Reaper," he scoffed. "It a legend that doesn't exist. Never has. Their ignorance is astounding."

"Are you denying you're a vampire?"

There was a glint in his eyes when he turned around. "Indeed. But not just a vampire. You and I are much more than just common Night Walkers. We come from the line that every inferior species mutated from, including those abominations that think they have a right to this city."

"There is no *we*," I said. "I'm ten times more my mother than you."

"Yes, you are." That glint got even brighter, sending a shiver through me. I had a strange feeling I was about to hear something that would shatter everything I thought I knew about my mother.

"It's your legacy, Morgan. Passed down from mother to daughter."

I did my best to hide my ignorance and act like I wasn't scared to death to hear the next words to come out of his mouth. But that was proving to be difficult as my lips stuck to my teeth and my mouth went exceedingly dry. "I think I need a glass of water."

Ignoring my request, he stood up and cocked his head. "You have read the journal?"

"Most of it."

He seemed to be having some sort of revelation and headed for the door. "I'll be right back."

A minute later he returned with the journal in his hand. He sat back down and scooted his chair closer to mine, then flipped the pages toward the end. "Let's finish it together, shall we?"

Katherine Winterborne
January 1, 1995

The women of Winterborne House have a dark secret. They keep it hidden so deep that it's rarely thought of and never spoken about, because just speaking the words carries connotations of a fate worse than death. Some aren't even aware of it because their mothers are cowards and refuse to arm their own daughters with the knowledge that might save them from an unimaginable fate. But I was one of the lucky ones. My mother told me about the legacy. That's why I knew the moment Ryker revealed himself to me that I would pass this knowledge on to you, Morgan. It's my duty as a mother. The day I found out I was pregnant, with a daughter no less, was one of the best and worst days of my life.

So, now for the truth. I tell it the way it was told to me. The way you will tell it to your own daughter if you choose to have children after reading this.

The legend goes that a Winterborne immortal woman took a vampire as a lover over two centuries ago. From that union, a rare pregnancy occurred, and the child became a carrier of a recessive gene. A vampire gene. From that moment forward, all females descending from that one fateful indiscretion carry the gene. Fortunately, our immortal genes are dominant, and they will stay dominant as long as a child is never conceived with a carrier of the same recessive gene. With a vampire from the original line.

Ryker comes from the same ancient line where the gene manifested and spread.

But it's just a legend. It's never been put to the test. No Winterborne woman has ever been foolish enough to sleep with a vampire, the enemies of the clan. Until now.

Legend or not, I'd do you a great injustice by telling you nothing will happen and it's just an old wives' tale handed down from mother to daughter. We'll take this journey together and find out. But if something were to happen to me before you're old enough to understand, I'll make sure you know the truth. But I pray every night that the legend will amount to nothing and the only legacy you'll know is to be the future queen of Clan Winterborne.

Katherine Winterborne
October 12, 2019

Well, so much for an old wives' tale. I've actually added to the legend, because there's another part of the story no one knew about. The days are getting darker for me, and my impulses are to the point where I fear I'll do something I can't live with. All these years I thought it was you I'd have to watch over to make sure your cravings didn't surface and give you away. I never knew I'd be the one who needed watching.

I've felt it for a while now, but lately it's been unbearable and I'm afraid I can't hide it any longer. My instincts are becoming harder to control, inciting an unspeakable hunger at the sight of blood, a hunger so deep in my bones I have to lock myself in the bathroom and draw my own blood to distract myself from the cravings. Jakob is the only one I trust. Neither of us understands it, but Jakob thinks it's because you grew inside my womb. Your blood is my blood, and after all these years, I'm no longer just a carrier. It's manifesting inside me.

I have to protect you now. By the time you read this, I'll be dead, drowned at the bottom of the ocean where the clan will never know what I've become. Or what you could become. You're a threat to the future of the Winterborne clan, and they'll kill you to preserve the bloodline. Trust Jakob. Let him help you. And whatever happens, don't let Ryker anywhere near you.

Now burn this journal and never speak of it again.

RYKER SNAPPED the journal shut and tossed it on the dresser. Then he headed for the window to glance out over the Hudson River. "I would have stopped her if I'd known she planned to kill herself. That wasn't my intent when I woke her thirst."

Still stunned by it all, I could barely speak. Then my brain caught up to what he'd just said. "What do you mean, you *woke her thirst?*"

He sighed and muttered something under his breath.

"Answer me!"

Without turning around, he headed for the bedroom door. "It'll be better if I show you."

As soon as he left the room, I stood up and started yanking at the damn jewelry again. I stopped when I heard a commotion down the hall, a moaning followed by a scuffle. Then the house went quiet again and I heard Ryker coming back.

I ran to the window and tried to break it with my fists, but they stopped inches away from the glass just like the chair had. Those rubies had bound me just as tightly as the twin's spell.

Ryker walked back into the room with a man wearing a white robe who looked like he hadn't shaved in a week. The man sat on the bed, his eyes fixed on the wall as if he were in a trance.

"We've been preparing for several days," Ryker said, taking the man's arm. "In fact, we completed a cleansing ritual this morning while you slept. An awakening requires preparation of the blood." He flipped the man's arm over and examined the vein that ran down his wrist, his brow furrowing as his face took on a thoughtful expression. "Maybe if I hadn't waited so long to wake Katherine, she'd still be alive and here with us now. But she resisted me for years until I finally insisted that it was time."

A sickening feeling roiled up from the depths of my gut as he beckoned for me to join him by the bed. "What are you going to do?" I asked, refusing to go near him.

"I'm giving you a gift," he said, running his thumb over the man's vein. "Just a taste and you'll become who you're destined to be. You'll wake up just like your mother did."

"You forced my mother to drink blood?"

"Of course. It's the final step. Until you drink consecrated blood, you're trapped between two worlds, neither to which you belong."

He crooked his finger at me, and I backed up, hitting the wall. With the rubies suppressing my power, I was trapped. My heart beat painfully against my chest as I shook my head and refused his order. Even the necklace couldn't compel me to peel myself away from that wall.

"Damn it, woman! Come here!"

He finally gave up and left the room, leaving me with the man sitting on the bed.

"Can you hear me?" I asked him.

The man slowly turned his head to look at me, but when he opened his mouth, nothing came out. His eyes looked vacant, like there was no one home inside his head.

"Don't waste your time," Ryker said as he came back into the room. "He's not here at the moment. I've given him some herbs to mask the pain." In his hand was a metal chalice. He set it on the nightstand and grabbed the man's wrist.

"You're going to kill him!" I yelled, unable to stand there and say nothing.

Ryker gave me a puzzled look. "Kill him?" He glanced at the man and then back at me. "He begged me to use him. They all want what we have."

"And what is that?"

He let out a sarcastic laugh. "Eternal life. But you wouldn't understand wanting that, would you? In a few short years, you'll be immortal." He dug his pointed fingernail into the man's wrist, puncturing his skin. The man flinched when his blood began to flow, but his eyes remained fixed on the wall. "He'll let me do whatever I want to him, with the hope of someday becoming one of us."

After tipping the man's arm to collect the blood in the chalice, he rubbed his thumb over the wound and it healed before my eyes. Then he stood up and offered me the chalice. "Drink."

I remained glued to the wall. "Fuck off!"

Ryker's eyes flashed red. "You talk to your own father with that foul mouth?"

He came toward me and grabbed my chin. I tried to fight but I was frozen, my will manipulated by his.

"Just a drop," he said as the cold metal cup pressed against my lips and tilted until the taste of warm copper spilled into my mouth. The urge to vomit disappeared as the taste suddenly changed to a sweet nectar that slipped down my throat as easily as fine wine. He kept tilting it until it was empty.

Ryker caught me as I slid toward the floor. He laid me on the bed, and I closed my eyes as the room turned on its axis and the sensation of flying filled my head. A bright light appeared, and a thousand voices whispered to me as I felt my arms fly open and catch the breeze in the valley I was soaring through.

"Enjoy this, Morgan," I heard him say in the distance. "You only transition once. It will never be this exhilarating again."

The bright sky went black, and I began to soar blindly through the darkness, trusting my instincts. Then suddenly I was on my back, the gnawing hunger in my throat making me so sick I thought I would vomit all the blood from my stomach. My eyes wouldn't open. I tried to sit up but felt his hands on my shoulders pushing me back down against the mattress as the whispers returned, growing louder until I could feel their lips against my ears.

Wake up, Morgan.

I couldn't breathe. A thousand thoughts bombarded my mind, filling my vision with images of blood and death and a world of never-ending darkness. "This isn't real," I said, trying to wake up.

The strange whispers became Ryker's deep, commanding voice telling me to open my eyes. But I couldn't. It was like sleep paralysis trapping me against the bed, with phantom limbs, dead and unresponsive. I fought back the terror that seemed to be eating me alive, and then my eyes suddenly popped open and I was standing at a window looking out over the river, the smell of grilled meat filling the air.

"Come and eat," Ryker said. "You've had a rough transition."

I turned around and saw him standing next to the dining

room table. "What time is it?" I'm not sure why I asked, but I was disoriented and needed something to anchor me.

He glanced at an old grandfather clock against the wall. "Half past ten."

I looked outside at the dark sky and realized he meant p.m. How had I lost an entire day?

Feeling weak, I approached the table and glanced at the steak surrounded by a pool of blood, and my stomach began to turn. "I can't eat that."

"You've expended all your energy. You have to eat or you'll pass out and I'll have to feed you more of Henry's blood. Shall I get him?"

Henry?

I stepped away from the table before he could force the nearly raw meat down my throat like he'd done with *Henry's* blood. "Then get me a muffin or something."

He laughed and picked up a knife, stabbing it through the center of the T-bone with enough force to shake the table. "From now on, this is your muffin!"

CHAPTER 28

Swallowing the last bite of my steak, I was shocked at how much I enjoyed something I'd sworn off years ago. I could have eaten a porterhouse.

Ryker watched me devour my dinner. "Unless you want to spend your nights hunting for human blood, that will have to become a staple in your diet."

I didn't want to believe what was happening to me, but it was hard to deny what I could see with my own two eyes. As a redhead, I was pretty fair, but my hands were paler than usual. When I turned my arm over to look at my wrist, my veins were alarmingly dark and looked like a map of a river telegraphing through my translucent skin. "What my mother wrote is true."

"It is now. All you needed was a little push. Blood to complete your transition."

The thought of looking at his smug face incited a violence in me I never knew existed. But with those rubies still hanging from my neck, ears, and wrist, I had no chance of escaping this prison.

I finally looked up. "You forced this on her, and she killed herself so the clan would never find out. She did it to protect me." To my surprise, he seemed a little remorseful. Maybe he did love her in his own perverse way.

"It was selfish of her." His smugness returned, and suddenly it was all her fault that she was dead. "If she had just trusted me and given herself more time to adjust to her transition…"

I never considered myself a violent person, but I wanted to hit him so hard his nose would shatter. Then maybe he'd feel an ounce of the pain he'd inflicted on me and my family.

"Speaking of trust," I said with a forced smile. "Why don't you take these rubies off me?" It was worth a shot. "I'm not really big on jewelry, and it's starting to make me itch."

He got up and stood behind me, grazing his hands over my neck before resting them on my shoulders. For a second I thought he was going to remove the necklace, but he dug his fingers into my skin and bent down closer to my ear. "I thought my own daughter would be smarter than to think I was an idiot. We were doing so well, but you just ruined all the progress we've made today."

"What happens now?" I asked, shrugging his hands away. "Do I stay in this apartment forever? Do I turn into a Night Walker and get hunted down by my own family?" The thought of taking on the Circle, night after night from here to eternity, ignited a feeling of dread unlike anything I'd ever felt before. What a bleak existence it would be to fight my own clan. Death was preferable.

He headed for the desk on the other side of the room and opened one of the drawers. "Until you earn that trust you asked me for, I'll have to keep you here. In the back room with Henry." He refused to turn around and look me in the eye as he delivered the rest of my sentence. "You'll feed from him exclusively until you no longer feel the need to go back to your old life. It's the only way to break your bond with the clan."

"No," I said, panic suddenly consuming me. "Don't do this to me! Please!"

He glanced at me over his shoulder. "It shouldn't take more than a few weeks. Maybe a month."

"You think the clan will just stop looking for me?"

"Not at all." He headed back toward the table with a key in his hand. "Once they know the truth, they'll hunt you, which is why it's so important that we break that bond. It'll be much easier to kill them that way."

I stood up and stumbled backward through the kitchen doorway, terrified to take my eyes off him as he followed me with that key in his hand. "You'll have to kill me before I let you lock me up with that... thing," I said as he cornered me.

"His name is *Henry*," he hissed through clenched teeth. "He's far better than some of the others I could put you with, so I suggest you remember his name. He'll be the only *thing* keeping you alive until you come to your senses, so be nice to him."

He grabbed my wrist and dragged me toward the door. I couldn't fight him off with the jewelry on, but I also couldn't live with the thought of being locked up with a blood slave until my humanity was gone. From the corner of my eye, I spotted a row of knives stuck to a magnetic strip along the edge of the kitchen island. I grabbed one as he dragged me past it, but as I raised it high into the air and brought it down toward him, my hand froze before the blade touched his back.

"Haven't you learned by now," he said, yanking me through the kitchen door and shoving me across the room.

I hit the wall hard, the back of my skull throbbing, the knife still gripped tightly in my hand. As long as I was wearing the rubies, I wouldn't be able to use it on him. But there was another way to free myself from the hell he was about to sentence me to. His eyes grew wide as I pooled every ounce of my courage and raised the blade to my neck. Then I smiled at him weakly as I slid it across my throat.

"No! You fool!" Ryker ran toward me, his face twisted with a look of disbelief. But before he reached me, the sound of shattering glass stopped him.

Barely conscious, I rolled my head to the side and saw something burst through the window and zero in on Ryker like a missile.

"Hawk," I managed to whisper, the cut not deep enough to kill me instantly. I was shocked as I reached for the wound and felt it healing under my fingertips. Either my transition had saved me or it was the rubies.

Hawk's wings spread wide as his talons shot out and wrapped around Ryker's neck, squeezing him tightly. He turned to looked at me when he heard me whisper his name, and Ryker used the distraction to sink his teeth into Hawk's fluttering wing. Hawk let out a piercing shriek and flew backward, tearing his good wing against the jagged glass of the broken window.

I grabbed the edge of the table and dragged myself to my feet. Hawk had shifted back and was staring at me wide-eyed from under the window where he'd fallen. I glanced down at my blood-soaked shirt and shook my head to let him know I was all right. He kept wincing and held his arm where Ryker had bitten him, but he managed to flash me a smile when he realized I was okay.

My relief faded when I saw a tall shadow against the wall. Ryker had disappeared, and I realized he was creeping up behind Hawk with something gripped in his hands that shimmered in the light coming through the window.

"He's behind you!" I yelled.

Hawk's smile vanished, but before he could turn around, Ryker had a silver chain wrapped around his neck. He pulled it so tight I could see Hawk's skin bulge and then start to turn red and smoke. Ryker's hands were nearly on fire, but it didn't stop him from pulling the chain tighter around Hawk's neck. I couldn't move or scream or do anything but watch as the silver seemed to melt into Hawk's skin and render him helpless.

Ryker looked at me as he lowered his lips to Hawk's ear. "You don't really think you're good enough for Morgan, do you? A two-bit shifter who thinks he's a vampire?" He laughed and went in for the kill, twisting the chain so tight I thought he was about to decapitate Hawk. "A fucking bird!"

Frozen in place by the rubies, I lowered my eyes. But when I heard Hawk's strangled voice, I looked back up.

"How about two birds?" he gritted out under the force crushing his windpipe.

Ryker let up briefly as the comment seemed to trigger his curiosity. "Two?" He snorted and eyed Hawk for a second.

A gust of wind blew through the broken window, and the drapes fluttered in Ryker's face, disrupting his attempt to sever Hawk's head. He grabbed the fabric and flung it away, his eyes growing wide as he caught a glimpse outside.

Hawk dove toward me as a giant black bird flew into the room and speared its bill straight through Ryker's neck, skewering him to the far wall. The bird's wings flapped wildly as it hovered to keep Ryker in place.

"Are you okay?" I asked Hawk. The wound wrapping halfway around his neck was deep, and I cringed as I imagined his pain.

He managed a strangled laugh. "Just a little silver poisoning."

Then I seized the opportunity. "Rip it off," I said, pointing to the pendant.

Confused by my strange request, he hesitated.

"Just do it, Hawk!"

He grabbed it and tugged, and it fell away from my neck with ease. Then he helped remove the earrings and bracelet, but I had to grease the ring with my own blood to get it off my finger.

"Is that *the* crow?" I asked, staring at the bird trapping Ryker against the wall.

Hawk hit the ground before he could answer. He was getting worse, and I knew we had to get him out of there before he lost consciousness.

"Let him go," I said to the crow, but not before making sure my power hand was good and hot. "He's mine."

The crow flew back toward the center of the room and shook its head to shed the blood covering its sharp bill. Ryker managed to stay standing and clutched the gaping wound that would have killed a mortal. He spat out a few mouthfuls of blood and leered at the giant crow. Then he turned his eyes on Hawk lying on the floor.

"Don't even think about it," I said, opening my hand to show him the blue light in the center of my palm.

He spotted the jewelry on the floor, and the bracelet started to shake. It seemed to come to life as if called by its master. Then the necklace lifted into the air. It flew toward me so fast I barely had time to react. I raised my hand and hit it with the light, smashing it into the wall. The ruby ignited in a burst of sparks that nearly set the place on fire.

Ryker dove for the smoking necklace, but I got to it first, blasting him with a ball of light that slammed him against the wall. It left a sizable dent as he slid to the ground.

"Uh-uh," I said, shaking my head. "I believe you gave those jewels to me." I intended to make damn sure no one would ever fall under their spell again.

He climbed to his feet and wiped the spit from his mouth. "How dare you use magic on your own father!"

"Father? You're not my father. You're nothing but a donor."

I had to admit his rage was frightening. But without those jewels locking me down, I had the upper hand now.

He must have come to his senses and realized he was

outnumbered and out of luck, because he eyed the window and made a run for it. The crow went after him, but Ryker still had a few tricks up his sleeve. He turned and gazed at the bird, his eyes glowing red, and it stopped in midflight before falling to the floor. It kept flapping its large wings against the rug as if trapped in a pool of oil as it shrieked in pain.

"Stop! Leave the crow alone and I'll let you go," I said, the knife I'd used to slit my own throat gripped in my hand.

His eyes turned black again. "You'll let me go?" He huffed a bitter laugh. "You're lucky we share blood. I should destroy you along with those winged abominations."

"You just tried," I said. "But you failed."

He glanced at Hawk with loathing in his eyes, and then he backed up toward the window. "The clan will try to kill you if they find out what you are. Then you'll wish you had me." In the blink of an eye, he disappeared through it.

I ran to the window, but he was long gone. Hawk was sitting up with the crow standing next to him when I turned around.

He'll die unless you feed him immortal blood.

"What?"

The crow was in my head again.

I remembered how Jakob and I had saved it the night I brought it home in a box. "We can use yours."

The crow slowly shook its head.

"Why not? We used Jakob's blood to save you. You're an immortal crow."

But I'm still a crow and only half immortal. The blood must be pure.

"I know you didn't kill Monoclaude," I said as it got ready to fly out the window. "I'm sorry I accused you, but when I saw that black feather caught in the conservatory door—"

You assumed I was the killer. I tried to save him, but I was too late.

"Are you planning to stay?"

That was Monoclaude's wish, so I'll stay if you'll have me. But on my terms.

The crow's wings spread wide, and it flew through the window and disappeared once again. I figured it would be back when it was good and ready. On its own terms.

Hawk moaned and tried to climb to his feet. I helped him up and got him to a chair while I went to the bedroom to grab the journal. Then I gathered the jewels and stuffed them in his pockets for the trip back.

"Let's hope this works," I said, standing Hawk up and wrapping his arms around my waist. "Hold on tight, and whatever happens don't let go." I focused on the wall until it fell away and all I could see was Mrs. Wells's living room. A moment later, Ryker Caspian's prison was nothing but a bad memory.

CHAPTER 29

I was relieved to step through the portal and find us in the apartment on the Upper East Side, proof that I was starting to master my traveling skills. I helped Hawk to the bed and told him to get some rest while I figured out how to get ahold of Jakob. Ryker had taken my phone, and Hawk didn't own one. If he made it through this—and by God, he would—the first thing I planned to do was bring him into the twenty-first century by buying him one.

"Jesus!" I barked, nearly slamming into Jules when I walked into the living room.

"Where the hell have you been?" she said. "I've been calling you since yesterday." She sat on the sofa and buried her face in her hands. "I thought your uncle locked you in the basement or something. I was about to go all commando and sneak into that damn building of yours."

"You're not too far off," I said. "I've got an interesting story to tell you, but I don't have time right now. Give me your phone."

"Where's the burner I got you?"

I glanced down the hallway and debated whether to tell her

about Hawk, but that call I was about to make would take care of that. "Just give me your phone!"

The desperation in my voice put a halt to her questions.

"It's on the kitchen counter."

I grabbed it and dialed Jakob's number, fully aware the clan could trace the call back to Jules, but it was a matter of life and death if I didn't get some of Jakob's blood inside Hawk fast. He had an hour, maybe two at best.

"It's me," I said when he answered.

After a pause, he spoke quietly into the phone. "Where are you?"

"Just listen, Jakob. Hawk is dying. He needs some blood. Immortal blood."

He let out a long sigh before responding. "Tell me where you are."

After giving him the address and handing the phone back to Jules, I rubbed my forehead and let out a shuddering sob. I pulled myself together a few seconds later and stuffed my emotions back inside. Breaking down wasn't going to help anyone, and it would only upset Hawk and make it worse for him.

"Is he in the bedroom?"

I nodded and sat down on the edge of the sofa. "I just spent the past twenty-four hours locked up in Ryker Caspian's house."

Her jaw went slack. "Holy shit! Your father?"

"Don't call him that." I stood up and started to pace the living room, wired and terrified for Hawk. "Where the hell is Jakob!"

"Calm down, Morgan. You just hung up the phone."

As I headed down the hallway to get back to Hawk, there was a knock on the door. We glanced at each other before she went to look through the peephole.

"It's him," she said, opening it.

He walked inside and embraced me. "Christ, Mora. You scared the life out of me."

"How did you get here so fast?"

His chest heaved against me as he laughed. "How do you think? I would have traveled straight into the living room, but I wasn't sure if you were alone." He let go of me and looked at Jules. "Thank you for taking care of her."

Jules shrugged. "She's my best friend."

"Come on," I said. "He's back here."

When we walked into the bedroom, Hawk was lying on the floor. He'd crawled halfway across the room, his bitten arm fully feathered and shifted into a wing.

"Hawk!" I dropped down next to him, lifting his head to cradle it in my lap.

Jakob got down on his knees and pulled a pocketknife from his jacket. "What happened to him?"

"Ryker bit him." The look on Jakob's face scared the hell out of me. "What's wrong?"

He stared at me like he was trying to make sense of what I'd said. "Ryker? Ryker Caspian?"

I nodded. "He was waiting for me in the penthouse yesterday. I went there to get the journal, and he kidnapped me and held me in his house. If it weren't for Hawk, I'd still be locked up. Ryker managed to get away." I decided to hold off on telling either of them about what Ryker had done to me. We had other things to worry about, like saving Hawk's life, and a conversation about my "transition" was going to require some time and a lot of alcohol.

"How did you get into the penthouse?"

"I traveled. By the way, you didn't do a very good job of destroying those rubies."

He gave me a suspicious look. "Why do you say that?"

"Because I woke up in his house wearing them. He also put that pendant on me."

"Where are they now?"

"Don't worry about that. I'll destroy them myself this time."

He gave me a wary look and opened the knife. Jules cringed as he ran the blade across his wrist and drew his deep blue blood before holding it to Hawk's lips. "A vampire biting a vampire is a tricky thing, but immortal blood should do the trick."

At first Hawk didn't respond to the blood entering his mouth, but suddenly his eyes popped open and he sat straight up, coughing violently like he was trying to expel something buried deep inside his stomach.

"What's happening to him?" I asked Jakob.

"I'm not sure, but I think we better step back."

I was reluctant to leave him, but Jakob grabbed my arm and yanked me up, stopping me when I tried to go back to him.

Hawk lurched forward and got on his hands and knees, gasping for air as something visibly crawled along the inside of his chest and moved toward his throat. His mouth stretched wide. He kept gagging like he was about to vomit, and then something black and shiny protruded from his lips. It pulsed like a beating heart, moving in and out of his mouth like it couldn't quite expel itself. Eventually he let out a strangled howl and it came flying out, rolling across the floor and squirming like a newborn *something*.

He collapsed and lost consciousness. Jakob grabbed my arm when I tried to go to him. "Let him be for now." He pulled a handkerchief from his pocket and grabbed the undulating blob off the floor. I followed him out the front door and up the stairs to the roof where he flung it into the sky. The strange creature hovered above us as it changed form, eventually sprouting wings before disappearing into the night sky.

"What the hell was that?" I asked.

He let out a long breath and stared at the spot where it had vanished, probably to make sure it was good and gone. "When a vampire bites a mortal," he began to explain, "it steals their essence and leaves behind its own. But when a vampire bites another vampire, the playing field is leveled. The two powerful forces create something very dark. An essence no one should ever have to face. Luckily for Hawk, my blood helped him expel it before it took up residence inside his body for good. He just got rid of what's left of it."

By the time we made it back downstairs, Hawk was sitting in the living room and Jules was getting him something to drink. The bright glow of his golden eyes had returned, and his skin was no longer pale.

"I think he'll live," Jakob said, getting a good look at the man who had stolen my heart.

Hawk got up, standing a couple of inches taller than Jakob, and extended his hand. "Thank you. I own you my life."

Jakob shook it and nodded once. "If Mora thinks you're worth saving, so do I."

He dropped Hawk's hand and looked at me. "Come home. We can spin this and make Hawk the hero."

"You've known all along about the legacy, haven't you? It's all in the journal."

"Yes."

"Why didn't you tell me?"

"I made a promise to your mother. She wanted to tell you in her own words when you were ready. When you were more… mature. Don't take this the wrong way, Mora, but until recently you *definitely* weren't ready."

Jules snorted. "Yeah, no shit."

"You should talk." I looked back at Jakob and wondered why he'd gone to all the trouble of commissioning that box with the auction house. "Why didn't you just give me the journal instead of putting me through the fiasco of trying to open that box?"

His brow furrowed. "I never had the journal."

"You didn't commission the box it came in?"

He shook his head. "I was as ignorant as you were when you brought it home. I just assumed your mother arranged to have it sent to you."

I tried to imagine her planning her own death and instructing someone to anonymously commission it with the auction house. But who?

"What's important is that you have the journal and it's safe where the clan won't find it." His face suddenly went grave. "You do have it, don't you?"

"Yes. It's in the bedroom."

His relief was palpable. "Good. Give it to Jules for safekeeping and come home with me. We'll worry about clearing Hawk of Rebecca's attack after we win him some points for saving you from the Reaper."

"They'll just lock me up again. And by the way, the Reaper doesn't exist. Ryker insisted it's just a legend."

"I'm well aware of that, but the clan believes what it wants to believe, so let's use it to our advantage. The Reaper abducting the queen of his archenemies will sit better with the clan than telling them he did it because you're his daughter. And don't forget, the real reason they locked you up was to keep you from warning Hawk, which you've clearly already done. What you have to remember, Mora, is you're the queen. And whether you want to acknowledge it or not, Ryker gave you something that makes you more powerful than even the twins. They couldn't lock you up now if they tried."

"You know what Ryker did to me? My... transition?" I cringed at his expression, which was consoling if not filled with a little pity—the last thing I wanted from him. "How?"

"I can see it in your eyes. Katherine had that same look after he forced her to drink the blood."

"Blood?" Jules said, leaning closer to look at my eyes. "What the hell is he talking about?"

I let out a shuddering breath and broke the news to her, hoping it wouldn't push her to the brink of leaving and never speaking to me again. "Ryker forced me to drink human blood. He called it my transition."

Jakob elaborated when Jules just stood there looking shell-shocked. "Your best friend is a vampire now. She's still half Winterborne, so she won't need human blood very often."

"Very often?" I said, taking a step back. "Like hell! Never!"

"I'm afraid you will," Hawk said, standing up to try to console me. "But only when the hunger becomes unbearable, and there are plenty of human volunteers who'll fall over themselves to offer it to you."

I thought about Henry back at Ryker's apartment. *He begged me to use him,* Ryker had said.

"Are you telling me you drink human blood?" I asked Hawk. "You told me you only drink from animals occasionally. Jesus, you said it was a choice!"

"It is for me because I'm a raptor. I get my blood from animal prey when I hunt. But it may not be a choice for you. Only time will tell."

I glanced at Jules and waited for her to say something. She already knew about Ryker and my vampire heritage, but the whole human-blood-drinking thing might be a deal breaker, and I wouldn't blame her if it was too much for her to handle.

She scratched her head and twisted her lips. "Okay," she finally said. "I think I can handle my best friend being a witch, an immortal, a vampire, and a queen. But promise me you'll go to Hawk if you start having those cravings."

I laughed halfheartedly. "I told you years ago you weren't my type." It was an old joke between us that seemed appropriate.

"It's getting late," Jakob said. "We should go."

"I haven't agreed to go back with you yet."

Hawk decided for me. "You should go, Morgan. They don't have any power over you anymore, and I can take care of myself now that I know I'm on their hit list."

I followed him to the door. "Where are you going?"

He turned around and smiled, his face a facade of confidence I didn't buy for a second. "I have a date with the queen Flyer. To convince her to testify in my defense. Now go home, Morgan."

CHAPTER 30

I asked Jakob to walk with me to the park before we traveled back to the Winterborne Building, because I wanted to show him the black opal and tell him what had happened with the Flyers. After listening to everything, he agreed that we needed the queen's testimony to make it stick. Without it, it was just my word against Rebecca's.

After that conversation, we traveled back to the penthouse and I headed straight for the bedroom to change into some fresh clothes. When I walked back out to the living room, Jakob was finishing a call.

"That was Cabot," he said, stuffing his phone back in his pocket. "He's requested our presence in chambers in half an hour."

"Half an hour?" Cabot's patience surprised me. "You mean he didn't tell you to get my ass down there immediately?"

He chuckled for a few seconds before getting an anxious look in his eyes. "Are you ready for this?"

I smiled uneasily. "I don't know if I'll ever be ready."

"Whatever happens down there, just remember I'll always have your back."

I took his hands and slowly released my breath. "You've taken care of me all my life, Jakob. How could I have possibly earned such devotion?"

"It's called love, Mora. You could have attacked Rebecca yourself, killed her with your own two hands, and I'd still love you like my own."

"Now I really feel like shit," I muttered, dropping his hands. "You know Cabot's going to have a field day with you when we get down there."

"Nonsense. You called me and I dragged you back. They'll probably throw me a parade."

With a humorless laugh, I said, "Well, I am still the queen. I'll just declare a royal pardon for you if they try anything."

He got that look in his eyes again. The same one he'd gotten back at Mrs. Wells's apartment when he was explaining how he knew Ryker had given me the blood. "It'll all work out in the end."

I wasn't as sure about that as he was. "What if they see what you saw in my eyes? What if they can tell that I've changed?"

"So that's why you look so worried," he said. "They won't see anything. The only reason I can see it is because I knew what was happening to your mother. I watched her change for months, and in those last few weeks before she disappeared, it was all I could see in her eyes. Cabot will only see fatigue, which is understandable. It'll fade in a day or two once your body gets used to the change."

I went into the bathroom to splash some water on my face and get a good look at myself. I looked like hell, which would probably win me some sympathy points if they bought the story about Hawk saving me from the Reaper.

Jakob called out to me when I took too long. "It's time to go, Mora."

"Coming." I dried my face and held my hands under the

faucet, releasing the excess energy into the cool water as it ran over my skin. I didn't want them to see my nerves.

We got on the elevator and headed down to council chambers. When the door opened, every member of the clan was staring at me.

"Samuel!" I couldn't believe my eyes.

My uncle from Edinburgh stood up and greeted me halfway as I practically ran across the room. He hugged me and whispered in my ear, "Don't let them see your fear." It was as if he could read my mind.

Samuel wasn't just my favorite uncle; he was my mother's favorite brother. They were so close they were practically twins, and Cabot had always been jealous of their bond. She hibernated in her room for weeks when he left for Scotland, thrown into a depression so unlike her that I wondered if she'd ever fully recover. I'd been shocked that he didn't return to New York when she disappeared.

He embraced Jakob next. "It's good the see you, brother. I was afraid they might have run you off by now."

Jakob glanced at me and grinned. "Not a chance."

"Are you back for good?" I asked Samuel.

He leaned in and spoke quietly. "Not here. Breakfast in the morning?"

Cabot interrupted our reunion and practically ordered me to take a seat. At first I wasn't sure if I should take my rightful place in that ridiculous chair at the head of the table, but then I decided it was time to show them that I intended to resume my role as queen whether they liked it or not. Let them try to ignore me now.

When I sat in it, Cabot shot me a look. I ignored him and focused on Jakob, who was giving me a very different look. One of pride and solidarity. The Elders made their grand entrance through the wall a moment later and took their seats on either side of me.

"Now that everyone is here, we can proceed," Cabot said with a little smugness in his voice. "Our queen has returned. The question is, what do we do with her now?"

"You'll do nothing," I said, hijacking his grandstanding opening statement. "That kangaroo court you held the last time I was in these chambers was a farce. I was abducted by the Reaper, and if it hadn't been for Hawk, the man you accused of attacking your wife, I'd be dead." At the mention of the Reaper, the room buzzed, everyone seemingly shocked by the thought that I had been a captive of the legendary assassin and managed to survive. "Hawk risked his life to save me, and I intend to prove he wasn't the shifter who attacked Rebecca."

"Hmm," Cabot mused. "Unfortunately, our misguided queen has forgotten that she's been stripped of her duties pending the outcome of a trial which has yet to take place. And now we can add aiding and abetting to her list of offenses because I'm sure her shifter friend has been warned." He nodded to Olivia and James, but Ramsey raised his hand.

"You say the Reaper took you?" Ramsey asked.

"He showed up in the penthouse and used some kind of magic jewels to control my will." That took care of the explanation of how I managed to escape the twin's spell. Now they wouldn't suspect Jakob had helped me.

Ramsey seemed skeptical. "Your experience with this vampire assassin will have to be documented so we can better understand our enemy. But I am curious. Why didn't he simply kill you?"

It was time to test my lying skills. "For the same reason, I assume. He wanted to get to know *his* enemy. When I refused to give him any information, he did try to kill me." I lifted my hair to show them the faint scar that had not completely disappeared from my neck. "He said it was an eye for an eye. For all the Night

Walkers whose heads had rolled at the hands of the clan. If Hawk hadn't found me and stopped him, the Reaper would have severed my head."

He finished examining my neck. "Is the Reaper dead?"

"No. He escaped through a window." I pulled the ruby ring from my pocket and laid it on the table. "This is one of the jewels he used to control me."

Cabot reached for it, but I grabbed it and shook my head. "Don't touch it. It's dangerous."

Ramsey seemed convinced, but Cabot still had a suspicious look in his eyes.

"I'll destroy the jewels myself," I said, shoving the ring back in my pocket before anyone got too good a look at it. Couldn't have them noticing the similarities to the earrings my mother used to wear.

"Let's get on with this," Rebecca said. "This has nothing to do with that shifter attacking me and Morgan helping him escape justice."

"Yes, I agree," I said with a cold smile. "Let's get on with this." I stood up and reached into my other pocket to retrieve the black opal. When I dropped it on the table, Cabot's eyes were expressionless. But Rebecca's were easy to read.

She clenched the spot on her neck where it usually hung and let out a small gasp. "Where did you get that?"

"From the Flyers. The queen confiscated it from the shifter you paid to frame Hawk. She returned it to me the other night, before I was abducted, and they've delivered their own justice to the real attacker. You're not denying that it's yours, are you?"

Her shocked expression eased. "Of course it's mine. Hawk stole it when he attacked me. Ripped it right off my neck."

"You're lying!"

Ramsey stood up to examine the opal. "Is the queen Flyer prepared to testify to this?"

And there went Hawk's defense right out the window.

"She would, but she's afraid to ruin the alliance with the clan."

He grunted and sat back down. "Then you have no evidence. It's all hearsay. Your word against Rebecca's."

"The word of your queen," I reminded him.

"A queen who committed a crime against her own clan," Cabot said. "You're still accused of attacking your own brother."

Ethan finally spoke up. "Can we just lay this *attack* to rest? It was an accident, for God's sake. Morgan would never intentionally hurt me."

It was about time he admitted that. I wished he had said something the day I got hauled in here and accused.

Cabot glanced at the others and smirked. "It doesn't matter. She was still helping the enemy. A vampire!"

He reached for the opal, but Samuel snatched it off the table. "I'll hold on to the evidence for now. You're not exactly impartial."

I thought Cabot was going to explode. There had always been animosity between the brothers, and it was clear Samuel's loyalty was with me.

"That's enough!" Ramsey bellowed. "Morgan may be cleared of attacking Ethan, but unless evidence proves otherwise, this vampire will be hunted down and executed."

"No, he won't." I stood up and faced the Elders. "I have proof that he couldn't have done it."

Ramsey gave me a suspicious look. "How can you be certain?"

"Because he was with me at the time." The room fell quiet, and I swear I could hear the hum of electricity traveling through the wires in the walls. "Hawk was with me the entire night. He didn't leave the penthouse until almost seven that morning. If you don't believe me, you can ask Avery. She stopped by early that morning and met him. But she didn't know what he was," I quickly added, lying to spare her from any complicity.

Cabot looked at me with disgust. "So you've been sleeping with the enemy as well as helping him. That in itself is a crime."

It was a risk to tell them, but at least it absolved Hawk of the greater crime. Now we could work on proving that Rebecca and Cabot were guilty of setting him up. Get that payback for Hawk and the Flyers.

"I told you before, he's not a Night Walker. I haven't broken any laws."

Not bothering to wait to see if the Elders took action, Cabot looked at the twins and nodded.

"Damn it, Morgan, I hate this," James said, sighing as he reluctantly stood up.

But Olivia grabbed his arm to stop him. The two had a silent conversation for a moment before he sat back down.

"What the hell are you waiting for?" Cabot demanded. "Bind her!"

Olivia looked at me for a few seconds before addressing our uncle. "I don't think so." Then she gave Rebecca a brief glance before looking back at me. "Something smells rotten in this room, and I don't think it's Morgan."

"That's my girl," Samuel muttered.

Rebecca glared across the table at Ramsey. "Who's in charge here?"

The Elders seemed lost for words, but Ramsey quickly recovered and sided with the voice of reason. "We seem to be at an impasse. If Avery can substantiate Morgan's claim that this… vampire shifter was with her at the time of the attack, then the council has no choice but to drop the charges against him."

"This is insane!" Rebecca jumped out of her chair and rushed around the table. As she came within arm's length of me, I turned to look her in the eye.

She stopped, her hands suddenly covering her ears, her eyes growing wide before she squeezed them shut. "Stop!" she screamed as the pain worsened. She managed to catch herself against the edge of the table and lashed out at me with one hand, the other still covering her left ear.

I held my hand up and sent her flying back. She hit the wall so hard the pictures fell, shattering the glass in the frames. After climbing to her feet, she quickly slid back down to the floor as I delivered another round of ear-piercing vibrations.

Resisting the urge to smile like a kid on Christmas morning, I marveled at my new powers and wondered what else I was capable of doing if anyone tried to challenge my authority again.

Cabot looked at his dazed wife, and his rage contorted his face as he raised his fist in the air.

"I'd think very carefully about that if I were you," I said, watching his fist wither. "Striking your queen could get you a death sentence."

He stared at his limp hand for a few seconds before glaring at me. "How did you do that?"

"She's our sister's daughter," Samuel said. "You remember what Katherine was capable of, don't you?" The wary look on Cabot's face suggested his memories of my mother's power were rushing back to him. "It just took Morgan a little while to discover her inherent talents. I'd remember that if I were you, brother."

When I looked around the table at all the faces that had been so quick to condemn me, I realized they were all victims of an antiquated guard that needed to be changed, which I was beginning to understand was exactly what my mother had intended for me to do. I was here to carry on *her* legacy, not Ryker's. Michael, Samuel, and of course Jakob were the only ones with proud grins on their faces.

"Your queen is back, and I'm going to show you all why my mother chose me as her successor."

Ramsey started to protest, but I shot him a warning look. "And by the way, I'll love whomever I want."

I headed for the elevator without looking back. In the morning, I'd find Hawk and figure out how to manage my new reality as the vampiric queen of the Winterborne clan. But at that moment, all I wanted was a solid meal and a good night's sleep.

⁓

My uncle Samuel arrived at eight o'clock to have breakfast with me. We sat at the kitchen table and caught up on all that had happened since the last time we'd seen each other almost a year earlier.

"I've missed you," I said. "I suppose you already know about everything that's been going on. Cabot isn't very keen on relinquishing his temporary power."

He laughed. "I bet he isn't. But that's not your problem, is it?"

Samuel was one of the most genuine people I'd ever known, and I understood why my mother loved him so much.

"Why didn't you come home when she disappeared?"

He lost his bright smile and took a sip of his coffee. "We have a lot to discuss, Morgan, beginning with your legacy."

A thick lump formed in my throat. "By my legacy, you mean…"

"Ryker Caspian."

The name coming from his mouth jarred me. "You knew all along? About her affair?"

He must have read the fear on my face, but instead of putting me at ease, he got to the point of our breakfast date.

"Caspian isn't just a surname," he said. "It's a dynasty. A race of vampires that make the Night Walkers look like weekend warriors." He pinned me with an intense stare. "Your race, Morgan. But lucky for you, you also have your mother's immortal genes, and they're stronger."

I looked away from him, terrified that he'd see what Ryker had done to me, but he took my chin and pulled my eyes back to his.

"I've spoken with Jakob. I know what Ryker did to you."

"Then you know what I am."

"Yes. You're a vampire. But you're also a Winterborne."

He stood up and went to the window, looking out over the city as he seemed to gather his thoughts. "You asked me why I didn't return to New York when Katherine died. Edinburgh is under siege. At war with the Caspians. I was in the middle of the fight and couldn't leave, and I'll always regret that. But your mother knew I wouldn't make it to her memorial service."

"She spoke to you before she did it?"

"We spoke every day, but I never thought she'd kill herself. She was too invested in the cause. The invasion here in New York that's already started." He looked at me over his shoulder. "But I guess your safety was more important than a war. I can't blame her for that. I probably would have done the same thing for James and Olivia."

I shook my head. "I don't understand what you're trying to tell me."

"You will." He turned around to face me. "Now, where's the box?"

"The box?"

"The one your mother sent you at the auction house. The one containing her journal."

I felt like my head was spinning as my heart began to beat faster. "It's in the bedroom. How do you know about it?"

"As I said, I've spoken to Jakob. There are two similar boxes out there somewhere. We suspect they're in private collections here in New York or in Europe, but we'll find them if and when they come up for auction. And if they don't, we'll hunt them down and take them. Those boxes are the key."

"Key? Key to what?"

"The key to ending this war. To destroying the Caspian dynasty." He walked back to the table and cupped my cheek, a grin spreading across his face. "Welcome to the *other* Circle, Morgan."

ALSO BY LUANNE BENNETT

THE FITHEACH TRILOGY
The Amulet Thief (Book 1)
The Blood Thief (Book 2)
The Destiny Thief (Book 3)

THE KATIE BISHOP SERIES
Crossroads of Bones (Book 1)
Blackthorn Grove (Book 2)
Shifter's Moon (Book 3)
Dark Nightingale (Book 4)
Bayou Kings (Book 5)

HOUSE OF WINTERBORNE SERIES
Dark Legacy (Book 1)
Savage Sons (Book 2)
King's Reckoning (Book 3)

Sign up for news and updates about future releases!
LuanneBennett.com

ACKNOWLEDGMENTS

This story started out a little shaky, but a few people helped me find the way. To my editor, Anne Victory, and my proofreader and beta reader extraordinaire, Jen Coleman. I also have to thank all my other beta and ARC readers for taking the time to read for me. It really does take a team.

ABOUT THE AUTHOR

LUANNE BENNETT is an author of fantasy and the supernatural. Born in Chicago, she lives in Georgia these days where she writes full time and doesn't miss a thing about the cubicles and conference rooms of her old life. When she isn't writing or dreaming up new stories, she's usually cooking or tending a herd of felines.

I love to hear from readers. Contact me at:
www.luannebennett.com
books@luannebennett.com

Printed in Great Britain
by Amazon